More Than Words

By

Maureen Hall Daly

authorHOUSE™

1663 LIBERTY DRIVE, SUITE 200
BLOOMINGTON, INDIANA 47403
(800) 839-8640
WWW.AUTHORHOUSE.COM

First published by AuthorHouse 10/08/04

ISBN: 1-4208-0162-7 (sc)
ISBN: 1-4208-0161-9 (dj)

Printed in the United States of America
Bloomington, Indiana

This book is printed on acid-free paper.

DEDICATED TO

Susan, Jimmie, Mom, Dad and Family
For all their insight, support and inspiration

My cheerleaders at Home Planners C3

Carol and Wayne
For taking the time to help me edit

And Ron
For taking the back seat to my writing

CHAPTER ONE

My Grandfather told me if I ever had the chance to live like a queen I should take it to the limit and beyond. After graduating from college, I decided to take advantage of my trust fund and went wild. Enjoying the life of the jet set, I bounced between a loft in DC, a beach house in Laguna, the lodge in Vail and various hotels abroad. Wherever my travels took me, I always had a few friends along so I was never alone. Loneliness in my mind was the kiss of death. Completely spoiled, I sported the nicest clothes, dined at the finest restaurants and indulged in some of the most expensive hobbies and interests. I wanted to live the rich life, at least until my money ran out before settling into a career. It was a fun and wild time and I didn't expect it to end on such a sad note.

One crisp spring day, after an exhausting game of tennis – I received terrible news. My best friend Karen and I were sitting in the clubhouse sipping martini's when I noticed a man heading in our direction. If leisure suits went out in the 70's, this guy had never been informed. The powder blue polyester clothed gentleman approached without a word and handed me a slip of paper. I stifled a laugh and glanced at the note. Thinking it was an invitation of some kind, but it wasn't.

Tess,
Your Grandfather passed away in his sleep. Please come home as soon as possible.
Jerry

It had to be a joke, a very sick joke. I looked up at the man who so boldly delivered the message. He gazed down with a look of pity confirming it was true. I let it slip from my fingers. Suspended in time, I sat there, no movement, no words, nothing - completely numb. The one person I trusted and loved was gone. Things would never be the same. Karen picked up the note, read it and began to cry. She didn't even know my grandfather and there she was shedding tears for him, as I sat there watching in amazement. I must have been going nuts. It was then time began to speed up as if I was in a dream.

I don't remember making the arrangements, but found myself on a plane heading home to Tucson. Surprisingly, the flight went by quickly. It was like everything was moving at warp speed, too fast for it all to sink in. My mind, my heart and my soul were empty. I couldn't process what I might face when I got home.

Arriving in Tucson, I rented a car and headed towards the large estate at the base of the Catalina Mountains where my family called "home". I gripped the steering wheel; nervous about the attitudes I would encounter from my brother and sister. I hadn't stayed in touch since the last family reunion when I stormed out of the house never looking back. I called my grandfather occasionally so he wouldn't worry, but as far as I was concerned, no other family existed.

The pavement disappeared and the familiar dirt road guided me to the entrance of the property. Grandfather loved the "wild west" concept. Even though he grew up in New York, he always fancied himself a true Arizona Rancher. Granted, the property was a ranch, but we didn't have animals…except the ones that would come down from the mountains to rummage through the trash. Along the property line was an old rickety fence decorated with rusty ranch equipment, animal skulls and mining tools. He would decorate with anything that looked as if it came out of a Zane Grey novel.

I breathed deeply to release the tension as I got out of the car. The night was amazingly bright and full of the desert sounds and smells I grew up with. Every light in the house was on, as if warning me of the number of people that must have already showed up to stake claim on the family fortune. I grabbed my bag and headed to the house. Standing at the door, I half expected it to fly open in welcome, and the other half expecting it to be bolted shut. I reached out and ran my fingers over the carved figures in the wood. Reflecting on the first time I ever touched that door…

Our parents had died in a car accident; my brother, sister and I were sent to live with our grandfather. I wasn't only the youngest of three children, but I was much younger then either of them. We were nervous about living with a man who seemed so severe whenever we saw him. Always arguing with my parents and never getting close to any of us. I didn't know what to expect living in his house. Oddly enough, it wasn't long before he and I grew very close. My brother Michael was about to graduate High School and head off to College, My sister Kathy was already enrolled in a Private College in California. I was the baby, the pest that always got on their nerves. My grandfather caught on to that and decided not to let me grow up to be the odd child out. Life with him was one big adventure after another. We'd go for long hikes in the mountains, ski trips to Colorado, shopping sprees in New York and so many others. Michael and Kathy were jealous of me for having such favor with Grandfather. They had each other, and I had him.

To my relief, there was no one there. I was expecting a full frontal attack from my family before I even settled in. Not wanting to jinx my good fortune, I quietly headed down the long hall to the back of the house where my room had been for the past fifteen years. It was just as I had left it, except it was wonderfully clean and the bed had been turned down. My suspicions began to mount.

I set down my bag and looked around the room taking in the wonderful comforts of home. It was my haven, and the only place I could go where no one was allowed to enter without permission. My sanctuary. It felt good to be home again; but then I remembered why I was there and my heart sank.

I decided to wander around to see who was home. Someone from the family must have arrived; I couldn't be the only one. I searched the main house to find lights on in every room, beds turned down and fresh flowers on every nightstand or dresser. It was unsettling; my grandfather never employed anyone on a full time basis. I chalked it up to a kind neighbor or my grandfather's lawyer setting up for another Kelly Family Reunion.

As I moved from room to room, I almost expected him to poke his head around a corner to catch me off guard. It was hard for me to accept that he was gone. I ran to his room, to make sure he wasn't playing some kind of cruel joke to get me back for being away for such a long time. Busting through the door I yelled, "Gotcha!" On the end of his bed sat a woman I'd never seen before. She was so startled by my sudden entrance I thought she was going to faint.

Staring in amazement catching my breath, I found my voice. "Sorry I scared you...I'm Tess, and you are?"

"Mary" she gasped trying to calm herself, "I'm a friend of Mack's."

Swollen red eyes told me she had been crying. Her delicate silver hair looked as though she had wiped her eyes with her hands and ran them through the fine strands. She had fragile features, light blue eyes framed by dark blonde lashes and tiny wrinkles that give the "tell-tale" signs of someone who likes to smile and laugh.

I thought she was about to burst into tears when she sprang from the bed and came over to deliver a warm and gentle hug. To my surprise, I melted into her arms and began to cry for the first time since I had found out my grandfather had died. She stroked my hair trying to comfort me.

"There now, let it all out." She coddled with a motherly tone.

I thought she was gonna break down, but she stood firm and let me have my moment of grief. Finally able to stop the tears, I stepped back.

"Thank you, I don't think it sunk in until now. I guess I was hoping it was all a bad dream. I'm sorry if I upset you." I wiped my eyes with the back of my sleeve.

"You must be tired and hungry. Come on, let's head to the kitchen for a snack and a drink – I think we both could use one right about now." Giving me a wink, she led me to the kitchen.

I wasn't hungry but didn't want to deny her the joy she seemed to get from fussing over me. Suddenly I realized for being "just a friend" of my grandfathers, she sure did know her way around his kitchen. She didn't have to search for what she needed. There was more to her than she was willing to reveal. I tried to think of a clever way to weasel out more information about her "friendship", but I was never one for beating around the bush.

Without warning, I blurted out… "How long have you been with my grandfather?"

Shocked, she spun around. "How'd you know? We never told any of the kids we were married."

"Married? Holy shit, I figured you guys were dating. Married!?...Married". My feet gave way and I slumped into the nearest chair. Shaking my head in disbelief, I looked up to see her about to break into tears. I got up and walked over to her, with a smile I extended my arms.

"Welcome to the family." She returned my hug. Although only moments, it seemed like hours before we were able to calm down. We sat at the counter tossing back drink after drink telling each other stories about my grandfather. We walked around the house turning off the lights she had on to make it feel less lonely. We said our 'Good Nights' gave each other one last hug and headed off to bed.

I woke up the next day with a slight hang over. Lying in bed I watched the reflections on the ceiling made by the pond outside my window. So much had happened in such a short period of time. I had a step-grandmother. It blew my mind they had kept it a secret. I swung my legs over the edge of the bed and rested a bit until my head stopped pounding. I got dressed and headed to the kitchen for a much-needed cup of coffee.

Mary was laying out breakfast for us in the courtyard. "Did you sleep well?" She said with a half smile, hinting that she was feeling a bit rough too.

"Tossed around a bit, but I finally nodded off, and you?" I was sure the dark circles under my eyes had already told the story.

"As good as could be expected, pull up a chair and have something to eat." She turned back to setting the table.

"I guess I should before the rest of the family gets here." Running my hands through my hair I pictured the series of events that were about to unfold.

"Tess, we're not expecting your family. They won't be here for another week. I thought you knew." She slapped her hand on the table. "Damn Cody, I knew I should've called you instead of sending word with that nit wit." She lifted the coffee to her lips rolling her eyes to the ceiling.

Amused, I asked, "Do they know I'm here first?" Wild images of my sister throwing the ultimate temper tantrum flashed through my mind.

"As a matter of fact, they do. Don't worry about all that yet, Mack's lawyer will be here later today to explain everything to you." Smiling, she passed me a plate of food.

I spent most of the day in my grandfather's study looking through some of his books. When I was young, we used to act out the stories and try to finish them the way we felt they should've ended. I developed a passion for writing because of those times together. I graduated with a degree in literature, but I never did anything with it. He was disappointed I didn't become a free lance journalist or go to work for a publishing company right after college, but he understood my desire to let loose and live the wild life. It felt good to have someone in my life that believed in me and trusted me to make my own decisions.

Mary kept herself busy cleaning and re-cleaning every area of the house. A big job considering it was cluttered with art and designed in a typical mission style where the rooms wrap around the courtyard connected by long halls and galleries. She made it look easy.

Jerry, my grandfathers lawyer arrived late in the afternoon. I had met him a few times before, but most our communications were phone calls, faxes or emails. I only had to see him once or twice a year to sign papers for one thing or another. I never paid much attention to the details; I just figured it had to do with my trust fund. I guess I should've taken more interest in matters, but I never had a head for legal mumbo jumbo.

I sat in an over stuffed rawhide chair across from a man I didn't particularly like. Feeling nervous, I swung my feet like a child. Jerry (a man who spent most of his money on plastic surgery) sat there flipping through files as I waited.

"Tess, I'm sure you're confused by all this." He leaned forward sucking air through his teeth.

"Last month, your grandfather called me to get his estate in order. I came over and went through all the paperwork with him and Mary. I bet you're pan caked they got married and never told you…but you have to admit, she's a nice lady." I nodded trying to figure out what he had said.

"Anyway… Mack discovered he had cancer about a year ago. Just after your last visit. Not being a man who takes things lying down, he went to New York to see some of the best doctors in the country. There he met Mary, fell in love and got married in Niagara Falls. A shock to me, I never thought he'd get married again. He loved your grandmother dearly."

"I never knew her." words finally coming out of my mouth.

"No, she died just after your mother was born…Well anyway, when they came back to Tucson he gave up on the doctors since they couldn't treat the cancer without putting him in more danger. The treatments would have only given him a few short months and even then he would've been too frail to enjoy them."

His eyes began to mist over, as he stood up and walked to the window catching his second wind. "He changed his will, Tess. He wanted to include Mary in the Estate. I know your brother and sister may have a problem with that, but I think they're gonna be more pissed off by other things he changed. That's why I had you come home first. He's got very specific stipulations for you in his will. They're a bit extreme, but he assured me you'd understand. Now… normally we'd have a funeral, everyone would attend and then we'd do the reading of the will. Well…you knew your Grandfather… convention was not his style."

He paused for dramatic effect; and walked over to a large portrait of my grandfather. Swinging it open he revealed a hidden wall safe. I thought "how typically Hollywood, a safe behind a picture." Grandfather did like the novelty of things. I watched in amusement as Jerry fiddled with the lock. He was trying to be professional – but his insecurities were written all over his face – almost literally.

"He knew he was dying, so he set it up to be cremated the day after he expired. He didn't want to have his body laying around for a wake and funeral, so he made sure that no one but the mortician and I knew of his plans. Even Mary's not aware he's already been cremated. I'll have the displeasure of telling her after you've left."

With a look as if he smelled rotten eggs, he gasped. "OOPS, I'm getting ahead of myself. Oh well, since we're already on the subject…why drag it out any longer. Your grandfather arranged for you to go and write like you've always wanted. However, where you're going is very secluded and you'll have to stay there a year even if you feel you've written all you care to. I've checked your accounts and you're almost out of money. The estate is divided equally between you, Michael, Kathy, and Mary. The house will belong to the entire family, but Mary will be the year round resident. The estate will be frozen for a period of one year before it's divided."

My head was spinning; it was too much to deal with. I stared at him in total amazement. A man who was as plastic as a pen cap telling me what I had to do to please my grandfather who wasn't even alive. My temper started to surface.

"Will you just get to the point and stop the bullshit!" I could feel my face turning red as my anger boiled my blood.

"Okay Tess, Jesus. There's no reason for you to go all wild." Placing a hand on his chest as if he was shocked I snapped. He was such an idiot.

"I know you could care less about the money, the house or the investments, but he really wanted you to do this for him and for yourself. He gave you complete control after college and last year when you ran out of money, he added to your accounts so you could go on."

"How could you let him do that? Why the hell didn't you tell me? I was supposed to stop when it was gone!" I began to feel that there was more than what he was telling me.

Clearing his throat, "Tess, okay, now who is being all dramatic over nothing. Shit, if I had that kind of opportunity, I wouldn't bitch about it. He did what ever he wanted to do plus, he loved you." He shifted his eyes over the documents on the table.

"Okay Jerry, I'll do it. I'll go away for a year and write, how hard can it be? I could go to Paris or San Francisco or…"

"Well that's the catch, you don't pick where you're going. It's already set up; your plane leaves first thing in the morning. Mary can drive you to the Airport."

He started to gather up the files tossing them in his briefcase, as if he was going to leave. "Jerry, I have questions. You can't just leave now, you have more to explain."

I chased him as he ran out of the office. "How do you expect me to believe all this bullshit? I want a copy of that damn will Jerry!"

Giving Mary a quick nod he dashed out and leapt into his car. Feeling the anger well up inside once again, I scream "You asshole" and slammed the door shut. Nothing made sense...no funeral, no wake, being forced to live somewhere unknown for a year, it was crazy. My grandfather must have gone completely mental before he died. I headed out to the courtyard and sank into the hammock where I let the drama play over and over again in my mind. I felt stupid knowing that I was going to give in and take on his adventure.

CHAPTER TWO

Mary had covered me with a blanket some time in the night. I woke up cold and sore from sleeping in such an odd position. As uncomfortable as it was, I didn't want to move. I thought if I stayed there long enough everything would go back to normal, but I knew there was no chance of that happening.

Feeling as disheveled as I looked, I headed into the kitchen. She was there with a fresh cup of coffee fixed just the way I like it. "Are you up for some breakfast before we head to the airport?"

"No thanks, I can't eat before I fly. It makes me sick, but I appreciate the offer." I took a sip trying not to burn my mouth. "I feel bad about leaving you here to face my family alone, I know how they can be."

"I'll be fine, I haven't met a person yet that could bring me down. No matter what they do or say, I will find a way to adapt and over come." She held up her fist as if she was going into battle.

I'd be leaving and there was nothing I could do to fight for more time. A strange eagerness started to build as I wondered what was in store for me. Fantastic ideas ran through my mind as I tried to imagine the kind of scheme my grandfather had cooked up. He was creative, but completely cracked. I knew what ever he planned was going to be different from anything I could have thought up.

"Tess? Tess dear? Are you okay?" Snapping her finger to bring me out of my trance.

"Yes, I'm fine…I guess I'm trying to get used to this whole crack pot idea. I think I'm getting a little excited about it.

Mary helped me pack before we headed to the airport. The drive gave me time to reflect on the meeting with Jerry. I was sure he got a kick out of the whole thing. He hadn't liked me since the time I kicked him in the family jewels for trying to get a little friendly during a family reunion. I should've mentioned his indiscretion to my grandfather, but I figured he wouldn't try again. I made the effort to wear pointed shoes or boots when I was expecting to see him. Needless to say, from that day on he never came within five feet of me.

The airport was bustling with busy travelers and the thought of having to fight the crowds made me edgy. To my relief, we pulled up to the curb in front of the executive terminal. I was grateful my grandfather arranged a private transport; commercial planes always made me sick. A private jet would be a much smoother ride.

Saying goodbye to Mary was difficult. We had only known each other a few short days and yet I felt so connected to her. She was the closest thing I had to a mother and I wanted more time. Standing at the curb watching her drive away made me feel abandoned.

I shook it off and headed into the terminal. There I came face to face with a ghost from my past. Scott Taylor... flyboy extraordinair. The punk college student who stole my heart and crushed it, the day couldn't have gotten worse? As if the pain of losing my grandfather and leaving Mary weren't bad enough, I was faced with reliving the pain of losing my first love.

"Hi Tess, I'm sorry to hear about your grandfather. I know it must be difficult for you." Lowering his eyes to express his sincerity.

"Thank you Scott, I appreciate that." For some reason I extended my hand "What brings you to Tucson? I thought you were a bush pilot in Australia."

Beaming confidently, "I'm piloting tours around Arizona, New Mexico, California and up the West Coast," with a sideways glance he continued, "but today...I'll be your personal taxi. I have strict instructions not to tell you where we're going – so don't even try to weasel it out of me."

He grabbed my bag and led me to the tarmac. Looking around at all the wonderful jets at the gates I wondered which one we'd be taking. I panicked when he led me to the plane farthest from the gate. I felt the blood drain from my face when I realized we'd be flying in a beat up single engine plane from hell.

The Cessna 172 was the first type of plane Scott had learned to fly. In college, we used to spend hours at the airport practicing touch and goes, trying to teach me take offs and landings safely in case of an emergency. He loved to fly; yet I think he was terrified of getting into an accident. Whatever his fear or obsession, he was one of the best pilots that graduated from his class.

He still had his good looks, wavy blonde hair, crystal blue eyes, and a strong but not overly muscular body. You could see the Swedish heritage in his perfect features. Looking as though he stepped right out of the 40's in his beat up leather flight jacket, new haircut and a close shave. Handsome was too weak of a word to describe him.

"Still know how to pre-flight?" He tossed me a checklist as if I was gonna do it for him.

"You can't be serious," I said, folding my arms across my chest.

"I'm not asking you to fly the damn plane Tess, just to be a second pair of eyes. You know I'm gonna do it again anyway."

"Always the safety boy!" I shouted after him as he headed back to the terminal to file his flight plan.

I looked down at the checklist and smiled. Doing the preflight always made me feel important. One slip up or small thing over looked could mean lives. To be trusted with such a huge responsibility used to be an honor. I looked at the laminated list not remembering a damn thing he taught me.

Always the professional pilot, he performed his preflight and instructed me on emergency procedures. I had heard him go over the same procedures hundreds of time and fought the urge to recite along with him. I knew it would've pissed him off, so I bit my tongue. Handing me a headset, he checked to make sure I was strapped in correctly. He leaned out the window and yelled "Clear Prop".

Flying with Scott was a full-blown production, but I knew we were in a safe craft that he trusted. It still didn't make my day any better, small planes are noisy and not the most comfortable rides in the sky.

I noticed we were heading northwest when I commented, "Don't you think I'm gonna figure out where we're going?"

"Hell Tess, I'm not an idiot. I know you'll figure it out. Just promise me you won't bolt when you do."

"Bolt? Makes me sound like a horse", I crossed my arms and sat back.

We didn't talk much during the flight. The drone of the engine made it difficult to carry on a conversation. From time to time, he would point out places that would help me determine our location. We had flown past Prescott and still headed northwest. I knew we'd have to land somewhere around the Arizona boarder to refuel. I was beginning to wonder how long the plane ride was gonna last. Occasionally I would glance at Scott as I recalled memories of us together in college.

Growing up the typical tomboy, I never cared much for makeup and frilly clothes. My grandfather tried to convince me I was pretty, but I knew he was just trying to make me feel better. I was chubby with red hair and freckles. It was Scott who made me feel beautiful for the first time in my life. I ran into him one day between classes, literally. As I was looking down trying to memorize a poem for a test I bumped into him sending his books flying out of his arms. He grabbed my shoulders to steady me. He flashed me a smile as I stuttered my apologies. Staring into his eyes, I was hooked, but it was his pick up line that reeled me in. "You've got the prettiest green eyes I've ever seen." He invited me to dinner and a movie, which was the beginning of our three-year romance. It was wonderful, but turbulent and it ended on a rough note.

By hopping from one airport to another, refueling each time, we made our way to a small airport just outside Seattle. I was relieved to discover the next leg of the trip would be in a nice comfortable SUV. Although the flight wasn't as bad as it could have been, it was twelve hours of being tossed around like a salad.

"We're gonna head up to my family's lodge. You can get a good nights sleep before tomorrow's flight." He said with a casual tone.

I mumbled "Crap…more flying." Not wanting to think about it, I tossed my bag in the front seat, hopped into the back and crashed. All the traveling had taken a toll on my nerves and I wasn't in the mood to talk.

Scott didn't bother to wake me when we arrived at the lodge. I didn't know how long I had been out there alone, but I did know it was dark and a bit chilly. I reached into the front seat for my bag but it was gone.

Heading to the lodge, I looked around at the thick dense pack of trees that surrounded the area. It smelled piney and fresh. Scott was sitting in an overstuffed chair leaning towards a very pretty lady with long dark hair. He always was a big flirt, couldn't get enough of the ladies. In fact, that was one of the reasons we split up.

I cleared my throat. "Hi, I'm Tess" extending my hand to her. Surprisingly she gave a firm handshake.

"It's so nice to meet you. I'm Monica, if there's anything I can do to make your stay more comfortable, just let me know." She was a natural at public relations. Curious to know who she was, I glanced at her nametag, M. Taylor, CEO Taylor Industries.

It didn't hit me right away…she was Scott's wife. I was completely shocked, but remained calm. With a smile on my face, I hid the fact that my heart was breaking again. I had no reason to feel that way; he had his life…I had mine. The ache I felt was jealously and I knew it.

It was uncomfortable during dinner. Not much conversation, just polite chitchats about nothing significant. I was sure he had told her we used to date in college. She kept glancing at me making me feel more insecure. I wasn't sure if she was trying to get my attention, or just curious about me.

After dinner, she led me to an upstairs room. It was smaller than my room at home, but very comfortable. Overly decorated in delicate laces and country flower prints, it oozed charm. I hoped to fall asleep quickly, the less I was conscious, the better my heart felt. If I had my choice, I would sleep forever just to keep dreaming. My dreams were always great…it was reality I had a problem with.

The thought of Scott married was hard for me to take. I always thought he'd remain the wild child. In college he had dreams of never staying in one place for too long. His dreams were to see every corner of the world without leaving any stones unturned. Seeing him with Monica was strange yet they were perfect for each other. With her long dark hair and dazzling smile next to his light features and sparkling eyes, she was the perfect ying to his yang.

CHAPTER THREE

I barely had time to collect my thoughts before Scott was rushing me out the door. Grabbing a piece of buttered toast, I dashed ahead of him. "What the hell's the rush? Your ass on fire or do you just like watching the chubby chick run?"

"Actually, we've gotta get to the seadrome to stay ahead of the weather if we have any chance to make it there today." I could hear the tension in his voice.

I shouldn't have asked in such a smart-ass manor. I knew it set his mood for the day and it wasn't a happy one. He said nothing during the whole ride and the look on his face was serious. I couldn't tell if he was worried or pissed. I'd never been in a seaplane, but decided I could handle anything after what I had already been through the past few days.

The seadrome was on a huge lake. Only a few float planes, a small shack and a couple of cabins. It would've been a good place to be stranded for a year, but a strange feeling told me I was headed for something more rustic. I'd be lucky if I had a roof over my head.

The beginning of the flight was amazingly calm, but as we headed further north, the sky grew dark. There was no question to the look on Scott's face... he was concerned. Finally getting the nerve to break the silence I said, "I don't mean to nag, but are we gonna land soon? This weather doesn't look good."

"Don't worry Tess, I know it looks evil – but we're skirting the edge of the storm, we're gonna be just fine. Our landing area is just over the next ridge." He pointed, but I couldn't see over the nose of the plane.

My heart began to race as I realized we'd have to land on a lake or river. As we cleared the ridge, I caught a glimpse of what was going to be my home for the next year. Surrounded by mountains and thick forest was a long narrow lake. The wind was calm and our landing was as smooth as gliding on ice. I let out a deep breath and looked down to find my hands clenched so tight my knuckles had turned white. I turned to Scott and let out a nervous giggle.

"You're such a baby. You know I'd never let anything happen to my plane." Giving me a sly smile and a quick wink he taxied to a small dock. "We've gotta get tied down before that storm pummels us."

I stepped onto the pontoon and balanced myself as we glided along side the pier. I grabbed the rope and jumped, pulling hard I secured the tie to a cleat. Tossing my bag to me, he stepped onto the dock, grabbed my hand and ran to a small cabin that was beyond the clearing near the tree line. I felt the same excitement he gave me in college.

As we approached the cabin, he took back his hand and turned to face me. "Welcome to your new home Tess." The realization kicked in as I looked around. It was charming, a bit rustic, but very charming. An herb garden to the right, veggies to the left – at least I wouldn't go hungry. The only thought that ran through my mind was that it better have running water and electricity. There was no way in hell I would survive with out electricity.

Determined to take on the challenge with a positive attitude, I headed in with Scott cautiously following behind. I knew he thought I would throw a fit at any moment. Looking around, I was completely amused. It was one big room divided only by the furniture scattered about. To the left of the door was a large picture window with a desk, I assumed it would be the place I was to spend most of my time since it was piled high with reams of paper and an old manual typewriter. A cup of new pencils and sharpener perched mockingly upon a stack of legal pads. I figured someone who knew me well had set it up as I notice instead of a waste paper basket there was a full size garbage can next to the desk. It didn't match the décor, but perfectly suited to the job for which it was intended.

As if in a trance, I wandered around the room to explore. Almost a wall by itself was the fireplace. It was huge and intended for use not just as a heat source but also a place to cook. The back wall was one huge bookshelf lined with books and boxes. The kitchen was like any other, but without appliances. The only other cooking source was a pot-bellied stove perched in the corner. I felt like I stepped into the life of Davie Crockett. It was too funny to be true. There would be no way I could last a year with out a fridge.

I looked around taking it all in and then it hit me…I didn't see a bathroom. "Where the hell's the can Scott? Do you expect me to stay here without at least a bathroom? – You've got to be stoned if you think I'm gonna spend a year squatting in the woods."

He dropped his bag and began to laugh uncontrollably. I was stunned, then embarrassed, and then amused. I must have looked stupid standing there bitching about a bathroom. I didn't even notice there was no electricity, but it soon became apparent, as the whole cabin grew dark in a matter of seconds. Suddenly a bright flash and crash of thunder stopped our laughter.

"We better get this place set up for the night." "Here," tossing me a book of matches, "go around and light the lamps. They should have enough oil to last the night. I'll go out back and get some wood for the fire." Suddenly he disappeared out a door I hadn't noticed.

The storm settled down by the time he came back and built a cozy fire. "You gonna be okay now? No more tantrums?" Nudging me playfully with his elbow.

"Yup, just groovy, but I have to ask…"Cutting me off before I finished, he grabbed my hand and led me out the door he went through to get the firewood. It was a mudroom with three doors. He swung open the door on the left, which lead outside to a large pile of firewood, an old tree stump and an ax. The door to the back led to a large storeroom that was stocked full of canned foods, blankets, lamps, flashlights, batteries and other item. The last door was what I was hoping for, the bathroom.

"You've all the comforts of home – well, kind of." Standing by me in the middle of the room, I turned around slowly. "See, you've got indoor plumbing, it's just different than you're used to." I knew it was the best I was gonna get. There was a pump at the sink, I already knew how to use a solar shower, and assumed what the bucket beside the toilet was for.

Kicking back on the couch, we warmed up in front of the fire. Playing "remember when", we caught up on what we'd both been doing the past few years. Getting comfortable, I stretched out resting my head against the arm of the couch and plopped my feet into his lap.

I was tired, hungry and a bit playful. "I assume you're staying here tonight to ride out the storm?"

"Yup, can't take off when it's dark." Suddenly realizing we were alone, at night, away from civilization, no way out – he sat up straight and looked at me in disbelief. "Don't you dare think I was planning to take advantage of the situation; hell woman, I'm married."

"Oh please, get over yourself. You think I'd even want some tired old pilot with no sense of humor? I just wanna make sure you're gonna to be here to cook breakfast in the morning. I'm just a lil' ol helpless woman." I said, batting my eyes as I brought my hand to my lips.

"Helpless my ass, you're a spoiled brat. You're sleeping up there," pointing to the loft. "I'm sleeping here." Laughing, he swung my legs off his lap. "Get your ass up there and go to bed, I've got a lot to show you tomorrow."

Saluting like a soldier I said, "Yes sir", grabbed my bag and headed up the stairs. The loft was small with only a bed and dresser. I knew I wouldn't need much more than that. The heat from the fire below radiated comfortably to the loft. I was toasty warm. "Scott?"

"Yup" he yawned.

"I like Monica; I can see she loves you. You're a lucky guy."

"Thanks Tess, She likes you too. Night."

"Night" I snuggled in.

Lying under the heavy quilt listening to the crackle of the fire, I looked back on all the images of the past few days. My mind recounted every moment as though it was happening all over again.

My heart went through every emotion as if I was trapped in a time loop.

When I woke up, I swore I smelled coffee and bacon. To my disappointment, it was just my imagination. I was hungry; I dreamt the fragrance and almost the taste. I quickly dressed and headed down stairs. Scott was still asleep, with his big-socked feet dangling over the edge of the couch and snoring like a buzz saw. The trip had taken a lot out of him. I thought it would be the best opportunity to use the self-flushing toilet.

By the time I had the toilet figured out and washed up, Scott was awake. I quietly snuck into the kitchen and watched him stretch shirtless in front of the fire. Man was he yummy. I couldn't help but stare; after all, I wasn't dead. He was the one who changed my world from girl to woman...from tomboy to debutante. It's true you never get over your first love, but I sure did try.

I knew that when we broke up, I'd never be able to have him again. There was no way that fly boy could stay grounded long enough for me to trust him. I always had the feeling he was off screwing around. It drove me nuts. I knew my suspicions about his playboy lifestyle were completely unfounded and came from my own insecurities, but it caused too much tension between us.

"Well, Mr. Taylor" I said with a smile, "I see you're finally up. Did you have a good night's sleep?" He grabbed his shirt and covered his wonderful body.

"As a matter of fact, you kept me up all night; I just got to sleep about an hour ago." At first I thought he was kidding, but then seeing the dark circles under his eyes I realized he was serious.

"I'm so sorry, was I snoring?" I thought I was gonna die of embarrassment.

"Nope, you were screaming, yelling, cussing and fighting. What the hell were you dreaming about?"

"Coffee and bacon." I said flatly as I walked to the storeroom to find something to eat.

"Damn, I'd hate to see you dream about Steak and Eggs" he shouted as I dashed out of the room.

I was determined to scrounge up a can of coffee and locate the root cellar to find out if I had any decent food. To my delight I found a make shift cooler with bacon, eggs, cheese and other little munchies. Locating the pans needed, I headed to the fireplace and cooked up a small feast for us to enjoy. It was a blast acting like mega mountain woman. I knew then I was gonna be just fine.

Scott showed me around the cabin and the grounds. I had a garden that needed very little attention, and herbs I'd never heard of. Around the side of the house was an open air shower and outdoor kitchen. Around the back was amazing - it reminded me of the Black Forest in Germany.

"Tess, I've gotta get going. We're expecting another storm and I need to head out before it starts to get bad." He gave me a strong hug, "Don't worry you're gonna be okay. Write the novel of the century." He turned and headed for the plane.

Without looking back, I went into the cabin and leaned against the door waiting for him yell "clear prop". It was taking too long; he should've already started the engines. My curiosity got the better of me as I opened the door running straight into Scott.

"What's the matter? Are you okay?" I looked into his eyes, searching for an answer. He looked stunned as he tried to speak.

"Tell me what's wrong!" I was about to slap him when he grabbed and kissed me. He bruised my lips as I melted into his arms completely forgetting he was married. My mind was spinning as I got caught up in the heat of his passion. I could feel every nerve in my body tingle. When finally he released me, I stepped back in shock but still tingling and craving more. I knew I couldn't act on my feelings. I reminded myself *"He's married you idiot. Don't dive back in knowing you'd be the other woman, it's not your style."* My mind was reeling as I came to my senses and realized he was walking back to the plane. I stood there watching as he performed his preflight, started the engines and took off. My lips were still numb from his kiss.

If there was ever a time when I needed a drink, it was then. There had to be something around the cabin. I could've torn the place up like a woman gone wild, but I was too dazed and confused. I threw a few more logs on the fire and sank into the couch. Thoughts running through my head like a freight train trying to understand what had happened. *Had he gone completely mad? What had compelled him to kiss me like that? What was it that held him back from saying anything to me? What was he trying to say?*

A crash of thunder jolted me out of my daze. I hoped he was able to avoid the storm that began to pummel the cabin. Pushing aside my worries, I relaxed. Loving a good storm, I tossed a few more logs on the fire and went to find some cocoa.

It was a nice size storeroom, much larger than any pantry I'd ever seen. Cold and dark, I assumed to preserve any perishable foods. The shelves were stocked with a good month's supply of food stashed, maybe more.

I was about to grab a packet of cocoa when I noticed a leather box with a brass latch at the back of the shelf. I had seen the same type of box before. A smile crept across my lips as I tossed aside the cocoa and grabbed it. Running my fingers over the leather, I closed my eyes and whispered a thank you to my grandfather. I just hoped there was a full bottle inside.

Grabbing a book from the shelf, I settled down with a glass of brandy to warm my soul. As I looked around I thought, how wonderful it would be if the cabin was not so secluded. A quick glance at the desk reminded me of my mission for the year. I raised my hand and gave a salute, then picked up the book and began to read. The brandy worked its magic quickly and soon I was fast asleep wrapped in the comforts of the couch.

CHAPTER FOUR

The first month went by slowly. I wasn't used to being alone. I always had people around to keep me up to date on the latest happenings. The first few days I stayed inside and sulked, but after awhile I ventured out discovering what veggies grew in the garden and what herbs were on hand. Being a decent cook I knew I'd have no problems creating some nice meals.

The lake wasn't as deep as I thought at first and stocked full of fish. The forest, although dense, had several paths to follow. I tried a new one each day to see where it would lead. I never wandered too far from the lake worried I'd get lost. It didn't take me long to learn to love the place.

Spring turned to summer and the thunderstorms became more sporadic. I never knew when to expect them, but when one would hit, I was cabin bound for a good day or so before it would let up. One day when I was tramping through the woods gathering up bits of bark for the fire one of the worst storms hit the area. I was lucky at first since the trees were so dense they shielded me from the biting rain. It wasn't until I got to the cabin that I realized how heavy it was pouring. Soaked from head to toe, I stood by the fire to dry off. The wind kicked up and the cabin began to creak. I looked up to the ceiling hoping the roof would be able to ride out the storm. It rained for two days straight before letting up. When I finally got the chance to go outside, I found the garden completely destroyed and the lake much higher than before. I was looking forward to a calmer summer.

Towards the end of the month I finally got a break from the wet weather. It hadn't rained in awhile and I was enjoying the warmth of the sun. After a quick swim in the lake, I stretched out on the dock and soaked up the rays. In the distance I heard a familiar buzzing. It wasn't in sight yet, but I could hear it was near. Looking up I spotted the plane. I got excited to know I was going to have some human interaction. I watched as it spiraled down to a smooth landing and taxied to the dock. I noticed Scott wasn't alone.

He had his usual pilot face on, serious with a touch of showoff. The other man I'd never seen before but at first glance I could tell he was a babe. He was about thirty six, dark wavy hair, electric blue eyes and dimples you can run a train through. He'd make a nice distraction to keep my mind off Scott. It was probably planned that way. I was sure Scott was nervous about seeing me again after what had happened the last time.

"Hey Tess, I see you're a bit short on clothes today…and you've toned up." A sly smile crept across his lips.

Just then I realized I was only wearing my bra and a pair of shorts. I grabbed the towel I was laying on and wrapped it around my shoulders. "So I guess you've come to bring me more clothes? Perhaps some food? Maybe a radio? It would be nice to have a little something to break the silence around here."

"As a matter of fact we did bring some goodies for you, but they'll have to wait until later. I want you to meet Ryan; he'll be flying your supplies in." He kept from looking at me.

I couldn't help but giggle, "It's nice to meet you." Shaking his hand and smiling. "I hope you had a good flight, the weather hasn't been this nice for awhile."

"Pleasure to meet you, hope you don't mind my coming along today. I thought it would be better if you met me first before I take over the route." His voice was deep and sexy.

"Not at all, you're more than welcome. Hope you guys can stay for dinner, I'm dying for some conversation. I'll run up and get dressed so I can help unload." I hollered over my shoulder as I headed to the cabin.

I ran up the stairs, got dressed and headed back to help. To my surprise, both of them met me at the door. "No help needed, there's not much this trip. We're mostly on a mission of mercy. Monica doesn't feel right about leaving you here for such long periods of time alone. So today we're just visiting and finding out if you needed anything special."

"You married a smart woman. She's right...it's not easy being alone. I was starting to go a little buggy. I got a list of things for you to bring next trip. Would you guys like something to drink?"

"Got a beer?" Scott said with a sideways glance knowing full well that I didn't.

"You can have tea, water or cocoa. That's all I got. Well, I do have a little brandy if you're interested." I had never realized how limited my choices were.

"No need, we brought our own." He opened the door and grabbed a red ice chest. Standing there with a confident smile on his face reminded me of the day we graduated college. He had that same look of satisfaction.

It was packed with beer and sodas, so I decided to barbecue to compliment the beverage selection. Scott had the same idea. After they had brought in the boxes of supplies, I noticed on the counter three steaks ready for the grill. I grabbed some potatoes and carrots from the root cellar and scrubbed them up in the sink.

Scott took off into the woods and Ryan fired up the grill. I grabbed a beer and headed out to get better acquainted with my new pilot friend. I wasn't sure what to say...he seemed a bit shy and a little serious. I figured I'd have to approach him cautiously.

"Thanks for getting this started" pointing my beer at the grill.

"My pleasure, I love to barbecue. Ever since I was a kid it fascinated me. I guess it's a guy thing." Shrugging his shoulders as he poked at the embers. "I think it's good to go, so feel free to bring out the food when ever you're ready."

After enjoying a wonderful meal, the guys headed back to civilization. It was a nice relaxing visit with no anticipation and no expectations. Although Ryan was a bit distant, I knew he'd warm up eventually. I watched the plane ascend into the twilight before heading back to the cabin.

I woke up every day telling myself I was gonna finally sit down and begin to write, but each morning I'd walk downstairs to see the desk still set up the same as before, I'd turn and find something else to occupy my time. I had already straightened up the garden, but still had boxes to break into and shelves to stock. Very important daily living tasks that I felt were way more important than writing a book I may never finish.

They had stacked the boxes in the kitchen for me to tackle. The first was full of food and dry goods. The second had some girl supplies, laundry soap and clothes that Monica had picked out for me. The third was the biggest surprise...Scott had packed a collection of music, a portable CD player with batteries, several bottles of wine, a big bag of popcorn and a note. I decided to wait until I had a chance to enjoy a glass of wine before reading it. There was one more box to unpack. It was the heaviest, so I left it on the floor to open. There was a ham radio, boxes of what looked like large blue Christmas lights and a lamp. Not an oil lamp, but a lamp that needed electricity in order to be of any use. There had to have been some kind of logic behind it and I was sure Scott's letter would tell all.

Later I settled on the couch with a glass of wine and read the note. He wasn't one for details, so I knew it wouldn't be anything exciting. It was short and to the point...

> **Dear Tess,**
>
> **Generator's on its way. We'll be setting up landing lights on the lake for night flights. Don't get too excited, it's only to be used on rare occasions. Dangerous machine in such a heavily wooded area is a bad thing. Can't risk burning the whole place down.**
>
> **Scott**

I leaned back and stared at the craftsmanship of the huge fireplace. I had to admit I loved the cabin, it was comfortable. I could feel at home living there the rest of my life, but the seclusion would drive me bonkers. I needed to have people around. I used to fight to find quiet and there I was drowning in it. I jumped off the couch and grabbed the CD player. Soft music radiated through the cabin for the first time.

My peaceful moment was suddenly broken by a loud bang. It came from around the outside where the grill was. A bit freaked at first, I gathered up my courage and grabbed the rifle. I decided to go out the front and peak around the corner. I panicked when I saw there was a bear licking the grate on the grill. It wasn't very large, but a bear is a bear no matter what the size. Figuring it would be best to leave the animal alone; I quietly backed away retracing my steps.

Back in the house, I went around and made sure all the doors were secure before I poured another glass of wine, enhanced my calm and sat down at the desk. The reams of paper were cloaked in a thin film of dust. I carefully brushed off each one and placed them in the bottom drawer. I centered the old typewriter in the middle of the desk so I would be able to look out the window at the lake. The cup of pencils and legal pads I pushed to the edge to get them out of my way. I was ready to go. Taking a big swig of wine, I reached in the bottom drawer, removed one crisp sheet of paper, rolled it carefully in the typewriter and set the margins just right. There it was...the very first page of the book I'd always wanted to write. I raised my glass to the typewriter confidently and then belted back the rest of the wine.

I sat there for at least an hour staring blankly at the page before I headed up to bed. Like a fallen soldier I sulked as I listen to the crackle of the fire. Perhaps somewhere in my mind I was afraid to work so hard for something that would end up being a complete flop. I hated rejection more than the idea of taking the time to set up to be rejected. I knew I'd have to get over that hurdle. I wished my grandfather were there to encourage me. He had a knack for making me feel invincible.

CHAPTER FIVE

The bear came every night for a week before it realized there was no more food to scavenge. I hoped it wouldn't get brave enough to come during the day. Finding a book on survival I memorized just about every page. I figured better safe than sorry. I wasn't up on the basics for living in the woods, especially alone.

The day the plane came back it was gently raining. I was surprised that Ryan or Scott would attempt any kind of wet weather flight. The plane approached in the usual corkscrew pattern. I stepped out to watch it land. Just as it was about to set down gently, a gust of wind seemed to whip up the tail section pitching the nose into the lake. As the plane righted itself, it landed with a loud thud, and glided along the water. I ran to the dock as it passed not seeing anyone in the cockpit.

The rain started coming down harder as I panicked, trying to figure out what to do. It was adrift in the middle of the lake. Gathering my courage I jumped in and swam straight for the plane. My clothes were making it difficult to swim, but I pushed on. Each time I got close, it would drift farther away. Finally I was able to grab a pontoon and lift myself up.

Lucky to have reached the right side, I swung open the door. Ryan looked like a rag doll carelessly tossed over the yoke. A deep gash on his forehead and torn seat belt indicated the incident was worse than it had looked from the dock. I hadn't taxied a plane in years, and never a floatplane – but I gave it my best effort. I tried to get the engine to turn over, but it was completely dead. Using the rudder petals helped guide the plane a little, but I still didn't know what to do. The storm was picking up and the wind began to push us around the lake. As I tried to steer in the right direction, we drifted beyond the dock. Not wanting to be stranded in the middle of the lake, I looked around desperately for something that might help. To my relief, found a large coil of rope in the back seat.

Balancing on the pontoon, I tied the rope to the strut, jumped in and with the other end twisted around my arm swam back to the dock. It was a lot closer than before and not as difficult to swim. My only concern was if I had the strength to pull it in. I lifted myself out of the water just as the wind shifted and drifted the plane right to me. I couldn't have been luckier.

I had to find a way to get Ryan out and up to the cabin. Having no idea what to do and worried that if I moved him it would make his injuries worse, I stood there and stared hoping he would wake up and walk his own ass up the path. Right then all the frustration that had built up over the past few months exploded. I wanted to scream so I did.

I screamed so loud, it brought him around. He was dazed, confused and weak. Without saying a word, he shifted his weight allowing me to help him out of the plane. Conscious enough to understand we were heading to the cabin, he leaned against me as we made our way up the path. The rain came down in sheets just as we reached the door. I helped him to the couch and I ran to the storeroom to grab the first aid supplies and blankets.

The gash on his head wasn't too bad but would need a few stitches. I hoped to find butterfly bandages in the kit and some kind of first aid guide to show me what to do. Scott had always been a stickler for safety and this time he hadn't let me down. Once the worst of his injuries were taken care of, I decided to inspect the damage the seat belt must have caused. Opening his shirt I saw the diagonal mark across his chest. Gently I removed his clothes and covered him with the blankets. A nurse I never pretended to be, but for some odd reason the nurturing instinct kicked in and I knew what do.

I knew I had to tie the plane down better and try to call someone on the radio. It wasn't until I'd reached the door that I realized my pants were missing. They must have been pulled off when I climbed onto the pontoon. There I stood in the doorway in nothing more than a tee shirt and underwear. Only in the middle of nowhere could I get away without feeling embarrassed. Shrugging it off, I headed out to secure the plane.

I got in and tried the radio only to find it dead. I should've already known, but at that moment my mind wasn't in a mechanical mode. Feeling like a complete idiot, I wanted to sit there and cry, but I couldn't muster the tears. Knowing it was going to be a long night, I headed back to the cabin to wash up and put on dry clothes.

Ryan spent the night groaning in pain. I sat on the floor and rested my head on the couch while he slept. From time to time, he'd wake up wild-eyed and shout out, "Sarah". I assumed it was the name of his girlfriend or wife.

Around two in the morning, he woke up again and grabbed my hand, "Tess, you must save my baby, she's in the plane." With that statement, I bolted upright. I didn't see anyone else in the plane. I was sure I would've noticed a baby. I thought; *maybe the blankets in the passenger's area had covered her. What if the baby hadn't survived? What kind of man would bring a baby on a plane?* My panic turned to terror.

I didn't consider he was dreaming up the illusion, I just headed for the door. It was still raining, but I could see the plane and ran for it, slipping on the mud as I got to the dock. I cautiously approached, hoping to hear the sound of a baby. All I heard was the rain pounding down around me. I grabbed a flashlight that was rolling around the floor of the cockpit and tossed the seat forward to aim the light over the passenger area. I found a bundle of blankets on the seat, Ryan's flight bag on the floor and some sectionals scattered about. There was no one there, and then suddenly a small whimper came from beneath the blankets. Climbing in further, I slowly lifted the bundle to reveal Ryan's baby.

There, curled up on the seat was a dog, not a very big dog, but still a dog... She couldn't have been more than six months. She was shaking, but her body felt warm. Bundling her in the blankets I carried her carefully up the path. "A dog, his baby's a dog", I mumbled. I couldn't help but feel silly about getting all worked up over a damned dog.

Ryan was still out cold and Sarah began to whimper as if she knew he was in the room. I brought her over and laid her gently by his side. She snuggled right in and quickly fell asleep. Without waking, his arm wrapped around and began to stroke her fur. I couldn't help but smile at the pure happiness on both their faces.

I knew I wouldn't be able to sleep, so I went to the storeroom and grabbed the bag of popcorn and some cocoa. I snuggled into the leather chair in the corner of the room to enjoy my munchies and watch over my guests. It gave me time to reflect a bit and try to formulate the first sentence to my book. I always had the hardest time starting a story, but once I wrote that first sentence, it just began to unfold without much trouble. I wanted my book to be more than words, I wanted it to have a life of it's own.

The warm glow from the fire made haunting images dance on the walls of the great room. I thought if I stared at them long enough, I would eventually fall asleep. Unfortunately I had no such luck. The hours went by slowly and finally around the time I saw it getting light outside, Ryan woke up. He didn't notice me sitting in the corner, as he quietly whispered to Sarah. I'd seen men go gah gah for animals before, but he was different. He talked to her as if she was really a baby.

Moving her off the couch, he swung his legs around and set his feet on the floor. Still not noticing I was in the room, he looked around the coffee table and then over his shoulder. "Looking for something special?" I said quietly trying not to startle him.

"My clothes, I can tell I'm naked." Shooting me a sideways glance and a smirk "and you call yourself a lady."

I chuckled. Someone in as much pain, as he had to be in, cracking a joke. I was amazed. I could see it wasn't going to be too difficult to include him in my short list of friends. He had a sense of humor and that was the most important tool I felt every person should carry around with them.

Taking a breath I confessed, "Yes, it was me...I did it...I'm completely guilty of removing your clothes. It was either that or hang you out to dry along with them. I figured you'd prefer the couch."

"Thanks Tess, I appreciate what you did for me and Sarah." He bent down and gave her a snuggle. "She's very important to me."

"Tell you what…I'll make a pot of coffee and a great breakfast… you just sit there and re-coup a bit." I turned and skipped into the kitchen with Sarah at my heels.

"I'd love to but…"

"I want no arguments from you, the plane's dead so you're going nowhere. Not another word, I've made up your mind."

"That's fine, but you better let me at least go to the bathroom." He rose from the couch and gathered the blanket around to cover up his handsome naked body.

"Well I guess if you gotta go, you gotta go. I'll bring your clothes."

Wrung out and hanging by the fire, I was surprised he hadn't noticed them. Then again, he did have a large gash on his head. I was a little nervous about him seeing what was under the bandage. It wasn't pretty, but it would heal without having stitches. I hoped he didn't have other injuries I wasn't aware of. Sarah on the other hand was perfectly fine, she may have been tossed about, but she didn't seem traumatized by it.

He took his time in the bathroom. Tired of waiting for him, Sarah went to the front door and whined. I took the hint and let her out. She must've been dying to run around and perhaps take care of a little business. She took off around the house and disappeared into the woods. She came back about an hour later scratching at the front door carrying my wet jeans in her mouth.

"I guess I wasn't the only one who lost clothes last night." Grinning he held up the jeans like a kid with a trophy.

After breakfast, I moved a chair out to the dock so he could sit and watch me unload the plane. As I worked, I told him what had happened the night before. He stood up and gave me a soft hug. "Thanks Tess, we'd still be in the middle of the lake if it weren't for you."

"Yup, but it wouldn't have happened if I wasn't here in the first place." I said as I turned back to the boxes I unloaded.

"If you weren't here, I would have never metcha", with that, he sat back down. I shook the thought out of my mind and went back to work. I had a little trouble lifting the generator out of the plane, but I wasn't gonna let him lift a finger.

Ryan enjoyed being the one in the chair with me doing all the heavy work. To my surprise he began cracking jokes at the speed of light. He was a lot more open than the first time he had visited. With all the razzing he was dishing out, I retaliated by dubbing him "King Ryan the Lame".

The day flew by quickly and before I knew it we were sitting down to dinner. I set out food for Sarah in the kitchen away from where we'd be walking. Ryan recommended not putting her dish outside because the wild animals would make a habit of coming around for food. That was the last thing I wanted. I relayed the bear story to him and he agreed we should find a way to lock down and cover the grill.

With a bottle of wine between us, we sat on the floor against the couch looking into the fire and telling each other stories about our crazy lives. Ryan was a wild child the same as most flyboys who didn't settle down until after college. He'd been in a plane accident one time before where he was the only one who survived. For about a year he wouldn't go near a plane, let alone entertain the thought of ever flying again. His father was originally from Ireland, but moved to the States when he was a little boy. He married a woman who was widowed young leaving her and her daughter to start a new life. Ryan was born a year after they married.

It was a warm and cozy moment I didn't want to end. I felt so comfortable with him. It had always been difficult for me to be myself around people until I had known them awhile. I was a better flirt than I was Tess Kelly. I guess maturity took over and I realized that someone in his condition would be in no mood for romantic undertones and a giggly ditz to talk to. It was late so I said my good nights and headed up to bed.

CHAPTER SIX

By the time I finally coaxed myself out of the cozy warmth of the blankets, Ryan was already working on the plane. I was fully awake, and eager to join him so I got up, dressed and headed out the door. Face smeared with dirt; he was completely focused on the engine. It took him a moment to realize I was standing there.

"I'll be able to fix it, but I need some parts. I think we need to set up the generator and get some help." He stood up wiping his hands on his jeans. "Taylor's not expecting me back for another week, so he has no idea there's a problem." It took me a moment to figure out that he was talking about Scott, I hadn't heard anyone call him Taylor since college.

"I guess we better head up to the cabin to make that call. While you're setting it up, I'll fix something to eat. Sound good?" For a brief moment, our eyes met sending tingles up my spine. His eyes were enchanting. I couldn't tell if I was really attracted to him or just feeling a bit lonely. Even dirt smudged and sweaty, he was handsome.

"Let's go, I'm starved." He turned and quickly walked up the path. I stood for a moment watching him, wondering if I should make a move. I knew he wasn't married, but he never really showed any interest in me. I decided then to let it go. If something was going to happen, it would just happen.

It didn't take him long to set up the radio and contact someone at the base. We found out Scott was on a cross-country, but they could send a plane with the parts he needed within a few days. As we ate, he told me it would take a day or two to make all the repairs. He worried about putting me out by staying, but I couldn't have thought of a better distraction.

"It's nice to have someone around; you're welcome to stay as long as you need." With that, I took up the plates and headed to the sink. I was about to pump the water, when he came up behind me and placed his hands gently on my shoulders. A warm sensation swept over me. I was as nervous as a high school girl on a first date.

"Mind if I use your shower?" He whispered. I could feel his breath brush the back of my neck. I wanted to melt into his body, but I held my composure.

Without moving a muscle I replied "Any time you'd like." I couldn't think. I just wanted him to stay; right there so I could enjoy the feeling a bit longer.

"Thanks Tess, you're the best." He said with excitement as he gave my shoulders a squeeze and headed out the door. I stood there unable to move. Just one touch turned me to jelly. I may have read more into it than was intended, but I didn't care. Standing there, daydreaming I finished the dishes.

The dog barking broke my trance. Grabbing a dishtowel to wipe my hands, I stepped out the door and went around the side of the cabin. To my surprise, there was Ryan, standing in the open air shower, covered with suds.

"I thought you were using the shower inside." Tossing the dishtowel over my shoulder. Although he was behind a small fence, I pretended to divert my eyes.

"Water's warmer out here. You mind getting me a towel? I forgot to grab one." He said tugging the cord to let the water trickle down his back.

With a smirk, I walked up to the fence and held out the dishtowel. "Here ya go."

He looked down at the towel, then up at me. "I'm sure it would amuse you if I paraded around in this scrap." With a wink, he took it and began to dry his hair. "If I ever get dry enough to put my clothes on, perhaps we can take a walk in the woods. I need to move around and work out these sore muscles."

"Okay, you talked me into it; I'll get you a bigger towel." I turned and headed back into the cabin.

Later we headed into the woods for our adventure. Deciding to make a day of it, I brought along a backpack with a nice picnic lunch. We chose a well-worn path that wound around the lake. It didn't take us too deep into the woods and we were able to look through the trees to the cabin. Not too close and yet just far enough to make it interesting. As we reached the opposite side of the lake from the cabin, we found another trail that took us deeper into the forest.

Just as it became difficult to follow the trail, we stumbled upon a small clearing. It was the perfect place to have lunch. Once the sandwiches were devoured, we sat back and gazed up at the leafy canopy. The dappled sunlight danced as the trees swayed in the breeze.

"Do you miss your family?" He said thoughtfully. I hadn't realized he was staring at me.

"I miss my grandfather and Mary. My brother and sister, I don't miss so much. They never really took the time to know me." Not wanting to continue this line of question, I rolled over on my side to face him.

"If you had a chance to go anywhere in the world- free of charge, where would you go?" I asked, trying to change the subject.

"I think I'd go to Ireland and visit my relatives. My sister lives here, but my cousins, uncles and aunts are back there. It seems to be the thing to do if you're Irish. He stopped only for a moment, to ponder the question a little more. "Actually, Tess, I like it here." Completely unexpected, he leaned over and kissed me, his lips gently brushed against mine. "Thank you for making me feel so welcome." He stood up and headed into the woods.

I could still feel the whisper of his kiss on my lips. Using the backpack for a pillow, I laid back. I couldn't figure out why he held back from what could have been a very romantic moment. I closed my eyes to think of all the possible reasons. I kept them closed when I heard him return. I felt his breath hot on my cheek and a soft brush of hair against my shoulder. A powerful desire for him began to consume me, I knew I had to have this man or go nuts.

Suddenly something didn't feel right and I began to panic. My eyes flew open and found myself face to face with a bear. It had to have been the same one that came to the cabin. I laid there frozen with fear. I knew bears were dangerous and the whole "act dead" thing was bullshit. My breath began to come quick in my chest as it sniffed around my face. Although it hadn't touched me, I was pinned to the spot. Just when I thought it was about to rear up to attack, Ryan came flying out from the woods waving his arms and yelling. The bear bolted in the opposite direction.

I couldn't move. My body began to shake as I tried to catch my breath. "Tess, are you okay? Did he get you anywhere?" frantically he checked me over. The whole time I stared at him, still in shock. Taking me in his arms he rocked me gently trying to bring me back to reality. I felt numb. Slowly I came around and sat up. He still looked concerned as he searched my eyes for some kind of response.

"I'm okay Ryan... I'm fine. Thanks." I took his face in my hands and pulled him to me. It was the most natural kiss I had ever felt. His arms went around my back as he drew me into his body. Tears began to stream down my face. Pulling away from me, he hesitated. He looked away and got to his feet holding out his hands to help me up.

"Let's get you back. A glass of wine will calm us down." We gathered everything up and headed back.

When we reached the door, Sarah came out of the woods and followed us in. I thought to myself, *where the hell was she when all that happened? Damn dog would've let the bear maul me to death.*

I felt like an ass. I should've never forced myself on him. After a cool shower I headed up to bed without a word. I looked down to see him lying on the couch with Sarah. The man and his beloved dog snuggled together reading a book. I felt oddly rejected, yet strangely caught up in my own fantasies. The traumatic bear incident didn't play as heavy on my mind as did the thought of Ryan pushing me away.

Sometime in the night, Sarah had come up to the loft and crawled into bed with me. Needing to feel any kind of affection, I put an arm around her and pulled her close. Giving a sigh, she settled in and fell asleep. The fire kept the cabin dimly lit and it danced shadows on the walls. Looking down at the couch, I saw Ryan wasn't there. I figured he had gone to the bathroom so I closed my eyes and went back to sleep.

A wet nose and whimper woke me up early. Sarah was eager for me to open the door and let her run. She only liked being inside at night, but once the sun was up – she'd take off into the woods for the rest of the day. She too, loved the adventure. That or she had some big secret.

Ryan was nowhere to be found. I checked to see if he had slept in the plane, but it was empty. Assuming he had gone for a walk in the woods, I made breakfast hoping the smell of bacon would entice him back to the cabin. I wanted to apologize for my behavior and thank him for saving my life. The need to get everything I was feeling out in the open was eating at me.

It wasn't until noon when I began to worry something had happened to him. Wondering if he had taken off in the middle of the night, I went to the couch to check to see if the blanket were laid out. My heart dropped when I saw them folded neatly on the coffee table. I didn't know what to do. If I went into the woods, I wouldn't know which way to go.

I sat down and stared blankly at the wall. As I sank further into the couch, I spied a piece of paper tucked under the blankets. I picked it up and saw he had written my name and nothing more. It looked as though he had planned to write me a note. As if struck by lightning, I got the idea to look to see if anything was missing from the storeroom. If he had planned to leave on foot, he would've packed some essentials.

The rifle was still by the door, but I noticed a flashlight and the pistol were missing. At least I knew he'd be able to defend himself if he had to. Worried he was lost or injured I looked around outside to see if I could figure out in which direction he went. It took me awhile but I found his footprints leading from the back door into the woods. There was a rough path but there were no more footsteps to follow. Taking a chance, I ventured in.

I walked a few yards before finding another clue he had been there. Part of the bandage that covered his wound was lying on the ground. I knew I was on the right track, but worried I would go too far and not know how to get back. The trees were getting thicker and it became more difficult to navigate the path.

I wondered what the hell brought him this far into the forest. As I was about to turn around to find my way back, I saw a clearing just beyond the dense pack of trees. Curiosity pulled me forward. It was beautiful, a large meadow of wild flowers that were waist high. The perfume floated on the wind. Like a child, I began to run through the thicket forgetting the reason why I was there, and began to gather up a large bouquet.

It was a nice surprise in the middle of a stressful day. Feeling a little more focused, I decided to head back. If Ryan wasn't there, I'd wait until sunset then call for help. The walk back went quicker since it was down hill. In the distance I heard a roar of thunder and noticed clouds had begun to fill the sky.

I was relieved to see he had stirred the fire and lit the lamps around the great room. I poked my head out the door and saw he was down by the plane, tinkering with the engine. Deciding not to disturb him I went back inside. I headed into the bathroom to set up a shower. The water was cold and not too relaxing. Wrapped in a towel I headed straight for the fire. Staring into the flames, I contemplated what to say to make things right between us. Feeling a bit warmer, I backed my way to the couch and began to sit.

His hands grabbed my waist and brought me down gently on his lap. With a laughing smile he said, "So, you went looking for me didn't you?" Tears welling up in my eyes, I nodded and threw my arms around his shoulders. "No reason to go to pieces on me. I just went on an adventure." He closed his arms around me gently.

After a few moments, I loosened my grip, sat up and turned to face him. "Do you have any idea what you put me through today? For all I knew you could've been injured, or worse, killed."

"I'm sorry, but I had to give you some space. You're supposed to be here writing and here I am keeping you from your work. Taylor would kill me if he knew I was having this much fun distracting you and not working on that damn plane of his." He looked surprised at his own words. I wasn't sure he meant to admit that to me.

"You're a wonderful guy and you saved my life. You can distract me as much as you like." I paused for a moment. "I know I am a bit bold, but yesterday when we kissed I felt there was something special between us…I'd like the chance to feel that again." My heart was pounding in my chest. I couldn't believe the words came out of my mouth. Had I really made such a bold confession?

He pulled me close. His lips were soft and inviting. There was no hesitation, only a sweet tenderness. As he leaned back to get more comfortable, he took me with him. We didn't eat, drink or leave the couch the rest of the night. We just laid there enjoying the feeling of our lips together and our warm embrace.

CHAPTER SEVEN

It was heaven waking up in his arms. Propping myself up, I gazed down at his handsome features. It was still dark outside but the fire cast a golden glow over the room. I couldn't help but smile as I watched him sleep. He had captured my heart, but I was afraid to loose my soul. My mind raced with hopes, desires and fears. I wanted to take it one day at a time and not let myself rush into anything. I messed up so many relationships by going too far too fast. He was so damn handsome; I didn't know how I was going to control myself.

My thoughts were interrupted when I saw his mouth draw into a smile. "I can feel you watching me." I felt his hand glide up my back as I brushed my lips along the curve of his neck.

"Did you have a nice nap?" I teased.

Drawing me into his body, he moaned, "Yes, but I think if we lay her much longer I'm not gonna be able to control myself."

"Me either" I whispered softly. "I think we should get up and watch the sunrise." Trailing kisses up his neck, across his cheek, over his lips.

I positioned myself over him, straddling his hips. I could feel how excited he was. Although we were both adults, I felt like a teenager experimenting for the first time. A bit scared to take it to the next level, but wanting to go all the way. His hands glided up my arms as he drew me back down to his lips. He reminded me, "You're right, we need to get up before this goes too far." his lips curved into sly grin, "Tess... I think I need a shower."

As he sat up, I wrapped my legs around his body. I couldn't help but laugh as he carried me like a baby on his hips to the kitchen. I kissed him one more time before lowering myself to the floor.

"I'll be back in five, think you can make some coffee?" He winked as he grabbed a towel and headed outside.

"Sure can, want me to bring warm water for your shower?"

Calling over his shoulder he said, "Nope, I don't think that would help right now."

I set the kettle by the coals in the fireplace and dashed into the bathroom. It was chilly, but it helped to shake me back to reality. The icy water soaked me completely in one big swoosh. It was all I needed to bring me back to earth. Teeth chattering, I toweled off and changed into fresh clothes.

When I came back to the great room I caught Ryan standing in front of the fire bouncing up and down rubbing his arms. As I approached, he put up his hand "stop woman, I can only handle one cold shower a day!" I couldn't help laughing...he almost looked serious.

I deciding to give him a break, "Okay, I'll keep my distance until you're a little warmer. Coffee?" I asked holding up the kettle of hot water grinning from ear to ear.

We headed outside to find we had missed the sunrise. A buzzing sound in the distance broke through the silence of the morning. We both knew what was heading our way. My heart sank as my hopes of spending time together were crushed. I grabbed onto the new hopes that the repairs would take a few days, or maybe the approaching plane didn't have the parts, or better yet it would fly right over and not give us a second thought! A lot of maybes were going through my mind, cupping my coffee; I looked up to watch the plane approach. In such a short time, I had gone from completely happy to royally bummed. Ryan must have felt the same way. He came up behind me and wrapped his arms around my waist, holding me tight as we watched it land.

Not wanting to face the reality of it, I headed back to the cabin leaving Ryan to deal with the visitor. I slumped onto the couch and listen to the muffled voices outside. I sat there and sulked like a baby forgetting my promise to take it one day at a time.

The day had dragged by and I didn't accomplish anything. I puttered around the cabin, occasionally peeking out the window to see what Ryan and the stranger were doing. About noon, I made some sandwiches, and headed down to the dock. With the echo of "Clear prop", a puff of smoke and a whirring sound, the engine turned over.

Leaving the plane running, Ryan stepped onto the dock and headed towards me grabbing a sandwich. "I'm starving...we didn't have breakfast remember, I thought you'd never bring us food." Leaning in a bit, he whispered, " I'll have to thank you later." He winked and grabbed another sandwich before heading back to the plane.

I didn't want to get in the way, so I put the tray on a crate and headed into the woods. I found a stump that was partially hidden by a tree; it gave me a perfect view of the lake and the guys. I sat there watching them work until it started to get dark. As they headed up to the cabin, I decided it was time to join them.

The stranger's name was Kevin, he couldn't have been more than eighteen. Red hair and freckles, didn't help his little boy looks, it only enhanced it. After soup and sandwiches, we sat in front of the fire listening while Kevin rambled on about something. I didn't hear a word he said my mind was dreaming about being alone with Ryan. Pretending I was tired, I said goodnight and headed up to bed. Lying there, I wondered what Kevin had said. I wasn't sure if he asked me any questions, but I knew I made a pretty bad first impression. The look on Ryan's face earlier told me he knew I wasn't listening. Not wanting to torture myself further, I drifted off to sleep.

All was quiet when I headed down to grab a cup of coffee, I figured the guys were out working on the plane. If they'd managed to get it airworthy, Ryan would have to leave. Knowing Scott, he'd want him back as soon as possible. The thought of being alone again, left me numb. I'd have to find things to fill my days, perhaps begin writing. I pushed the thought out of my mind. The least I could do was to pull myself together and enjoy what time we had left.

When I got to the dock, both of them were taking a swim. "I guess I slept in?"

"Well if it isn't her Royal Highness, yes, it's almost noon...feel like taking a dip with a couple of good looking guys?" Ryan said as he floated on his back.

"Humm, sounds real tempting...I better not, might be dangerous." Putting my hands on my hips and grinning.

"For who, you or us?" shouted Kevin. I was surprised to find that he too was a classic smart-ass. I would've known that if I paid attention the night before; I probably missed out on a good time.

We finished off the day with a fish fry and game of poker before Kevin took off leaving us alone. I was thrilled that we would have some private time together. There was so much I wanted to say and do, but I didn't know how long he'd be able to stay.

As if he read my mind, "I'm leaving tonight too; in fact, I've gotta go before it gets too dark." He said grabbing my hand. "Tess, I want you to know I have no regrets. I've loved spending time with you and hope we can do it again...I'll come back." He looked into my eyes searching for any sign of what I was thinking.

I was speechless, but knew there was no way to make him stay. "You just make sure you do." Smirking, I added "and bring me presents."

He threw back his head and laughed. Taking me up in his arms he kissed me playfully spinning me around. "I am gonna miss you! Don't forget me while I'm gone"

"Fat chance of that, I don't know if you've noticed, but it's not exactly party central around here. Who could ever make me forget you?" Giggling like a teenager.

"Well Tess Kelly, I must be off. Write something special while I'm gone." Nodding I mustered a smile. The lump in my throat didn't allow me to say a word. I lifted up on my toes and kissed him. We hugged for a short while before he called out for Sarah and loaded the plane. I stood on the dock watching it disappear over the mountains.

Alone again... was such an odd feeling, as if I'd lost everything in a matter of minutes. I stood there hoping to hear the plane come back, but it didn't. I waited until it got dark and headed back inside. I opened the door and the emptiness inside hit me like a ton of bricks. I made up my mind to be strong and do what I was sent there to do.

I went to the pantry, grabbed a bottle of wine from the top shelf, snagged a glass from the kitchen and flipped on the stereo.

With a new attitude, I bravely sat down at the desk, positioned the typewriter and began to let all my thoughts and feelings flow through my fingers. I wasn't aiming to write anything in particular, any structured sentences, no paragraphs...just pure unadulterated crap. I wanted to get words on paper knowing I would sort it out another time.

I'd been typing for at least an hour when I realized the cabin had become cold. Afraid to stop for fear my thoughts would freeze up and I'd be right back where I started, I tried to trick my mind into believing it didn't matter and I went on until my fingers began to cramp. The tap tap tap of the typewriter drowned out the music and I hadn't realized the batteries had rendered their last bit of juice. I gave in and threw some logs on the dying fire stirring it until I had a large blaze going.

As I stared into the flames, my mind began to draw images of Ryan, his bare chest, his handsome face, his dazzling smile. I was completely hooked on his memory. Closing my eyes, I wrapped my arms around me pretending they were his. Picturing everything I could about him made my heart ache. I hadn't felt that kind of longing for someone since Scott.

I laid down on the couch and snuggled into the pillows. Still smelling Ryan's cologne imbedded in the fabric, the images began again, only stronger and more defined. I must have been dreaming because the next thing I knew, the room was growing cold again and it was morning.

CHAPTER EIGHT

For days I stayed at the typewriter, letting all my thoughts flow freely. I was consumed by it. It helped to make the time fly by and kept my mind off my growing feelings for Ryan. Occasionally, with pen and paper in hand I would walk down to the dock to dangle my feet in the water and write a letter to him.

The days were getting warmer and it rained less. I'd take short walks in the woods, never venturing too far from the lake. Being alone, I kept myself company by talking aloud as if there was someone else with me. As silly as it seemed, it helped me to stay sane.

The area around the cabin became so familiar; I could navigate it in the dark or with my eyes closed. I began to embrace my solace. The cabin and surrounding areas would've made a great a resort for people who liked nature. It was a thought I pondered on some days and rejected on others. It was becoming my home, my haven. I had spent years traveling around the world to see all there was to see. No matter what exotic location I could think of, none compared with the freedom I found at the lake. There was no shopping mall, no friends within calling distance, no hustle, no noise; it was a place I could let my hair down and just be me.

Peace and serenity, how long could I possibly stand it before going bonkers? That question plagued me every day I opened my eyes to see the sunrise. I'd heard stories about people who were lost and survived several months alone. They'd go completely mad. I knew I had to keep myself grounded. My writing kept me busy, but

I needed to find other avenues of entertainment. I decided to tackle some of the books that sat on the shelves.

One night, I grabbed a stack and set them on the table in front of the couch. It was unusually hot in the cabin so I kept only one lamp lit. The first book on the top of the stack was well worn as though someone had carried it around rubbing off the gold title. Even the words on the binding were unreadable. I ran my fingers across the fabric to see if I could feel the letters that used to be there. I always loved the look, feel and smell of old books.

The pages were aged and browning, but the print was still readable. Surprised to find they weren't brittle, I leafed through each barely skimming the contents. I must have been about halfway through the book when I turned a page and found it had been altered. The center of several pages had been cut out and a block of wood rested snugly in the space.

Careful not to tear the pages, I removed the block of wood and put the book aside, The rounded edges, rich grain and the high polish made it look almost plastic. In the dim light, I couldn't tell if there were any markings or seems that would allow it to open. Putting it on the table, I picked up the book to see if there was some kind of clue to its meaning. I leafed through the rest of the pages and found a sealed envelope with my grandfather's name on it. It seemed to be as old as the book itself and appeared to have never been opened.

The glue on the envelope was crusty and came away from the paper without ripping. Inside was a crisp note card with the letter "S" printed on the front and lined in silver foil. Parting the folded paper, I saw a beautifully handwritten message. I felt like I was snooping into the private world of my grandfather. As I tried to read, the words began to run together. My head started to hurt and I realized the room was blazing hot, it was making it hard for me to concentrate. Running my fingers through my hair, I tossed the note on the table and slumped back on the couch.

The letter would have to wait. I knew I needed to get some sleep and find a way to cut through the heat. I went into the bathroom, took off all my clothes and doused myself with a shower of cool water. Feeling a bit more refreshed; I wrapped myself in a towel and headed out to the dock where I could sit in the night air and hope for a cool breeze.

The moon was full and the water looked inviting, so I dove in. Never before would I've had the guts to skinny dip. I floated on my back and gazed up at the stars. The type of moment I wish I had someone to share with. Again I began to think of Ryan. I was missing him. I knew someone would be coming soon, the supplies were almost gone and he had promised to come back as soon as he could. He had to be coming. He couldn't have just forgotten me. As I began to panic, I remembered the radio. I swam quickly back to the dock, jumped up and raced towards the cabin. *Why hadn't I thought to call before? What was I thinking?* I must have been going mad!

I found the power and clicked it on, but nothing happened. I didn't hear fuzz or see any lights. *How could it be more complicated then flipping a switch*? I thought to myself. "Damn things broken." I screamed as I slammed my fist on the table. Paranoia began to sink in as my mind went wild. Giggling, I said aloud "It can't be broken, Ryan used this same radio to call for parts. How could it be broken now?" Biting my lip, I began to pace the kitchen tapping my fingers against my mouth. "Maybe he didn't make the call? Maybe he's not who I think he is? Maybe he broke the radio after he made his call?"

My panic turned to terror as I convinced myself I was stranded. "I could die and no one would know I was here." The more frantic I became, the hotter the room got. Sweat streamed down my face and into my eyes. Everything in the room began to blur, I screamed out "Blind! I'm going blind". The room was spinning as my leg went limp making me fall to the floor.

I laid there, barely covered by a towel. I couldn't find the strength to stand up. Giving into my weakness I closed my eyes against my fears. My mind went wild with images and flashes of light. I wasn't sure how long I laid there before hearing muffled noises outside the cabin. My throat was dry and I couldn't scream for help, so weak I couldn't open my eyes to see if it was day or night. I just remember thinking I was going to die.

Not knowing if I was dead or alive, I had the sensation of floating and then ice cold against my skin. I tried to open my eyes, but it felt like there was something heavy on my face. I couldn't tell if what I was experiencing was real or if I was dreaming. My skin was on fire and then suddenly I felt a moment of relief, as though I had stepped into a cold bath. Not able to fight against it, I gave in to the experience.

When I came around, I was still unable to move, open my eyes or speak. I could smell the flowers outside and hear the birds in the trees. I knew I was alive and somehow had managed to make it to the couch. I began to feel a little stronger and realized I had a wet dishcloth over my eyes and a sheet covering my body. My arms felt like lead as I tried to remove the cloth from my face. A bright light burned through my closed eyelids. Squinting against the glare, I slowly opened my eyes to see it was the light of day that had caused my pain.

I gathered my strength, and scooted my legs off the couch. Rolling onto my stomach I used my arms to push myself up. My legs were weak, but with my knees together, I was able to stand. At that moment, the door flew open startling me. Before I knew it, I was falling backwards and then blackness.

"Tess? Tess? You okay?" a panicked voice rang in my ears. "Damn it Tess, you've gotta open your eyes!" Suddenly a strong foul odor penetrated my senses and my eyes flung open. Everything was blurry and my head was throbbing. I reached up to find the cause of my pain.

"Keep your arms down Tess; you've got quite a bump on the back of your head." The voice was muffled but seemed familiar.

I dropped my hand to my chest and realized I had no clothes on. Laying there in front of God knows who bare ass naked. "Clothes, I need my clothes" my voice sounded weak and far away.

"Here, this should cover you. It's not like I haven't seen you naked before." Just then I recognized the voice.

"Scott? Is that you?" I reached my hand up to the fuzzy blob beside me.

"Yes, now shut up and drink this." He brought a glass to my lips and let the cool water trickle down my throat. I wanted more, but my stomach began to twist as I pushed the glass away. For no reason at all, I began to cry. Rocking me in his arms, he comforted me.

"I'm sorry, I just feel so weak." I managed to say. I tried to focus my eyes, but everything was fuzzy.

"You've been very sick Tess, you need to relax and let me take care of you until you get your strength back." He slowly got up and helped me to sit. The sheet fell to the floor. I tried to grab it, but my arms were too weak.

"Could you please cover me up? I feel stupid sitting here in front of you half naked." I brought my hand to my head trying to stop the throbbing.

"Half naked? Geeze Tess. I had you laid out full naked for the past three days. No need to be modest with me now." Hearing the sarcasm in his voice, I tossed out my hand trying to land a slap on his face.

"You're such and asshole! Give me a little dignity." I reached around trying to find the sheet. He draped it over me, bent down and kissed my forehead. "Your fever's broken, I think you're going to live."

I managed to smile, "Thanks Doctor Scott, you saved my life." Trying to be a smart ass.

As he walked away I heard him whisper "Yes I did."

CHAPTER NINE

My strength returned a little more each day, but I still had trouble seeing clearly. Not wanting Scott to make a big deal of it, I kept quiet. When I knew he wasn't in the room, I felt my way around trying to memorize where everything was. I even went so far as to sit in front of the typewriter and crank out a few pages of pure crap.

One night he told me Kevin had returned from his flight with a serious illness that he must have passed on to me. Ryan came down with a slight cold, but recovered quickly. He had arranged for someone to deliver my supplies once a month and figured I would have contacted base if I were in trouble. I was too sick to realize the generator needed to be on for the radio to work. I had been wild with fever and completely out of my mind.

A week had gone by and I began to wonder why he hadn't left. Normally his schedule wouldn't permit him to take so much time off and I was sure his wife wouldn't approve of his extended stay. If he was concerned with my health, he would've flown me to a Doctor or at least contacted someone on the radio. I wondered if there was more to his visit. Not wanting to butt into his business, I kept my mouth shut.

Taking advantage of having him there, I decided to do something special for the man who "saved my life". Searching through the unpacked boxes in the storeroom, I found some emergency candles and bottle of champagne. I grabbed a package of smoked salmon from the shelf and headed into the kitchen. Gathering some veggies from the garden, I set to work making a fabulous meal for us to enjoy. Scott had brought a propane stove for the kitchen. It made it a lot easier to prepare meals and wouldn't heat up the whole cabin.

I hadn't seen him most of the day and figured he was giving me some space. Feeling a bit spunky, I flicked on the stereo that had been refreshed with brand new batteries and cranked up the tunes. I cleared off the table in front of the fireplace, set up the candles and laid out the food. Once everything was perfect, I headed to the door to call Scott.

Just as I was about to reach for the handle, the door flew open. "Tess! I have to go, there's been an accident." Before I could say anything, he grabbed his bag and ran back to the dock. I raced after him.

"Scott, slow down, what accident? Who?" I ran towards his blurry figure.

"One of the planes went down, I need to get back to base." He said tossing his bag in the plane.

"Wait, you can't fly when your all wound up like this. You could crash yourself." I grabbed at him hoping to catch his arm. I must have been further away than I thought, because all I felt was air.

"You still can't see can you?" I couldn't read his expression, but I heard the concern in his voice. "Why didn't you tell me? Shit, what the hell am I going to do now?" He paused for a moment, "Get your shit, you're coming with me. I can't leave you here alone"

"I can see fine, it's just a little fuzzy." Not wanting to be the cause of more stress, "Go, I'll be fine. Just be sure to fly carefully."

I could feel him staring at me trying to look for some kind of spark that would set his mind at ease. I flashed him a smile "Don't worry, I'm a tough broad!" He grabbed me by the shoulders and gave me a hug. "I'll be back soon and if not, I'll send someone up to stay with you." With that, he jumped into the plane.

As I stood there hearing the engine turn over, it occurred to me that Scott had a small fleet and only a few pilots. My heart sank, as the thought of Ryan being the emergency became a possibility. Once the sound of the plane faded into the distance, I went back to the lonely cabin.

Starring down at the meal, I no longer felt hungry. I cleared off the table and popped open the champagne. The whole year was becoming a nightmare. Reflecting on that, I took a big swig from the bottle and settled in for the night.

Two weeks passed before the plane came back. My heart leapt as I ran to the dock to watch it land. In my heart, I hoped Ryan was the pilot. I was worried that he hadn't missed me as much as I had him. I didn't tell Scott about us, afraid that he would get upset. Even though I knew he was married, the memory of that intense moment we shared when I first arrived haunted me. I wasn't completely sure Scott would accept the idea of Ryan and me together.

My heart raced as the plane drifted towards the dock. I couldn't make out the faces clearly, but I could tell it was two people. One had light hair the other dark. I dropped to my knees and felt for the tie downs to help secure the plane. My attempt was in vain; I was too excited to focus my eyes.

"Tess, let me help. You'll never find it that way." Scott grabbed my arm and lifted me up.

"I'm glad you came back…and in one piece." Casually tossing my hair to one side. "Who'd ya bring with you?"

"Well, I kinda had to bring him. It's Ryan. I figured he could keep you company, and you can help take care of him." He said without so much as a quiver in his voice, so I didn't think too much about it.

"Well then, I'll head up to the cabin and fix us something to eat, unless you need my help here?" Not even bothering to wait for a response; I took off up the path. I could hear him laughing as he watched me go. I knew the guys could unload the plane without me, and I wanted to make sure that I looked just right for Ryan.

I stared at the fuzzy blob looking back in the mirror. Concentrating hard, I was able to make out my features a little. I ran the brush through my hair and rinsed my mouth with mouthwash. It wasn't necessary, but I wanted to be minty fresh just in case we were able to steal a moment alone. I could hear their voices in the other room and figured they had finished unloading. I waited a few moments before making my entrance.

From where I stood, I could see the images of Ryan sitting on the couch and Scott making his way over to me. "Just a sec Ry, I'll go get Tess...want a beer?" Scott patted his shoulder and walked over to me. Without a word, he grabbed my arm and took me back into the bathroom.

My heart began to beat fast as I felt the urgency in his actions. "What's going on? Is Ryan sick or something?" Choking back the tears, I waited for him to explain.

"It's nothing Tess, he's just in shock. He was the one who found the pilot that had gone down. The kid died. It must have brought up memories he wasn't ready to relive; I guess it kind of hit him hard when he saw Kevin in that crash." He took a deep breath and sighed. I could tell he was trying to control his own emotions. "The NTSB report's not in yet, but I know it wasn't pilot error. It was the same plane Ryan ditched in the lake; I've had it grounded since the day he landed back at base. He was lucky to have made it back at all. Kevin shouldn't have been up in a plane in the first place."

The tears I'd been holding back ran down my check. He shook my shoulders, "I need you to stop that, you can't be around him if you're gonna fall to pieces. I don't want a lot of blubbering, it'll only make it worse for him and he'll never snap out of this funk...So wash your face, slap on a smile and come out and join us. Don't worry about cooking; no one's hungry right now any way."

I couldn't tell if I was crying because Kevin was dead, or because I was relieved it wasn't Ryan. Scott was right, I had to suck it up and play perfect hostess. I dried my tears and headed out to join them.

He hadn't moved an inch from where he sat on the couch. Scott had gone back down to the lake to fuss with the plane. I was given a moment to be with the man who had filled my thoughts for the past few months. Coming up behind him, I leaned around to give him a kiss. "I've missed you."

I draped my arms across his chest and rested my chin on his shoulder. He didn't say a word. I couldn't tell if his eyes were open or closed. I was about to get up when his hands reached up to hold me in place. He didn't want me to move; just then I felt the tears rolling down his cheek. I knew at that moment, he needed me.

I knew he needed time to work through his memories. The three of us stayed out of each other's way. I kept busy writing, Ryan ambled through the woods and Scott spent the days reading or fishing in the lake. Once again I had the feeling there was more to Scott's visit than what I had assumed.

On a balmy day, Ryan had fallen asleep on the couch so I headed down to the dock where Scott was lazing in the sun. "Want to take a walk in the woods? You'll find it's a lot cooler then being out in the open." I reached out my hand to help him up. I wanted to see if he would confess what was really bothering him.

"Sure…it'll give us a chance to talk." He grabbed my hand and we headed into the forest along the path that led to the meadow. As we walked along the trail, I wasn't sure what to say to break the silence. Suddenly I felt uneasy with him. There wasn't the usual feeling of security. His grip on my hand tightened like a vise, as he started walking faster almost dragging me along the path.

"Stop! I can't see where we're going…slow down." I got scared. I could feel his anger, but didn't know what I had done to make him act that way. "What are you doing?" I screamed.

Suddenly he stopped and let go of my hand. Not expecting it, I fell back and hit the ground hard. I sat stunned, trying to concentrate my eyes to see where he was and what he was going to do. He stood over me with his head buried in his hands. I clawed my way up to my knees. "What the hell is going on with you?" I screamed, tears running down my face. "What did I do to you to make you treat me like this?"

In a panic, he reached down and pulled me up into his arms. I could feel his heart racing in his chest. "Tess, I'm so sorry. Forgive me. So much is going on I just exploded… I didn't mean to take it out on you." The tension in his voice, and his crushing hug told me he needed to get a lot off his chest.

"It's okay… just relax. Tell me what's wrong." I tried to raise my arms to comfort him, but his grip was too tight.

More gently this time, he moved away from me. "Please… let's just walk a bit further." I took his hand and lead him further down the path until we reached the meadow. He stood there as if amazed at the abundance of flowers. I think he was more impressed there was such a large clearing in such a dense forest. I let go and walked to a fallen tree to sit and collect myself. My heart was still racing from what had happened.

As I rested, he walked out to the middle of the meadow. He looked up and yelled. Startling me, I jumped from the log and ran to him. "What the hell is wrong with you damn it! You're freaking me out!"

Staring up to the sky he calmly said, "Tess, there are times when you just have to let loose." He looked down and grabbed my shoulders, "You've been on my mind since I picked you up in Tucson. My first true love. It took me years to get over losing you and even then I always held out the hope that we'd get back together…When I met Monica, I was finally free of you. I do love her with all my heart, but seeing you has me so confused. I don't want to hurt her so I've basically stayed away from the lodge. I thought she'd eventually get pissed, but she's too busy to noticed I've been gone."

He dropped to his knees and pressed his head against my stomach. I couldn't help but wrap my arms around him. "There's no reason to get so worked up. She's perfect for you. I could tell that the day I met her. When I saw you look into her eyes, I knew you'd found the right woman. I'm sure she's noticed, but maybe she thinks you've been busy."

I hoped my words would help, but since I was never able to keep any of my own relationships together, I knew I wasn't the best person to be giving advice. "I'm an emotional mess and you've known that from the day we met. We had something special, but we couldn't hang on to it." Raking my fingers through his hair I knew what he was going through. I had the same feelings for him not too long ago. I finally accepted that I couldn't comfort him without admitting I was crushed when I found out he was married.

He pulled me down. "Tess, I don't know what to say. I've loved you from the first time we met…I've never stopped loving you. We should've been together. What changed? What tore us apart?"

Confused, I was unable to find a valid explanation. Without warning, his hands came up to my face and pulled me to him. His lips burned against mine, as old feelings began to stir inside me.

My stomach began to flutter as I melted into his arms and responded to his kiss. It was just like the first time he had ever held me. Memories of us flashed like lightning through my mind. All my inhibitions were fading. I went limp in his arms as his hand came up and cupped my breast.

"What happened to us Tess? How could we have lost each other?" His breath was hot against my mouth.

"I don't know." Sharp pains began to tear through my chest as I came to my senses. I pushed him away. "Scott, stop. We can't bring back what we've lost; we need to move on with our lives." I held up my hand to shield his advance. I sat back on my heels and ran my fingers through my hair.

"This is too confusing for me, I can't do this." I looked up with tears in my eyes "Not only are you married, but I..." I bit my lip to stop from confessing my feelings for Ryan. It wasn't the right time and I knew it.

"What the hell am I doing?" He leaned back and brought his hands to his head grabbing his hair in frustration. "Go away Tess, I need to be alone."

Without a word, I got to my feet and walked down the path. I couldn't bring myself to look back, ashamed I let it go that far. I could've brushed it off as a harmless kiss, but I felt his heat and it drove me wild. There was a point when I wanted him as much as I had in college. It hadn't been just a kiss that would happen between two friends, it was desire.

My heart was heavy as I tried to find my way back to the cabin. My mind reeled *How could I still have feelings for Scott? It was Ryan I wanted.* I didn't want to face either of them after that. I feared Ryan would figure out what had happened, and I knew Scott would treat me like a leper.

The cabin greeted me as I emerged from the woods. Not ready to go inside, I trailed along the trees until I came to the spot that was directly across the lake from the cabin. Sitting at the base of a tree, I stared out trying to focus on the scenery. As I sat there, I let the scene with Scott run over and over in my mind. My head began to ache so I leaned back and nodded off.

Frantic shouts woke me up. "Tess, damn it, if your out there, you'd better answer. Tess!" Scott's voiced boomed through the silence. Just as I was about to holler back a few obscenities, I heard Ryan calling out from behind me. I peered around the tree to see him coming up the path. "Shush, I want to stay hidden a bit longer." He spied me and crouched down placing his hand on my face.

His voice trembled, "Have you been here this whole time?" I nodded. He caressed my check checking to see if I was hurt. He shouted out " I found her, she's fine! I don't need help; we'll be there in a bit."

I didn't want to go back just then. I grabbed his hand and pulled him down next to me. He wrapped his arm around me and sat there looking at lake. It was dark and the moonlight shimmered on the ripples of the water. After a few peaceful moments, we headed to the cabin. Once inside, I went straight up to the loft and toppled into bed.

CHAPTER TEN

The smell of bacon and fresh brewed coffee wafted through the cabin reminding me of Mary and the short time we had spent together. It seemed strange that I had pushed her and my family completely out of my mind. I rolled onto my back and stared at the rafters running through the memories. If only she could visit, if not to ease my loneliness, but to keep me away from the guys. I felt I needed her to ground me and help me focus on my book.

Still dressed in the clothes from the day before, I headed downstairs and straight to the bathroom. There were too many emotions to deal with; I didn't want to talk to either one of them. I needed time to myself, or perhaps wanted them to suffer for some deranged reason... Scott, for his almost successful seduction, and Ryan for being so distant.

I could hear them talking in the kitchen as I opened the bathroom door. I tiptoed a little closer to hear what they were saying. Scott said something about heading back to base when Ryan broke in; "I'm staying here for a bit if you don't mind. I want to get started on those projects..." he dropped his voice to a whisper and continued, "I'm just not ready to fly."

"If you can clear it with Tess, I'm all for it. I'd feel better if she wasn't alone. Someone needs to keep her safe and since I can't I'm glad to have someone here I trust. I'll head out and do my pre-flight." He popped a piece of bacon in his mouth and headed out the door.

I reached back and jiggled the handle on the door to warn Ryan I was coming. His eyes followed me as I grabbed a mug and filled it with coffee. Keeping my gaze to the floor, I headed into the great room and sat down at the desk. I could still feel him looking at me as I stared out the picture window.

He moved to the stairs and sat down. "I know I've no right to ask, but what happened yesterday?" Keeping my eyes trained on the blurry images outside I tried to think of what to say.

"I needed time to come to grips with some issues. It's not as wonderful as you think living here, especially alone." I choked on the words as I held back tears. "I don't want to talk about it." I straightened up and squared my shoulders.

He stood and walked over to me placing his hands gently on my shoulders. "If I promise not to push the issue, will you let me stay here for a bit? I promise to stay out of your way while you work." I reached up and touched his hand.

"I'd like that." Sniffling, I looked up over my shoulder. He came around and knelt beside me holding my hand to his chest. "But if you want to spend some time together, we could perhaps take a stroll through the woods or maybe a picnic or two?" Leaning forward he whispered, "I promise no bears this time."

I stifled a giggle taking his face in my hands. "I would love for you to stay, if you don't mind my strange mood swings." Guiding him closer to me, I place a light kiss on his check, I could feel him smile. I pictured his dimples and longed to see his face clearly again.

We were interrupted when Scott cleared his throat. I stiffened up like a child who was caught playing with matches. Sure he had witnessed a good portion of our intimate moment, I could only imagine what was going through his mind. We stood up and Ryan headed out the door.

Scott stood there not saying a word. I couldn't read his expression so I wasn't sure how he would take what I was about to say. "Before you go, let' get something straight between us. What happened yesterday was too much for either of us to handle. I don't know what's going on in your life and it's none of my business. I know I got lost in the moment right along with you. As tempting as it was, it can't happen again. I do love you, but we both have changed. I haven't always made the right decisions in my life, but this time I am not gonna blow it for both of us." I stepped closer to him, "I'll always be your friend and I'll always love you, but the passion that we had in college can't ruin the lives we have now." I waited for his response half expecting him to explode.

"I'm not sorry for yesterday. It had to happen and it helped me to realize exactly what you're saying. I don't want to lose you Tess. If you'll have me as a friend, I'll always be there for you." Holding out his arms, I stepped into his embrace. With a gentle squeeze, he turned and headed down to the dock.

I went up to the loft and flopped down on the bed finally letting my body relax and listening to the sound of the plane heading off into the distance. When I heard Ryan return, I sat up and ran my fingers through my hair to make myself look a little more presentable. He was standing at the landing looking up as I came down. Draping my arms around him, I breathed gently against his neck, "I'm so glad you're here."

He lifted me off the last step and held at arms length. Gazing down at me, "I'm glad you want me here, but you still need to keep your focus on writing and I've got things to get done before the next plane arrives." As my smile faded, he continued. "I promised time together and we'll have that, we need to make sure we both do what we came here to do."

With a quick kiss, he turned away. I was floored; I couldn't find the words to respond. I watched him walk to the couch as I stood there feeling like a fool. Taking the hint and feeling a little hurt, I grabbed a notepad and pen and headed out the door. I spent the rest of the day on the dock writing meaningless phrases.

He spent his days working behind the cabin putting together something that had been delivered one box at a time. It looked like plane parts and since I was trying to stay clear and give him space, I didn't ask what it was, I didn't really cared. For some reason, he was keeping me at a safe emotional distance. I searched my mind every night going over what I might have said or done for him to push me aside. I'd look down from the loft to watch him sleep on the couch every night. We'd talk during meals, but usually about things that didn't really matter.

For days I stayed inside glued to my typewriter. I tried to focus but my heart wasn't in it. I had to find a way to get him to open up to me. We hadn't gone for a special picnic or an adventure in the woods like he promised. He was too into whatever it was he was building. To help ease my mind, I set my thoughts to paper. It never occurred to me to read what I had written until I had cranked out a full ream of paper. Grabbing the stack, I survey the large room and started to tape each page end to end along the shelves. By the end of the day, I had the walls completely covered.

Cranking up the stereo, I poured a glass of wine and headed over to the pages. In order to read the words; I had to hold my head within inches of the pages. Using a red marker, I crossed out sentences and circled others. Dancing to the music as I went around the room, marking and slashing. At the last page, my glass was empty so from across the room I hurled it into the fireplace. Holding my arms up in victory I twirled about singing to the music. Out to the corner of eye I saw shadow by the open door. Embarrassed, I stopped and lowered my arms. There was Ryan leaning against the jam with his arms across his chest. I couldn't see the look on his face but I was sure he was amused.

Clapping his hands, "Bravo Tess, a writer and performer. You've got a great future ahead of you." He walked around the room eyeing the red marked pages. Once he finished the complete circuit, he came over and swept me up in his arms. Still a little out of breath and feeling lighter then air, I hugged him as tight as I could. He swung me around letting my feet leave the floor. We spun around a few times and then slowed as the music changed to a soft dance song. He bent down and kissed my cheek. I rested my head against his chest and felt his heart beat.

"I almost gave up a few times, but I think by tomorrow we may be closer to having a form of electricity available without the generator." I was too wrapped up in the moment to hear what he was saying "Taylor figured you'd appreciate real light instead of candles." I noticed when he said Scott's name his voice seemed a little rougher.

His words sank in. "Electric light?" I jumped back and clapped my hands like a child who just got a new toy. "That's great! What did you build?"

"Wanna see?" He reached out his hand. Nodding with excitement, I followed him out and around the cabin. Even fuzzy, I could tell it was a windmill. Considerably smaller then the ones I had seen in Tucson, but it was perfect.

"It's great Ryan. How does it work?" Amazed, I walked around looking up at the streamlined blades

"Well it doesn't right now, but the rest of it will be arriving on the next few planes. When the wind's up, the blades rotate creating energy which will be stored..." I held up my hand.

"Wait... don't tell me. All that mechanical mumbo jumbo will take away from the moment." Laughing I looked over at him, "This is too great for words. We need to celebrate." Skipping, I passed him and slapped him on the butt.

"Oh...that's completely unfair!" He hollered as he turned to chase after me. I looked back to see him closing in. Excitement raced through my veins as I headed to the dock, just before he could catch me, I jumped in and began to swim as fast as I could. I stopped and turned to look back. I couldn't see him. I knew he must have jumped in after me. Treading as best I could with the weight of my wet clothes pulling me down, I searched the water to see if he was coming.

Fear crossed my heart when he still hadn't surfaced. "Ryan! Where are you?" Suddenly something grabbed my legs and pulled me under the water. My panic vanished as I felt his hands come to my waist and his lips to my mouth. I wrapped my legs around him and grabbed his neck as we came to the surface. Breaking off the kiss, we gasped for air.

Laughing, we bobbed for a bit. "Thought you'd get away with smacking my ass did ya." He said playfully.

"Yes, as a matter of fact I did." Dipping my head back into the water to get it out of my eyes. I heard a loud ringing in my ears. I leaned back and let my hair float in the water. When I brought my head up I looked at Ryan and for the first time since he had come back; I was able to see all the features of his face clearly. With a gasp I said, "Ryan, I can see you!" excitement in my voice I stared into his eyes. "I can see everything clearly, you're not a blur anymore." Guiding him closer to me, I pecked kisses over his face. His hands came up stopping me in mid pucker. Holding me still, his eyes searched mine. I was still wrapped around his waist and he began to struggle to keep us afloat.

A smile crossed his lips as he was dragged under the water, when he came back up he tossed me away from him. "Come on, we should get out of these wet clothes." He turned and began to swim back to the dock. I couldn't help but laugh as a wicked thought crossed my mind. Just then I created a plan. I swam after him and when I was about five feet from the dock, I stopped and stood up.

The water came up to my neck. "Hey you, don't go just yet. You owe me this swim and some quality time." He was just about to hoist himself onto the pier, when he turned to face me.

"Woman, I'd love to take a swim with you, but these clothes make it too hard to stay afloat." He pulled at his shirt to demonstrate his point as it stuck to his chest.

As I watched him, I removed my clothes and let them drift away. The sun had begun to sink below the trees and the lake had taken on the golden glow of twilight. "I can solve this little problem you're having." Seductively, I walked forward…my body became exposed as I reached the shallow water. When I got to him, the water was to my waist. He leaned against the dock staring at me in amazement. He didn't say a word as I reached out and to remove his shirt.

His bare chest was bronzed and muscular. My eyes floated over every inch taking in the wonderful sight of his body. With the lightest touch, I caressed him. My hands slowly made patterns over his skin. His hands come to my waist and I thought he was going to push me away again, but he didn't. He caressed my back following the rhythm I created. I looked into his eyes as he pulled me close. His body was warm and inviting as my breasts pressed against his chest. He worked his hands up my back until they tangled in my hair. Cradling my head in his hands he brought his lips to mine. Softly we kissed. I could feel the heat racing through my blood. Our bodies pressed tight together, our kiss became fevered breaking away only to catch a breath.

The sounds of the forest began to come to life in the night. We hadn't noticed it had grown dark and a full moon illuminated the lake. Slowing down our kiss, we melted into each other. "Are you sure you want to do this Tess?" He questioned as he trailed his kisses from my mouth to my check down my neck to my shoulder. My desire for him was too strong to stop.

I leaned my head back giving him access to my breasts. The heat of his tongue trailed across my skin as he reached down and removed his pants. Finally free from his clothes, we were able to move around easier. He straightened up and guided me back into the deeper water. When we were at the point where the water came to the top of my breasts, he turned me around and began to nibble on the back of my neck. Tingles went up and down my spine as he brought his hands around my stomach. With a gentle caress, his hand explored me. No man had ever brought out my desires like that before.

It felt like a romantic dream. I arched my back as his hands came up to my breast and drew me back until I was floating on the water. "You're even more beautiful in the moonlight." I kept my eyes closed and enjoyed the feeling of being light as a feather. I let my legs sink back down into the water and found the bottom. I stood and turned to face him. His body glistened. "You're not so bad either." Standing toe to toe I lifted myself up to wrap my legs around his hips. Never before had I been so bold with a man. We teased each other with kisses as we made love. It was a dream that I didn't want to wake up from. Wrapped up in the moment, we hadn't noticed the sky had clouded over. A flash of lightning and loud crash of thunder brought us back to reality.

Laughing, Ryan said, "We better get out of the water before we become stew." I nodded and followed him. With no shame, we headed back to the cabin hand in hand completely naked.

CHAPTER ELEVEN

Still wrapped in his arms, I woke feeling extremely secure. "Ryan, you awake?" I whispered quietly hoping he was still asleep. I didn't want the night to be over.

"Yes I am. In fact..." he breathed into my ear, "I don't think I want to move from this spot."

Giggling, I snuggled closer. "Me either, but we'll have to eat sometime don't you think?"

"Well...that's a matter of opinion." He kissed my neck and I rolled over to face him.

"If you keep that up, we'll never get out of bed." There I was, laying in bed staring up at one of the most handsome men I had met in my life. Holding me in his arms and loving me, I felt completely happy.

A concerned look crossed his face. "What are we going to do about Taylor?" The tone in his voice was serious.

Surprised by his question, I propped myself up and looked down at him. "What does Scott have to do with us?" I brushed the hair from my eyes. "Because he's your boss or because he's my ex-boyfriend?"

Looking as confused as I was at that moment, he sat up. Sitting face to face he held my shoulders and stared deep into my eyes, searching intently. "You mean you and Taylor haven't been together since you came here?"

I shook my head in disbelief. "What the hell made you think that?" Feeling insulted I pushed his hands away. "Scott's married and what we had was a long time ago. We may have shared a few uncomfortable moments since I've been here, but I'm pretty sure I made it clear to him we could be no more then friends." I looked away, not sure if I should confess what happened in the meadow.

He lifted my chin and kissed my cheek. "Tess, I saw you and Taylor together. I didn't hear what you guys were saying, but from where I stood..." My heart began to pound in my chest.

"I can imagine what you must have thought, that's why you've been so distant with me isn't it?"

He nodded. "It wasn't just that. Let's go down and talk about it over a cup of coffee." Brushing my hair from my face, he continued with a smile. "Perhaps we can even have a little breakfast?"

Trying to break the tension we created, I flipped my head from side to side, "Well, if we must we must." I grabbed the sheets from the bed and wrapped myself up.

"Hey! Sensuous." He called out as I headed down the stairs. "Can you toss me up some clothes?"

"You got it." I reached in his bag and pulled out a pair of his boxer shorts. Tossing them over the rail, "Here... the perfect outfit for breakfast."

Over a plate of eggs and a hot cup of coffee, he explained what had been going on since he had left. I sat and listened intently without interrupting or asking questions so I could understand every detail.

The flight back had been a series of hops from one lake or river to the next. There were more problems from the accident than he had realized. He had to fight the plane to stay aloft. When he finally made it back to base, Scott was waiting to hear every detail of what happened while he was stranded at the cabin. Being the gentleman he was, Ryan told him about the bear, but little else. While celebrating his safe return, Scott had too much to drink and confessed that he still had deep feelings for me. He was confused because he loved his wife desperately, but seeing me again stirred something inside that drove him to a new level of insanity.

Ryan decided he'd back off not wanting to get in the way. Ryan took as many flights as he could to keep himself as far away from me as possible. He didn't know I had been alone at the cabin for so long or that I was sick.

He'd left Sarah with Kevin while he ferried a plane to San Francisco. Kevin wasn't suppose to fly because he was still recovering from his illness, let alone a plane that was still grounded for mechanical repairs. They had no clue as to why he took off or where he was planning to go. It wasn't until the next day that anyone knew he was gone. Ryan spied the plane tangled in the trees about fifty miles from base. It had crashed into a dense patch of forest. He radioed his findings and met up with officials to lead them to the area where he saw the wreckage.

They weren't able to reach the plane by truck, so they spread out and went in on foot. It was Ryan who found Kevin's mangled body. When he turned from the sight, he heard a faint whimper. Digging frantically, he found Sarah trapped under the wreckage. He kept digging until he was able to pull her out. She was limp, but he knew she wasn't dead.

He gave his contact information to the officials and with Sarah dangling in his arms headed to the nearest animal hospital, but she died on the way. Ryan couldn't find the courage to fly after that. Scott had been at the cabin and was radioed about the accident. When he came back, he couldn't get Ryan in the air. Figuring some time away would help him come to his senses; they came back to the lake.

On the way back, Ryan was sedated so he could relax during the flight. Scott had regaled him with the story of how he found me naked on the kitchen floor and how he took care of me as I fought against the virus. He told him everything in full detail. He admitted that the sedative made him groggy, but he heard every word. He was sure he had no place in my life.

When he finished, his eyes had misted over. I could only sit there with my mouth hanging open in disbelief. My mind was reeling. It was almost too much to take. Scott was still in love with me. He shared intimate and embarrassing details of my illness and my body as if he was still a stupid college kid bragging to his friends. Ryan thought he had no place in my life even after the night we had shared on the couch. Kevin was dead and Ryan witnessed his beloved dog die. What cosmic event could have caused all this drama to happen? I sat there shaking my head in disbelief.

I looked up and realized Ryan's heart was in pain. I stood and held him in my arms mustering as much strength as I could to try to comfort him. "I'm glad you told me, this makes everything so much clearer." Rubbing his back, I felt his muscles tense. He gently pushed me. Not wanting to show weakness, he gave me a gentle kiss and headed to the bathroom.

I made up my mind I wouldn't speak of the accident again, but knew I had to clear the air about Scott and me. We got comfortable on the couch and I told him everything: Starting in college and how we met, our reunion at the airport, the bizarre kiss, waking up naked and blind with only Scott to relay on, and the episode in the meadow. I was completely honest with him and didn't skirt around the issue of how I felt. Everything was out in the open and no more secrets or misunderstandings stood between us.

The weeks flew by quickly. I began to enjoy working on my book and Ryan finished wiring the cabin for electricity and running water. A plane flew in every week to deliver supplies and building materials. Worried that Scott would show up and create tension during his visit, my heart sank each time I heard a buzzing in the distance. The pilots who flew in would only stay to make deliveries and pick up letters I had written to Mary and friends as well as receive instructions from Ryan or wish lists I had drawn up.

A month went by and the cabin had completely transformed into a semi-modern home. We not only had lights, but hot and cold running water. The windmill could only produce a minimal amount of electricity, so we did our best to conserve. Using the lights for a short time at night and taking showers together. Not all conservation was for the cause, but I still liked to use it as an excuse. It did help to make living there more comfortable.

The outside world was forgotten most of the time and we enjoyed the life we created for ourselves. My book began to take shape in the form of a solid outline. I kept the pages taped to the shelves and added to them each day. From time to time, I'd walk around the room skimming each to find anything I might be able to use. Every night, we sat on the couch holding each other as I rattled off ideas to him. Always reminding me that he was no writer, I found that much of what he'd suggest inspired a new idea or path to take. He became my muse.

One night we were sitting together staring at the page-covered bookshelves. The cluttered mess had me feeling claustrophobic so I decided it was time to clear the deck. As he sat on the couch, I went around the room removing the pages and stacking them carefully in my arms. When they got too heavy, I'd put them on the table and returned to collect more. Amused, Ryan leaned back and propped his legs up knocking over a stack. He bent down and gathered up the papers.

"Don't worry, I can straighten them out later" I said and turned back to pulling pages from the shelves.

"Hello?...what's this?" I turned to see him lying on the floor reaching under the couch.

"What'd ya find?" I walked over as he pulled out a book.

He placed it on the table and sat back. "How did this get under there?"

I flipped it open and pointed to the block of wood. "I found this the night I got sick. There should be a letter." I picked it up and tossed the block to Ryan. He sat there turning it around looking at it as I flipped through the book carefully. "It's not here." I held it by the spine and shook it hard. We dropped to our knees and searched under the couch and around the floor.

"Are you sure there's a letter?" he asked as he tossed up the rug in front of the fireplace.

"Yes, there's an envelope and a note with an "S" and silver lining or something shinny...it's gotta be around here somewhere. I can't believe I forgot about it." I searched again under the couch finally hoisting it up to get a good look. "Damn it to hell!" I shouted letting it fall.

"Take it easy Tess, it's just a note." He came over and calmed me with a hug. "We'll find it if it's still here. It may have been tossed by accident."

He put the couch back in its proper place and pulled me down onto his lap. "Here, take it out on me." He said opening his arm for a full assault. The teasing smile on his face told me to give in. I fell into his arms and kissed him as I felt around the cushions of the couch. Knowing I was not paying full attention, he reached under my arms and tickled me, I jumped up and in my hand was the envelope. I held it up. "See, I was right!" I smiled down at him straddling his waist.

"Good", he said, grabbing the note from my hand and tossing it across the room. "Let's celebrate." He pulled me back down and we spend the rest of the night teasing each other.

CHAPTER TWELVE

We placed the book, block of wood and letter in a safe place on a shelf like a shrine, wanting to keep it a mystery a little longer. I needed to keep my focus on my writing. I had the beginnings of a good story, but there were still pieces missing that would make it great.

Ryan's last few tasks of setting up landing lights in the lake and chopping a cord of wood were completed and we both knew Scott would want him back to work. The nights became warmer in August and we took full advantage of the clear weather with moonlight swims, or laying in each other's arms in the meadow. During the days, we both worked apart, but the nights were ours.

With weekly deliveries, we had an over stock of food, supplies and emergency equipment. I knew Scott would arrive soon. He'd want to make sure everything was set up right. The only connection he had with us was by radio. Since we didn't keep it on unless we were going to call base, Ryan had made a habit of contacting him on certain days at specific times. I hoped he had come to grips with his feelings so we could feel more comfortable around each other. I could tell he loved his wife. In the short time I saw them together, he was completely different with her than he ever was with me. I remember feeling jealous watching them together.

With Ryan, I felt complete. I was hopelessly in love, but couldn't bring myself to tell him. I felt it would destroy everything we had developed. I knew in time I would confess, but it wasn't something I could plan. Not used to having such feelings, I didn't know if there was some kind of protocol that needed to be followed. In college, my friends and I would joke about the "Dating Rules". I made up my mind to let him make the first move.

During his last radio call to base, Scott announced he would be coming to check out the windmill and to pick Ryan up on the last day of the month. We'd only have a few days together before I had to go back to living like a hermit. I stopped writing and spent every moment wrapped in his arms not wanting to let go.

When the day finally came we watched the plane land, as I choked back my tears. Grabbing my hand, he whispered, "I won't be gone for long this time, I promise Tess." I gathered my strength as the plane floated to the dock. This time it was Monica who stepped out first. Surprised to see her, she ran up and gave me a hug. "Tess, it's good to see you. We brought a surprise." She turned to Ryan and gave him a kiss on the cheek. With a wink she commented, "Nice tan handsome, this vacation's been good for you." Squeezing his arm, "and I see you bulked up a little."

She locked my arm in hers as we headed up to the cabin leaving the men to tend to the plane. "Let's have a drink" she patted her bag and giggled. A little relieved she was there, but also feeling a bit guilty at the same time. Not knowing if Scott had told her what happened between us, a twinge of anxiety sweep over me. I decided to push it out of my mind and enjoy having another woman around.

As we walked in, she gazed around the room. "Tess, this place is great. It's rustic and unpretentious." She spun around and looked me. "A romantic place for lovers, don't you think?" Raising her eyebrow suspiciously. I didn't know if she was talking about me and Scott or me and Ryan. I felt a little trapped not knowing how to respond.

"You can't tell me that you've been alone here with Ryan for two months and nothing's happened?" Placing her bag on the floor giving me a concerned look.

Relieved, I smiled. "I've gotta admit, he's great company to have around. I'm gonna miss him when you guys leave." I walked into the kitchen and grabbed some glasses from the counter. She walked around browsing the books on the shelves.

"I'm sure of that, but he won't be gone for long. Scott has him set up for a few short hops to get him back in the air, but after that he should be free to visit as often as the weather allows. The winters are pretty nice here, but we get the occasional storm that can really sock us in." She flopped down onto the couch and stretched out her arms. I came around with the glasses as she whipped open her bag to reveal a bottle of my favorite bourbon.

"You're a life saver!" I said holding out a glass. "There's only so much wine a person can drink before it begins to taste like Kool-aide." I took a small sip and let the warm liquid gold trickle down my throat. "Good stuff!" I said smacking my lips.

"I love a woman who knows her booze!" She held up her glass. "I don't have to worry about staying sober; I'm not the one flying. Plus...I'm on vacation for the next two weeks." She held up two fingers victoriously.

"How'd you manage that?"

Motioning me to lean closer she whispered, "I got Scott to agree to run the lodge for me...We got into a fight about him never being around and not knowing what I do for our company. So we're trading places, for the next two weeks I do all the schedules for his pilots while he preps the lodge for the winter season." She turned to face me. "I actually started doing his job about a month ago… that's why you had a plane fly in every week. I know a girl needs to have some kind of outside contact. Scott did all the shopping for you so I'm sorry you didn't get anything too exciting."

We belted back a few more glassfuls before the guys came in mumbling to each other with serious expressions on their faces. "Well I see you two didn't waste any time." Scott said with an accusing glare. Monica and I looked at each other and burst out laughing. "Drinking...at this time of day! I'm shocked at both of you!" Dramatically bringing his fist to his chest. Ryan just stood there laughing along with us. "We better be careful Ryan, these women might go wild on us." Grabbing each other pretending to be scared, "It's okay, we'll be strong and fend them off with hot coffee and…" they both raced for the door and came walking back in both holding a box. "Cake!" In sync, they began to sing *They say it's your Birthday*.

I completely forgot! I covered my face embarrassed as they continued to sing and dance towards us. Monica didn't stop laughing. I peeked through my fingers as she gave me a nudge. They set the cake on the table and finished the song. I clapped, "Bravo...what a show...what singing...you guys should take that act on the road."

They bowed and took a seat on the floor behind the table facing us. I was still giggling. "When did you guys cook this up?" I asked.

"We had this planned for a week." Ryan winked at me from across the table.

"To be honest, I completely forgot about it." Shaking my head and smiling at how stupid it must sound for someone to forget her own Birthday.

"If it weren't for Scott, no one would have known." Monica raised her glass to her husband in toast.

Raising mine too, "Here's to Scott, a man who likes to remind a woman how old she's getting."

"Not true, not true!" he shouted in his own defense. "I don't remind, I rub it in...so Tess, tell us...how old are you?" He mocked me with a grin.

"I'm old enough to know what I want...and young enough to get it." Taking a swig, I looked at Ryan over the rim of the glass and noticed that he had a smile plastered on his face.

I discovered that cake and bourbon didn't mix well, so I switched to the coffee the guys were drinking. Monica slowed down a bit too. In between bites, Ryan explained the changes he made around the cabin. We headed outside to see the improvements. Beaming with pride, he led them around showing off his accomplishments. I held back to let him have a glory moment. He deserved it; the work he'd put into the modifications was incredible. During the tour, I excused my self and went back inside. I was inspired to grab a note pad and jot down all that I could remembered about the day. It was fun to see the guys clown around. It helped to take my mind off the fact that I would be alone again.

Monica had sobered up a little by the time they came back. She went into the kitchen and gulped down a large glass of water. We all watched as she bolted for the bathroom holding her mouth.

"I guess my wife had a little too much cake?" Scott said stifling a giggle.

I smacked his arm, "don't make fun, I bet you've had a few moments like that in your life." I began to laugh, "Hope she figures out the toilet. You should go help her butt head."

He patted my shoulder, "You're right, I'm such a shit!" He headed to the bathroom. "Honey?...You okay in there?...Let me in baby." The door opened and he disappeared.

Taking advantage of being alone, Ryan grabbed me leading me out the door to steal a kiss. Hearing someone come back, we quickly straightened up and turned to the lake pretending to gaze upon the scenery. When Scott joined us, he looked a lot more serious then when he first went in to help her. "I don't think she's up to making the flight back, do you mind if she stays until tomorrow? I can have someone pick her up in the afternoon."

"Sure she can stay." Feeling concern for her. "I didn't realize she was that toasted."

"It's probably the drinking and eating cake after flying more than anything. She's never liked flying in the puddle jumpers." He stifled another giggle.

Thrusting my chin forward, I looked him square in the eye. "I've changed my mind." He caught his breath and his face became vacant in disbelief, "No need to send for her tomorrow, she'll stay the week!" In shock, he blinked his eyes a few times and then squinted at me suspiciously.

"You wouldn't mind her sticking around for a week?" He questioned accusingly.

"I think she needs some time here. This place is the perfect getaway. If she wants to leave sooner, we'll call you. Sound like a plan?" I watched his face soften.

"You've got a point." He looked over my shoulder at Ryan and gave a nod. "We should start out then before it gets too dark. I'll let Monica know she's saved." He vanished back into the cabin.

I turned around to find Ryan looking at me in amazement. "You're an incredible woman Tess!" He picked me up in his arms and spun me around bringing his lips to mine. As he set me down, we shared one last kiss. My heart felt heavy, I didn't want him to go. We had made a perfect life together at the cabin. I knew it would be at least two weeks before he could come back. We were only able to get one more hug in before Scott came bounding out the door.

He gave me a quick squeeze, "Thanks Tess, I hope you girls have a good time. Call if you need anything." He turned and raced to the plane calling over his shoulder. "Come on dude, we better get out of here before they change their minds."

We gazed into each other's eyes searching for a few last words to say that would ease our hearts. No words powerful enough existed to say it all. With a knowing smile and a quick peck on the cheek, he left. I stood at the door and watched as they taxied to the end of the lake and took off. I closed the door behind me and headed to the bathroom to help Monica.

I found her hunched over the sink washing her face. Completely embarrassed by what happened, she moaned as I entered. "At least it got me out of getting on that damned plane." With a grateful smile, "Thanks Tess, for letting me stay."

"You need a break, and this is just the place for it. Take a quick shower and I'll bring you some fresh clothes. Good thing you sent some up, I wasn't very prepared when I came here." I smiled and headed upstairs.

The guys were gone and it was just us. While she collected herself in the bathroom, I cleaned up the cake and put up the half empty bottle of booze. I figured neither one of us wanted to finish it off at that moment. When she finally joined me, she looked completely refreshed.

"Feeling tired?" I asked.

She shook her head letting her dark hair fly about. "Not a bit. How about you? Has the liquor hit you yet?

"Nope, actually I feel energized." I stretched my arms up and shook my hands.

She came over and sat down. "So, what do you do for fun around here?" She laughed knowing that there was nothing but books for entertainment.

"Well, not much...but if you're behind on your reading...we're well stocked for the challenge." I waved my arm around the room pointing out the abundant number of books on the shelves.

"Well, I did find something that looks interesting. What's that for?" She pointed to where the forgotten book and block of wood perched on the shelf.

"You know, that's been a mystery I haven't yet explored." I walked over and grabbed the items. Putting each one on the table, I told her how I found the book and forgot about it until Ryan found it under the couch.

"Why haven't you read the letter?" She asked as she turned the block around in her hands studying it.

"I've no idea... every time I think about it; I get an idea for my book and forget. I guess there's no time like the present." I grabbed the envelope and pulled out the letter.

It got crinkled when it was hidden in the couch, but still in pretty good condition.

I flipped it open and read it out loud...

My Dearest Love,

Our time together draws to an end and I can't bear to say goodbye. These past few month we have spent together has meant the world to me. I came here a girl and leave a woman. As I look around this wonderful place we have built together I can hear you toss in your sleep.

I will always treasure this time together and will reflect on it throughout my life. If you are reading this, you will have already seen me take off. Don't be worried my love, I will have the plane returned to pick you up. I couldn't bear to look you in the eyes one more time and have my heart torn from my chest. I love you and I will always love you. If only there was some way we could stay together always. I left the box that has the key you asked for.

My heart will be yours always,
Sofia

By the time I finished the letter, tears were rolling down both our faces. I brought it to my heart, reflecting on the loving words that still rang in my ears. I knew this woman's heartbreak. It brought back the pain of saying good bye to Ryan.

I felt that Monica knew the same pain. She picked up the block of wood and studied it even closer. "How can this be a box, there's no seams, no openings. If it is, there's no way to open it...Perhaps it's some kind of puzzle box." She kept studying it while I read and re-read the letter to myself. It made no sense. My grandfather built this cabin. I didn't recall a story about a woman helping him. All kinds of thoughts came to my mind.

I got up and went to the bathroom. I looked in the mirror searching my memory for some clue that would unravel the mystery. My grandfather must have revealed something to me about it. Perhaps he was the one who rubbed the letters off the cover of the book. I splashed water on my face and feeling refreshed I went to the storeroom and grabbed a bottle of wine and two glasses. When I came back into the great room, Monica had flipped on the lights and was holding the box up trying to find a way to open it.

We stayed up most of the night sipping wine and making up wild stories about the different possibilities that would answer the questions we had. Like girls at a sleep over, we giggled and tossed the box back and forth to each other. It got late and the wine had taken its toll. She headed up to bed and flicked off the lights as I snuggled into the couch.

CHAPTER THIRTEEN

We slept in late, a little hung over from the night before. I woke up and started a strong pot of coffee and soon after Monica slowly came down the stairs. "My head's killing me, but I'm starving." She pulled her fingers through her hair and sat down. "That letter haunted my dreams." Grabbing the mug of fresh brew, she cupped it staring into the black liquid. "I did get an idea last night that I want to bounce off of you to see what you think..."

Curiously, I grabbed a mug for myself and sat across from her. "What's on your mind?" I asked, burning my tongue on the first sip.

"Now, this is just an idea and I wouldn't be hurt if you thought it was way out of left field, but I thought I'd pitch it to you anyway." She paused for a moment to blow across the coffee to cool it down. "Have you ever thought about making this place a rustic resort of some kind?" She looked up to capture my response.

"Actually, I have a few times. I don't really have a head for that kind of thing and I'm not too good at planning stuff like that." My lip curled into a smile as I realized that I was sitting across from a resort manager. "Perhaps if I had someone to help me with the details and the lay out so long as the plan didn't destroy the charm of this place, I think it would be a pretty good idea." I took another caustic sip and looked up at her.

Her eyes beamed, "Tess, if we can come up with a layout that you like would you really consider it?" She pleaded.

"Sure, I think it would be nice to see a little more around here then just a cabin.   If all goes well this year and I get my book finished, I'll have the funds to support such a project." The thought was exciting and I was glad she wanted to develop the idea.

I cooked up pancakes and she went over some of her thoughts. She told me she and Scott had gone to Hawaii for their honeymoon and stayed in tree house structures that she thought would be perfect and unique for the area. It would bring a flare that other resorts didn't normally have. I was in awe of how quickly she came up with everything.

After we finished eating, she headed out to explore with a note pad to jot down her inspirations and I went back to writing. I looked over the pages of my outline and like a woman possessed; I placed a crisp sheet of paper in the typewriter and let my fingers fly. The old typewriter was difficult to use at first, but once I found my rhythm I couldn't stop. I had cranked out almost half a ream before I realized it was getting dark and Monica hadn't come back. I finished the last sentence on the page and pulled it from the roller placing it on the completed stack.

A habit that Ryan taught me, I grabbed the rifle and a flashlight before I headed out to find her. I looked around to see if she was sitting at the dock or somewhere around the lake. "Monica!" I shouted, but no response. I decided to take the path to the meadow since it was the easiest to navigate. Calling out as I went, I flashed the light from side to side. When I reached the meadow I called out again as loud as I could. I heard a faint whistle far off in the distance. "Monica! Are you out there?"

I strained to hear her above the crickets, "Yes, don't worry I'm fine. Shine your light ahead and I'll come to you." Doing as she asked I waited.

"Girl, you scared the shit out of me." I said as she approached. "If something had happened to you, Scott would kick my butt." I laughed in relief.

Holding up her hands, "Don't shoot Annie Oakley!...geeze, what kind of mess did you think I got myself into?" Laughing as she lowered her hands. "I grew up in a place a lot like this Tess, I know my way around these kinds of woods better then most people."

Patting my shoulder in comfort, she guided me back to the path. "Come on, I have so much to tell you."

We decided to set up a campfire by the lake to enjoy the night. "This place has so much potential...there's a lot here." She looked into the darkness and I could see that she was imagining each idea she had. "This lake is fed by a stream to the north..." she pointed to the right. "And empties into smaller stream to the south". She reflected a bit.

"There are clearings up and down along the water that would be perfect for little cottages, and you have that large meadow that can be built on or left as is to allow for a helicopter to land. I came across an old access road, but it's a bit overgrown so I'm not sure it's been used in awhile." She caught her breath and continued. "If we could find a layout of where your property lines are, I would have a better scope for my imagination." Her eyes glittered with excitement.

"Maybe we should call Ryan and see if he can do a little research for us." She clapped her hands and sprinted to the cabin to make the call. I leaned back and put my hands behind my head, stretching to imagine her vision. It was going to be a huge undertaking, but with her help it would all come together nicely.

The night before the plane came to pick her up; we sat in on the couch and went over the plans one more time. She still had a week left on her vacation and said she would put together a presentation to show the guys and me before moving forward. With the winter ahead, there was no way we could start the project, plus we still had to find out how much of the property was owned by my grandfather.

"I wish we had figured out that box while I was here, it will drive me completely nuts not knowing." She picked it up again and walked around tossing it up in the air. "I used to be great at these types of puzzles when I was a kid. My mother had them all over our house." She turned and her eyes widened as if she had figured it out. "It's a balance puzzle...look." Holding her arms out to me, she opened her hands to reveal the box had fallen apart. "By tossing it around, I off set the balance and the pieces just came apart. This is so cool!" She placed it on the table and we sat down side by side staring at the pieces. There was a key and a wad of paper among them.

I handed her the key and picked up the wad of paper. "You think this is a clue?" I was about to open it when she stopped me.

"No, that's the balance trigger for the box, you open that and we may never get it to work again."

She held up the key so we both could see it clearly. It was old fashioned about two inches long with a filigreed "S" engraved on it. It looked like something you would see hanging from Ben Franklin's kite only smaller. "What could it possibly go to?" She asked as she handed it to me.

"I've seen a key like this...I think it belongs to a cigar or jewelry box of some kind." I placed it back on the table and sat back, drawing my knee into my chest and wrapping my arms around my leg. "The mystery continues."

The plane arrived early and I was crushed that it wasn't Ryan. We packed up her sketches and after a quick hug she took off. I stood on the dock rubbing my arms as I watched her go. I was alone again, but completely rejuvenated by her visit. I could hardly wait to see her presentation.

Over the next week, I fell into my usual routine of writing, cleaning the cabin and going for inspirational walks in the woods. I was always amazed that each time I ventured out, I found something new that would inspire me. Although I missed Ryan, I knew he would be coming back soon...I could hardly wait to see him. I would close my eyes and picture every detail of his face; his dark wavy hair, crystal blue eyes that could express a thousand different emotions, and the dimples that would form on each side of his mouth when he smiled at me.

With the weather still warm, I was able to take showers outside without the fear of frostbite, the water was chilly, but it felt refreshing first thing in the morning. On the day the plane arrived, I had just stepped in the shower as I heard it land. Knowing it would take time to dock and unload, I took my time.

Once I dried off, dressed and had just wrapped my hair up in a towel I heard Ryan's voice calling out to me. "Tess, are you gonna come down here and help or make me haul all this crap myself. As I rounded the corner, he let out a wolf call making me blush.

I was glad he was alone. I ran down and jumped into his arms. His lips responded to mine as we devoured each other. My mind was completely focused on him and nothing else, until we were interrupted by a familiar voice calling down from the cabin. "GET A ROOM! Geeze you guys need to learn how to come up for air occasionally." My heart sank as I realized we weren't alone.

To my surprise, it appeared Scott knew about us and seemed okay with it. Ryan grabbed me around the waist and rested his chin on my head as we watched him come down the path.

"Don't look so sick Tess, I'm okay with you molesting my best friend." Giving me a peck on the cheek, "but make sure you leave enough of him behind to help lug these boxes. We've got some unpacking to do, you guys can...well...do what ever it is you do later." Motioning us to get to work.

We made quick work of unloading the plane and stole a moment behind the cabin. "How long can you stay?" I questioned between kisses.

Trying to respond as I nibbled at his neck, "I'm here for as long as you want me." I stepped back and looked deep into his eyes to make sure he wasn't kidding. "Are you serious?" As he nodded, I leapt into his arms. We knew we had to help unpack, but were too wrapped up in each other to let go. Finally realizing our behavior was rude; we went inside and joined Scott in the kitchen.

Placing my hands on my hips and surveying the mess we unloaded, I asked "So, what's all this stuff? I've got enough food and supplies to last me a year." They looked at each other with confused expressions.

"You mean you don't want this stuff? We could take it all back if it's in the way?" Ryan teased as he ran his hand along the top of one of the boxes. Knowing full well my curiosity wouldn't let them do that.

"Okay, you have my attention, let's open these suckers up and see what goodies you brought me this time." My eyes were wide as I rubbed my hands together greedily.

"Well, these are things you'll need for the winter. We don't want you up here freezing." Popping open the first box, Ryan pulled out a black lace nightgown and held it up. Scott sat back and chuckled as he watched him pick on me. I grabbed the gown and held it up.

"I like the color – but I think it might be a bit drafty." Peeking over the edge of the box, I was curious to see what other "cold-weather clothes" they brought. Scott smacked my hand away. Giving in to their fun, I hoisted myself on the counter and dangled my legs like a kid as they took turns pulling items from the box and modeling them against their chests to make a show of it. I was completely amused. By the time they emptied the box, I had a few nightgowns, a new bathing suit, a satin robe, some flip flops and satin bed sheets.

I clapped my hands, as the guys took a bow. "What a show, bravo! What style sense you have!" I picked up the satin sheets and rubbed them on my face. "I'll never get out of bed with these."

They shot each other an amused look, "What a challenge that would be." Scott muffled a laugh as he slapped Ryan on the back. "Guess you have your work cut out for you…don't you old buddy?" Ryan turned red as he looked at me with a shy smile. It was a look I hadn't seen cross his face before.

"Okay, now that you've both had enough fun teasing me, show me what you really brought." I gazed over at the next box hoping it was more fun stuff.

"Well to be honest, this one was filled with your belated birthday presents from Monica, Mary, Me and Ryan…well, Monica picked out my gift.

He held up the flip-flops. "Well thank you I love them all!"

Ryan tossed the empty box on the floor and opened the next one. Inside were real winter clothes: sweaters, a snowsuit, boots, gloves, scarves and other items that seemed appropriate for the weather I was expecting. The last three boxes weren't opened. Scott said they were for a new project that Ryan would be working on while he stayed with me.

"Ry, would ya do my preflight? I want to have a chat with Tess." He asked in a low tone.

"You got it Taylor; just be sure to make it sound good if you're gonna talk about me." He kissed me quickly on the cheek and vanished.

My stomach began to twist not knowing what he was about to say. I hoped the affection Ryan and I showed in front of him didn't piss him off. I looked down at my feet and watched them swing as Scott positioned himself in front of me. He lifted my chin and looked into my eyes as if he was searching for answers to questions he hadn't asked.

"Tess, I'm happy you and Ryan got together...really, I am. The shock of seeing you again was overwhelming, but I'm back to normal. Yes! In case your wondering... I'm completely jealous of him. I try not to think about him touching you in any way, shape or form, but I let you go a long time ago and I have no right to come between you guys. He told me you two had become very close the last time he was here. He was brutally honest with me about his feelings. I just wanted to let you know face to face that I am okay with this." I tossed my arms around his neck.

"Thank you Scott, I couldn't ask for a better birthday present." Leaning in close to his ear I whispered, "Monica's a lucky woman to have a fantastic guy like you." He pulled me off the counter and we joined Ryan down at the dock.

What needed to be said had been said. There was no reason to drag it out any further. Ryan and I watched the plane fade into the sunset. Grabbing my hand, he led me back to the cabin.

CHAPTER FOURTEEN

We spent the entire night lying on the couch in each other's arms reliving one of the first moments we shared together. When the sun finally came up, we decided to leave the comfort we found in each other's arms. I made a quick breakfast and watched as he opened the boxes left from the day before.

"Whatcha gonna build now? I can see by the tools it looks like a major project." I took a bite of toast and peeked over the table trying to get a better look.

"Yup, this will help me make man points." He looked up raising a brow.

"Well that sounds yummy. You've got big plans, perhaps I could help?"

"No way woman, this is a surprise that I've worked long and hard on and I won't let you steal my thunder." He stood up and took my hand, pulling me gently to my feet. I stepped over the box and followed him to the desk in front of the picture window. "This is your project, make sure you do what you came here to do. I know you pretend to have it all started, but I know better." He bent down and gave me a fast peck on the cheek, "Don't forget why you're here, I don't want to have to leave because I'm distracting you. We'll still have nights together." He winked.

I sat down. "Okay, I promise not to peak, if you keep your promise." He bent down and kissed me deeply.

"I wouldn't promise anything less." I couldn't help but smile as he walked away.

My curiosity was peaked the day I heard a helicopter arrive outside the cabin. I ran out to see as it lowered a pallet of planks to the open field. After it was safely on the ground, Ryan scurried to unhook the cables. The chopper landed and Monica, of all people, jumped out from the cockpit. I had no idea she was a pilot. I was under the assumption she hated to fly. I watched as she gave Ryan a hug and kiss, before grabbing a large bag and ran over to me.

"Hey Tess, I've got loads to show you." She pulled me along with her to the cabin. Tossing her things to the floor, she turned and gave me a hug. I stood there still shocked she knew how to fly.

"I thought you hated flying." Shaking my head and laughing at her energy.

She tossed her hair over her shoulder, "Oh, that. Well I don't like planes, but I love choppers. They make me feel powerful and in control." She grabbed the bag and headed to the couch. I walked over to see her pulling out rolls of blueprints and setting them on the table. "I've discovered so much about this place it'll blow your mind." She began to spread out plans.

I sat down eagerly looking at what she laid before me. "What's all this?" I bent over and flipped through the pages.

"Well, this is a layout of the property…from what I can tell, your grandfather owned most of this range. He purchased it in the 30's to stop the lumber mills from destroying the area. When I was here, I discovered areas like the meadow throughout the forest. A lot smaller, but great places to build small cabins." She rushed her words as I tried to keep up. "I haven't said a thing to the guys, but here's my idea." She unrolled another plan. "I don't know what you want to call it, but here it is…this cabin will be your residence, but I think another cabin should be built as a main lodge. It'd be bigger and would allow for group gatherings. The large meadow would have cabins circled around just where the trees start. We'd clear paths to the main lodge and create a few safe nature trails through the woods. We could still leave the meadow open to allow for Helicopters. You'd still want to use the lake for hoppers, but you'll want to keep that traffic to a minimum to preserve the pristine condition and to keep it clean for fishing." She sat back raking her hands through her hair.

I looked down at the layout; amazed she was able to draw it up in such a short time. "It's great...you really put a lot of work into this." I ran my fingers along the paper following the lines she made showing all the paths.

"What...What's wrong?" She looked at where I was tracing. "Tess, if there's something you don't like, just tell me. I can change anything that you feel's out of place." She picked up the plans and held them up giving them another look.

It never crossed my mind that such a quiet place could become a booming resort. I was nervous it would change too much. The peace that I had found would be broken; but then again it would bring it a new life. "It's great. I don't know how to take it all in." I ran my hand across my mouth to keep from saying more.

"I have to get going before it gets dark, so I'll leave these here for you to look over. Just promise me you won't tell Ryan until I've the chance to pitch the idea to Scott first." I nodded still looking down at the plans.

"Good than, oh...I almost forgot..." She reached back in her bag and grabbed a large envelope. "I haven't had time to look over these papers, but I had your grandfather's lawyer Jerry send them up." She rolled her eyes, "Man that guys a real jerk, hope you get rid of him when you get back to Tucson and settle the estate."

Back? I forgot that I'd have to go back. I longed to see Mary again but the thought of leaving the cabin was something I hadn't thought of. *What would happen between Ryan and me? What was I gonna do?*

"Tess, geeze...snap out of it!" She waved her hand in front of my eyes. I blinked returning her gaze. "I need to go, make sure you keep these in a safe place."

"Thanks for coming, it was nice to see you again." She stood up, gave me a warm hug and headed out the door. Looking over her shoulder with a concerned look. "If you need anything, you'll call me, right?"

I nodded and smiled, "Yes, I promise."

I sank back down on the couch and began to roll the plans up securing them with the bands she left on the table. Looking around, the only place I could find to put them where Ryan wouldn't get curious was under the desk. He always avoided poking around that fearing he would mess up the pages I had strewn about.

My mind was still questioning the idea of the resort. I could still hear Ryan working outside so I took down the bottle of bourbon that had been sitting on the shelf since Monica's last visit. I flicked on the stereo, grabbed a glass and poured a nice big shot. I needed to lie down and relax from the overwhelming excitement and flood of thoughts that were running through my mind. Heading up to the loft, I removed my clothes and laid down on the bed. I stared into space running the images of the potential resort through my mind. I tossed down the shot and let it burn my throat, hoping it would make my mind go numb.

I listened to the soft soothing music as it lulled my senses. Dozing in and out of reality, I felt a warm liquid on my back and then strong hands caressing it into my skin. I didn't hear him approach and became relaxed at his touch. The sheet I'd covered myself with was drawn away from my body. I opened my eyes to see the cabin bathed in the light of candles. My head was still spinning from the bourbon. I remained still and let my senses take over.

The smell of baby oil filled the room. His hands gliding over my shoulders and down my back sent shivers up and down my spines. I could feel my skin prickle under his touch. It was more of a tickle than a message as his hands glided to my waist, over my ass and down my legs. My skin tingled when I felt him leave me. I heard the rustle of his clothes as they dropped to the floor. He kneeled at the end of the bed and began to rub my ankles gently. His chest against my feet, I could feel his heart beat grow rapid as his hands moved up my legs to my thighs. When he moved I felt his body brush against me. He reached my waist as he pulled himself up on his knees to straddle my legs. He continued his massage as I melted beneath his fingers. Brushing my hair from my neck he leaned forward to deliver a burning kiss.

My heart was pounding in my ears as he lifted himself up slightly to let me roll over. I looked up to see him bathed in the soft glow illuminating the cabin. His body was tan and inviting. I reached up and ran my hands and my fingers across his chest, as he leaned back enjoying my soft touch. As I explored his muscles, he reached down and cupped my breasts. The electricity in his touch sent heat through my veins.

I brought my arms up and I arched my back. He rolled to his side propping his head in his hand while the other traced patterns on my skin. I watched his eyes as they followed his fingers over my skin. My desire for him was unbearable. I turned to look into his captivating blue eyes, bringing our faces close, I could feel his breath against my lips. As we kissed, he covered me with his strength and we gave into our passion.

CHAPTER FIFTEEN

I didn't get to see Ryan during the day. He spent most of his time putting together what ever it was he was building. I kept my promise not to peak. Since the days were getting colder, I stayed inside most of the time. When I got stir crazy being cooped up, he'd take me for an adventure in the woods. Wandering around, I discovered all the places that Monica had pointed out on the plans. I could picture her vision, but kept my promise not to tell Ryan about the resort. Even though I had thought about doing the same thing before Monica even mentioned it, I still had my doubts about changing things.

When the end of September rolled around, I pushed aside all the pages I had finally written. Reading them over and over again, I realized it was the same kind of story everyone else was writing. It felt formatted and full of empty metaphors that wouldn't mean a damn thing to anyone but me. Writing as if I was in the 17th century with a lot of "wilt thou's" and "hence forth's". I had read and re-read the pages and decided it was pure crap!

Since I couldn't find what I was looking for in my writing, I turned to something that wouldn't make my brain hurt. Moving all the furniture to the walls I hauled the area rugs outside tossing them over the rail on the porch. I felt like a true pioneer woman as I rolled up my sleeves, grabbed a broom and beat the crap out of the rugs. It felt good to take out my frustrations. Once my arms became tired, I stepped back. Sweat dripping down my face, I pushed my hair out of my eyes feeling satisfied with the job I had done. With the broom still in hand, I headed inside to sweep. Deciding that it would be best to start at the fireplace and work my way to the door, I swept across the room. In my haste, I tripped over something sticking up from the floor landing flat on my face. Feeling stupid, I was glad Ryan was still outside and didn't witness my graceful tumble. Wondering what I tripped over, I felt around and found the culprit. Right where the largest area rug had laid was a small trap door. The latch must have been pulled up when I lifted the rug.

I tried to pull it open, but wouldn't budge it. Taking a closer look, I noticed a keyhole about the same size as the key Monica and I found. Scrambling to my feet, I hurried to the shelf where we had set the pieces of the box. I grabbed the key and ran back to the lock. My adrenaline was racing as I steadied myself and tried the key. It was a perfect fit. Inside was a large box covered in dust. I reached in and gently pulled it from its hiding place. Knowing Ryan would be coming in soon to wash up and eat dinner, I put it under my desk, closed the trap door and put the key back on the shelf.

It was another mystery I wanted to enjoy alone. Putting it out of my mind, I went back to cleaning. By the time he came in, I had the cabin swept, dusted and put back together. "Nice job!" he commented as he looked around the room. "Your talents are beyond my scope of imagination."

Brushing off his teasing, I went into the kitchen to start dinner. "Before you get cleaned up, could you get a fire going for me? It's starting to get chilly."

"A man's work is never done." He said with a lisp, tossing his hands limply in the air as he walked by the kitchen to grab a few logs of wood.

Once he had a nice fire going, he headed into the bathroom to clean up. As I sat at the table, my hand brushed up against the radio accidentally turning it on. I reached to turn it off when a panicked voice came across loud and clear "Are you there?" and then static. Ryan heard it from the bathroom and rushed out dripping wet and wrapped in a towel.

"What the hell was that?" His eyes wild with concern. I stared at him with the same look.

"My hand brushed against the power switch and it just came on." I shrugged my shoulders not knowing what more to say.

"This is set for transmission between here and base." He fumbled with the dials and called into the mike hoping for a response. We stood there listening in anticipation.

An hour went by and no response. We ate quietly listening intently for anything to come across. It was late and I could tell that Ryan was tired from working all day. Reluctant to leave the radio, I suggested he lay down on the couch and keep the radio on the rest of the night.

It didn't take him long to fall asleep. I covered him with a light blanket and brushed the hair from his face. It was still early and I was cloaked in an inch of dirt. I hadn't noticed I was a complete mess. Before heading into the bathroom, I went upstairs and grabbed one of the nightgowns I got for my birthday. So as not to use more electricity, I lit a candle that illuminated the bathroom in a soft golden glow. I took my time in the shower letting the water trickle gently over my skin. My hair had grown past my shoulders and half way down my back. I hadn't paid much attention since I normally wore it up in pony tail. I enjoyed the feel of it as it covered my back.

I toweled off and put on the nightgown. The cool white satin felt good against my skin. I wished Ryan hadn't passed out on the couch. I felt sexy and wanted to seduce him. Giving up the idea, I blew out the candle and headed upstairs to sleep alone.

I woke to the sound of the radio still crackling in the kitchen. Ryan was nursing a cup of coffee and listening intently for any noise that sounded like a voice. He did a double take as I swept past him. "Wow! Look what I missed out on last night."

I turned swiftly letting the satin fabric billow out and wrap around my legs. "Yes, I dressed up just for you, but don't feel too bad. You didn't miss much, I fell asleep the minute my head hit the pillow… have you heard anything yet?"

"No, not a damn thing." Sounding frustrated as he ran his fingers through his hair. "We'll find out soon enough…Scott's weekly radio call…remember?"

"Well then," I leaned over and kissed him gently, "I'll leave you to it and you can do that male bonding thing you like so much." Giving a twirl, I grabbed a piece of toast and headed back upstairs to get dressed.

Ryan's call never came in. He sat by the radio most of the day before giving up and heading out back to continue what he was working on. I could tell he was stressing over the panicked call. Everyone back at base knew we only had the radio on during set times, so hearing that transmission didn't make sense. I was sure that's why it tormented him.

Trying to wipe it from my mind, I reached under the desk and grabbed the large wooden box. It had the same type of lock as the trap door and was made of the same type of wood as the puzzle box. I got the key and tried it, but it wouldn't turn. Frustrated, I pushed it behind the typewriter and grabbed the envelope Monica left for me to look through. Over stuffed with papers, it was difficult to pull the pages out without ripping the envelope.

At the top of the stack was a note from Jerry the lawyer from hell.

Tess,
Here's everything I could find about the cabin. I didn't have time to read through it, but I hope it helps.
Jerry

Even though his letter was sedate, the thought of him turned my stomach. I looked forward to the day when I didn't have to deal with him. I crumpled up the page and tossed it into the fire. Flipping through the documents I found a copy of the property deed, sketches of the cabin and furniture, a bunch of letters and a hand drawn map of the area. It was interesting, but I didn't know where to start.

The letters looked the most interesting, so I gathered them up and got comfortable on the couch to read each one carefully. I hoped they held some kind of explanation to the locked box. The first was from my grandfather to his lawyer requesting particulars about the area. He mentioned wanting to build a group of cabins around the lake with the intent to sell and make a profit. The second was also written by him, but harshly worded and addressed to a lumber company demanding they cease the traffic along the access road at the back of his property line.

Before I had a chance to read the rest of the letters, Ryan came in and sat down beside me. "I think I'm done for the day. Did you hear anyone come across the radio yet?" I looked down at the letters and shook my head. He let out a sigh as I looked over at him. The stress was beginning to show on his face.

"Don't worry babe, if there's an emergency…they'd find some way to contact us." I placed my hands on his face and gave him a gentle kiss. Putting the letters on the table I patted my lap inviting him to rest his head. As he laid there, I ran my fingers through his hair lulling him to sleep. I reached for the letters and continued to read. Half way through the stack I found another note card with the letter "S" and silver foil lining. It was more business like than the first one.

> *Dear Mr. Kelly,*
>
> *With regrets, I am unable to accompany you to survey your property. I will be able to fly up the following week to deliver your crew. Should you require additional assistance, let me know and I will see what I can do to help. Once again I would like to thank you for allowing me the opportunity to work with you as Project Manager. I will do my best to complete this job to your satisfaction.*
>
> *Sincerely,*
>
> *Sofia Sartori*

I laid the letters back on the table and shifted my weight slowly trying not to jostle Ryan awake. Placing my hand on his chest, I felt the calm rhythm of his breathing. I leaned my head back and stared up at the rafters wondering about Sophia and what happened to the idea of developing the land. If it had gone like my grandfather intended, there'd be people around instead of the peaceful quiet. I let the questions swim in my head until I fell asleep.

CHAPTER SIXTEEN

Ryan couldn't shake the missed radio call thinking it was more then just someone on the wrong frequency. We conserved as much electricity as possible so we could keep the radio on. Going back to living the way we did before the windmill. The nights got colder so we kept the fire going not only for light, but to help keep us warm. September was coming to an end and I made no real headway on my book. I couldn't find the right story. I lost my inspiration. Ryan had been working hard on his project and was usually too tired to do anything but sleep.

Expecting the next plane to arrive any day, I couldn't stand to sit behind my desk and stare out the window. I read over the rest of the letters hoping to find more clues to help solve the mystery of the locked box, but discovered nothing more than a woman had designed and help build the cabin. I decided it would have to remain a mystery. Frustration began to exhaust me and I once again went stir crazy. I wanted Ryan's attention and was getting antsy about his big secret. Just as I was about to turn the door handle to finally take a peek, he came crashing though, knocking me against the wall.

"Oh, geeze Tess," he reached out and caught my arm, bringing me to my feet. "Gosh babe, I'm sorry, I didn't know you were standing there." He looked me over making sure I was all right.

I smacked his hand away; "Yes…I'm fine." My voice was harsh. "Just…" I smoothed out the front of my shirt roughly. "Give me a sec, would ya?" I looked up. The frustration on my face must have hit him like a ton of bricks. He stepped back with a confused look and he held up his hands in defense. "Chill out wild woman. Just trying to help."

Feeling like a complete ass for acting like a bitch, I looked down at my feet. "I'm sorry, it's not your fault. I'm just pissed and getting sick of this place." He lifted my chin and brushed a kiss across my lips.

"I think I can take away some of that frustration." His words sent shivers up my spine. It had been days since we had slept together. The idea made me feel giddy. "I've got a surprise for you…" his smile grew wide. "I finished your present."

It wasn't what I had in my mind, but I was excited to finally see what he had been keeping from me. I caught a peek a few times when I went for walks in the woods. It looked like he was building a shed or a room onto the back of the cabin. He covered my eyes and led me out the door. A step down and a few steps forward, he turned me and lifted his hands from my face. I was right; it was some kind of shed.

"It's great…but…" I ran my hands over the door, "What's it for?" I turned around, tossing my hair over my shoulder.

"Well my dear…"he reached around and pushed it open. "This is the answer to all your stress and tension." He pushed me forward gently. "This is your birthday present from me!" He stood behind me and I saw it was a sauna. "It'll keep us warm in the winter and provide another way for us to enjoy each other." He brought his lips to my neck and ran his tongue up to my ear. "Wanna try it out?" I swung around and kissed him deeply.

He'd worked so hard to give me a wonderful gift and I spent the whole time feeling abandoned by him. I felt ashamed of how selfish I had been. "Thank you Ryan, it's wonderful! I'm sorry I snapped at you." Searching his eyes for forgiveness. "You did all this for me and I acted like such a brat." He reached down and scooped me up in his arms.

"Well, then…you'll have to make it up to me." Kicking the door shut, he brought me to the bench.

The heat from the sauna intensified our passion bringing us to new heights of ecstasy. My heart ached for him to tell me he loved me. I held my own confession remembering my vow to let him make that critical step. The moist heat made the air thick. He rose and opened the door letting cool air hit our bodies. I leaned against the wall and let it caress my skin. He stood in the doorway taking in the sight of me enjoying his gift.

Suddenly, he turned as if startled and ran into the cabin. I hadn't heard anything that could have caused to him to rush away like that. I picked up our wet clothes from the floor and followed him. Creeping through the door, I listen carefully as the radio crackled over the sound of Ryan's voice. I wasn't able to make out what he was saying. Heading into the bathroom, I hung our clothes on the peg behind the door and strained to hear the call. I wrapped myself in a towel and headed into the kitchen trying to be as quiet as possible.

He flipped off the radio and sat back in the chair. "So? What happened?" I tossed him a dishtowel.

Looking a bit amused, he dabbed his chest and explained. "It was a kid." He looked up smiling. "He was channel surfing...he uses the radio to try to make friends across the country. I guess he was disappointed to learn we were only a few states way." He laughed as we both realized that the one tiny transmission he had worried about for almost a week was nothing more than a kid trying to make his way across America on the radio.

He twirled the towel and gave it a snap in my direction. I let out a playful scream and ran past him up the stairs. He followed catching me as we fell onto the bed. We awoke to the sound of a plane landing in the lake. Feeling tired and spent, we dragged ourselves out of bed, dressing slowly, as if our bodies were made of lead. As we descended the stairs the door burst open making us both jump. "Honey...I'm home!"

There stood Scott with his hands on his hips looking amused. I gave him a hug and peck on the check before heading into the kitchen to toss some logs in the stove. "Tess, I need to steal the old man for a bit if you don't mind." His voice turned serious.

"Sure, I'll just fix something for us to eat." As they headed out the door I went to the storeroom to grab what I needed. Sick of pancakes, I grabbed a large can of corned beef and a bag of powdered eggs. Getting creative with the herbs that grew around the cabin, I was able to make them taste more like eggs than paste. It was a beautiful day, so I made up my mind to eat alfresco.

I cleared the desk and pulled it out to the porch. Draping a clean sheet for a tablecloth and grabbing the only three chairs in the cabin, I set up and waited for the guys to come back. After an hour, the food had gotten cold, so I went ahead and ate without them. I didn't know where they had gone, but as I sat there I started to get pissed. They knew I was planning to fix breakfast.

I made up my mind to really lay into them when they came back. After two more hours had passed, I gave up. Clearing off the desk I whipped up the sheet and tossed it over the rail and lined the chairs against the wall. Just as I hoisted up the desk to bring it inside Ryan came around the side of the cabin. He didn't say a word as he passed me and headed up to the loft.

I brought the desk inside and put it back in its place. I looked up to the loft to catch him packing his bag. It was the first time I ever saw him that upset. I watched as he fisted his clothes into the bag as if he were punching someone. He looked around one last time and with a quick zip he tossed it over the rail. If I had been two steps closer, it would've hit me.

I stood there in shock as I watched him come down the steps. He stopped and stood staring into my eyes with a cold look. "I've gotta go Tess, I'll be back. I just need to take care of something before it gets out of hand." I searched his eyes for answers to his anger. "I'll try to be back next week." His face softened a bit. "I wouldn't leave you if it wasn't important. Just trust that I'll be back." He pressed me against him bringing his mouth down hard bruising my lips. As I stepped back, he grabbed his bag and ran to the plane. Without waiting for Scott or performing a preflight, he took off.

I stood on the porch completely stunned trying to absorb what had just happened. Suddenly it dawned on me that Scott was still somewhere around. I yelled out, but there was no response. I decided to look for him. I knew Ryan had come from the back of the cabin so I took the familiar path to the meadow, calling out as I walked along. When I came to the clearing, I saw Scott slumped over the log in the middle of the meadow. His body was lifeless.

I approached cautiously. "Scott, are you okay?" He still didn't move. I reached out my hand and placed it on his shoulder. Rubbing my hand along his back I could tell he was breathing. I grabbed his shoulder using all my strength and turned him over. Blood trickled from his mouth and nose; I gasped and fell to my knees. "What the hell happened?...Scott, wake up!" My heart raced with panic as I tore the bottom of my shirt. Using the ripped cloth to dab the blood from his lips. He winced as he opened his eyes. Reaching up he pushed my hand away.

"Tess, stop." His breath sounded weak and forced. "Don't, I deserve this pain. Don't try to make it better."

"What the hell happened?" I demanded an answer and was pissed that he tried to brush me away.

"Just help me up, would ya?" He reached out using the log to steady himself. I grabbed under his arm and helped him to his feet. He stood there a moment than pushed me away and headed to the path. I followed watching him sway like a drunken man towards the cabin. I could hear him cussing under his breath when he saw the plane was gone.

He looked at me and flipped his hands above his head. "My plane...he took my damn plane." Shooting a hateful look at me, he stomped up the path and into the cabin slamming the door behind him.

Not wanting to deal with his drama, I headed to the dock to dip my feet in the water. I tried to figure out what could've happened to make Ryan go ballistic on him. He was normally a very passive guy; and didn't seem like the kind of man who would beat the crap out of someone. No matter how curious I was to get answers, I knew it would be best to wait until Scott was ready to talk.

I sat there most of the day until I heard a rumble of thunder in the distance. My heart leapt as I prayed Ryan was already safe on the ground. I figured he had flown back to base. I couldn't let myself feel unwelcome in my own home, so I got up and brushed off my pants and headed up to the cabin. Standing at the door I looked around not seeing Scott anywhere. I headed to the kitchen and cleaned up the mess I made earlier.

Once I had dried the last dish, he came out of the bathroom. He kept his head down as he passed and headed to the couch. "Tess, I don't want to talk about it so don't even ask."

"Fine" I said tossing a towel on the counter. My blood began to boil and I knew I was gonna explode. "If you don't want to talk than I won't force the issue, but I'd like to go on record and say that this bullshit today is completely unappreciated. You and Ryan have this little game of keeping me in the dark about everything and it's really starting to piss me off." Being brushed off again brought up the frustration and anger I had kept to myself way too long so I let loose.

"I've had enough of this place, this stupid quest to pull a story out of my ass and all the secrets everyone thinks they should keep from me. Ever since I came here I've had to face one drama after another. When's it gonna stop?!" I stomped into the room and began to pace behind the couch as he sat staring into the fire. "I was having the time of my life and then, BAM!, I learn my grandfather's dead...I go home to grieve and find that he's married....oh...but that wasn't enough! I had to have my life tossed like a salad by Jerry the jerk who informs me I have to live like a hermit and write a damn book to fulfill my grandfather's wishes. Being the sap I am, I agreed to do it...and then...and then I get to the airport thinking I'm gonna finally have a moment of peace and there you are! Standing there all handsome and confident ripping my heart right out of my chest." I turned and pointed at the back of his head, catching my breath. "You shit...you flew me in a piece of shit plane to meet your wife... YOUR WIFE...did it ever occur to you to at least let me know you got married...I told you everything! EVERYTHING! Even after we had broken up. I sent letters to your damn PO Box...never getting one damn response. I never gave up on you...you dumb ass."

I dragged my hands through my hair and looked over to him. He hadn't moved so I continued my ranting, "Don't get me wrong, I like Monica...I think she's great! She's your perfect fit damn it! I hate that I couldn't be that for you. You brought me here Scott, you were the one who left me here. You were the one who kissed me... not once, but twice. You confused the hell out of me, but I found something special. I finally found a man that filled every empty hole in my heart. You come here today and suddenly I'm here with you and not him. How much more of this shit do I have to take?"

I stood there waiting for him to say something. His shoulders tensed up, but he still didn't turn around. "Fine, you just stay there and be the asshole you are. Just be sure to stay the hell away from me!" I reached down and took off my shoe sending it sailing barely missing his head. He turned sharply as I stormed up the stairs.

CHAPTER SEVENTEEN

It felt good to finally get everything off my chest. I was glad Ryan wasn't there to witness my rage. At that moment, I couldn't care less what had happened between them. All I knew was that he had done or said something to tear Ryan away from me again. I was sick of being stuck at the cabin, trying to find things to keep myself busy. Even with someone around, it was getting to me. I missed all the world had to offer.

I laid there dreaming of all the wonderful food I had no access to, all the stores there were to shop in, all the places to go and people to see. I was missing everything at that moment. I wanted out. The book was going nowhere and I felt too boxed in. I had to find a new atmosphere and fast.

When the light from the fire was taken over by daylight, I wrapped myself up in the bed sheet and headed down for a shower. By the time I was done, Scott had started a fire in the stove and put on a pot of coffee. He went outside to shower in the cold morning. I hoped he felt miserable. Pouring a cup of coffee I sat down at the desk. Reaching down I grabbed the plans Monica had left for me to look over.

I went to the couch and unrolled them on the table. Searching through the pages, I found the map of the area and carefully folded it up. I rolled up the rest of the pages and tossed them back under the desk. In the storeroom I found a backpack and stuffed it with a med. kit, some food, a large hunting knife, compass, and other emergency supplies I thought might be helpful. I packed up a blanket and secured it to the bottom of the pack with rope. Storming into the great room I headed out the door and grabbed the rifle. I paused, realizing I was about to create the same kind of drama I bitched about the night before. I went back in and sat down realizing my idea was stupid.

I stashed the backpack and rifle behind some boxes in the storeroom and went back to my desk to lay out a better plan. Looking the map over, I discovered another large clearing only a few miles south of the cabin. I formulated my escape, but would have to find a way to reach Monica for it to work.

Knowing Scott wasn't going to come near the cabin for awhile, I sat down at the radio and prayed Ryan had left it on the same settings from the last time he called the base. I flicked the switch not knowing what to say, I mumbled "Hello, is anyone there?" Surprised to hear Ryan. "Tess? You okay?" I leaned back, staring at the mic. I didn't want him knowing my plans.

"Yes, it's me and I'm doing just fine. Is there anyway you can get Monica for me? I need to talk to her privately…is that possible?" There was a long pause before he responded.

"Is Scott around?" His voice was cold.

"No, he took off earlier. Haven't seen him for awhile. It's a girl thing babe; I just need to talk to Monica. I don't mean be rude, but I need to talk to her alone…just me and her. If you don't mind." My heart sank as I heard the hurt in his voice.

"Yeah sure, if you can hang on for a minute. I'll get her…Tess, before I do, I just want to say I'm sorry for taking off like that. You didn't deserve it, especially from me. I miss you… I can't talk about it right now, but I'll explain when I get back…I promise."

There was another pause and then I heard Monica say Hello. "Monica, do me a favor and make sure there's no one around to hear us."

"I'm in the office and the door's closed, Ryan went to get a soda…what's wrong?" Her voice was vacant.

"I want you to come get me…before you say anything listen to what I gotta say." The radio remained silent and I knew that she was listening. "I've gotta get the hell out of here and you're the only one I know who won't talk me out of it. I'm going to take off down stream tonight after I know Scott's asleep. I looked over the map you left and there's a huge clearing about five miles downstream."

She broke in excitedly, "Yes, I know the spot you're talking about."

She paused. "If you have any money you can loan me I promise to pay you back." I waited anxiously for her response.

There was a long pause before I heard the radio crackle, "Tess, if you think you can make it by sunrise, I'll be there."

Excitedly I smiled, "I'll see you then!" I didn't hear a response so I turned off the radio and went back to the desk.

Knowing I had a definite way out, I decided to pack a little better for the trip. Retrieving the backpack, I went to the loft and dumped it out on the bed. I picked out clothes that would pack tightly, to be on the safe side, I re-packed all the emergency supplies, knife and compass and grabbed the flashlight that was on a shelf over the bed.

I only went down to grab a quick bite to eat for lunch and again at dinner. Scott didn't return until it had grown dark. He looked up to see me sitting on the bed pretending to read; he disappeared coming back with a bottle of wine.

I watched as he belted back the whole bottle. Staring in anticipation, I waited for him to pass out. He couldn't have picked a better night to get drunk. A few hours passed before he had gone through two bottles. Finally his head fell back and he began to snore.

Waiting another ten minutes just to make sure he wouldn't wake up, I grabbed the pack and tip toed down the stairs. I grabbed a pack of matches from the kitchen and spied the radio; realizing it would be a matter of minutes from the time he discovered I was gone for him to get help. I had no idea what to break to make it useless, so I pulled the mic and stuffed it in my pack hoping that would be enough.

I opened the door quietly keeping my eyes on Scott's lifeless body. Once outside, I took out the flashlight and headed to the far end of the lake where I knew there was a rough path that lead along the stream. The moon was full and helped to illuminate the water as I walked along. At first I went quickly fearing he had discovered I was gone.

The path that led to the clearing began to veer away from the stream and lead me deeper into the forest. I sucked up my fears and pushed forward. After about two miles the flashlight began to dim. When I smacked it against my hand, trying to get it to work the cap came off spilling the batteries on the ground. I fell to my knees to grab them landing on a sharp rock. An intense pain shot through my body as I jumped up sending the flashlight into the air. I hopped on one leg trying to get the pain to settle.

Once I had collected myself, I realized the flashlight was a lost cause. I stood up and let the pain shoot through me as I put my weight on both legs. My eyes grew accustom to the darkness and when I could see far enough ahead, I pushed on.

At some point the pain in my knee turned numb. It became easier to walk. I was happy to see the path lead back to the stream. Stopping for a moment, I bent down to get a sip of water. I was tired, but eager to push on. Determined to make it to the clearing before sunrise and compelled by the excitement of the adventure, I pushed forward along the path.

Hours had gone by and the clearing wasn't too far ahead of me. The blood from my knee had dried on my jeans and I could feel the hard fabric scraping against the wound. I reached the clearing just as the sun began to rise. A fine mist cascaded over the landscape. Setting down the pack, I tore off my sweater letting the cold air hit my body. I went to the stream and splashed water on my face. All the stress and anxiety from the day before melted away.

I heard the whirring of the helicopter as I changed into fresh clothes. Tossing what I had been wearing, I grabbed my bag as she landed gently in the middle of the clearing. I ran to the craft and jumped in. Excited smiles on our faces, we gave each other a nod and took off.

She handed me a headset. "You know the minute Scott finds you gone he'll radio base." I shrugged my shoulder, bent down and pulled the mic from my bag. She threw her head back and laughed. "Well, in that case…where you want to go?"

"Just take me the hell away from here." With a nod, she flew us just above the trees. I looked down trying to figure out where we were. Normally I could tell what direction, but I was completely turned around. Monica was right; it was a lot more fun then a puddle jumper. I watched in amazement at how easy it looked for her to handle the craft.

"You been a pilot long?" I shouted, hoping I didn't blow her concentration.

"All my life, it runs in the family. My grandmother paved the path for us all. There isn't a person at my family reunion that doesn't fly. I didn't have the chance to know her like you did your grandfather, but the stories my mother told me made her a hero in my eyes." She smiled as she reflected on those memories.

I sat back and enjoyed the ride. It wasn't long before we came upon an airstrip next to a lake. Once on the ground I recognized it, we were at the base. "Are you nuts? Ryan's gonna take me back!" I looked at her in disbelief.

"Don't stress." She said calmly as she powered down. "Ryan's been gone since last night and the only guy here has no idea who you are or where you came from."

Realizing she was a very smart woman. I grabbed my bag and stepped out on the solid ground. At first I felt heavy, but found my land legs quickly. I waited as Monica secured the helicopter. Once in the office, we sat down and enjoyed a hot cup of coffee. She kicked her heals up on the desk and looked across at me. "So, where do we go from here?"

"I know you're way too busy to jump me from place to place, so I figured if you could loan me some money, I could rent a car and just head out." I took a careful sip from the mug.

Flinging her feet off the desk. She sat up looking shocked. "Nobody told you a thing did they?" She stood and began to pace. She was pissed. I didn't know what to say so I kept my mouth shut.

She pounded her fist on the desk. "Tess, once again those assholes have you completely in the dark. Now I know why you wanted to leave." She made another circuit of the room before plopping back down across from me resting her head in her hands.

"So much has happened." I saw tears forming in her dark eyes. I put my cup down and leaned forward to show she had my full attention. "Scott and I got into a huge fight and I left him." Her words didn't sink in at first, but then it hit me like a ton of bricks. Stunned, I sat back and listened.

"He didn't spend two weeks running the resort, he hired some chick named Becca to do it for him. I came back to find this woman doing my job. I tried to brush it off, and concentrated on our project instead. At first I thought it was great having the time to explore a new venture. I got so caught up in what I was doing, I wasn't seeing who was doing who when my back was turned. A week ago, I was heading to the library when I realized I forgot my notes. When I got back to the lodge, I walked in on Scott in the arms of that slut."

She choked back her sobs and went on. "I was crushed." She looked up accusingly. "I know the two of you had some tense moments together and I was able to understand. At least he told me about it and we worked through it, but this was completely out of left field. I packed my things and moved into Ryan's house. He wouldn't be there while he was staying with you, so I knew he wouldn't mind." Her eyes shot up to the ceiling and she lifted her hands to wipe away the tears.

"The day before Scott flew up to the cabin, he came to the house and begged me to come back. He told me he fired Becca. He had some lame story trying to make me believe nothing happened. He was drunk off his ass and got physical. I kicked him in the nuts and the minute he hit the ground, I grabbed my keys and drove off. The next day I was surprised to see Ryan show up and pissed as hell. He told me he beat the crap out of Scott." She leaned forward again, grabbed her coffee taking a big gulp. "Just like my brother to come to my defense."

I bolted back in my seat as if struck by lightning. "Ryan's your brother...Holy Shit! I didn't know that!"

"Damn girl, I thought for sure you knew" She looked as shocked as I was. "We may have had different father's, but we shared the same mother."

"Oh shit, he's not coming back any time soon is he?" I panicked. I didn't want to him catching on I had left.

"Don't worry, he took off on a cross country before I went to pick you up. He'll be gone most of the day." She gazed out the window with her arms folded across her chest, "So, since I've no where else to be…where should we go?"

Still in shock, I shook my head. "I have no earthly idea, you got any?"

"Well…" She spun around holding up a credit card. "As a matter of fact I do…how'd you like to experience a little tropical getaway and do a little research?"

I had always known there was something about her I liked.

CHAPTER EIGHTEEN

We left a note for Ryan telling him we took off, but not giving a clue to where we were planning to go. Neither of us had the guts to just leave the guys hanging wondering what could've happened. I was running away, if not for good…at least a week or two until I found my sanity. Monica was running not just because her husband turned into a complete asshole, but because she loved an adventure.

We went to the bank and got traveler's checks before driving to the local airport. It took most of the day before we finally reached LAX. Tired and hungry, we got a room at a hotel to relax and get cleaned up. Once we were settled in, we headed down to the gift shop and bought some appropriate clothes and other necessities for the trip. I was enjoying being around people again. At first it was a little overwhelming, but I quickly adapted. I felt free and wanted to take in all the sights and sounds of the city, unfortunately, our flight was leaving early the next morning.

Over martinis, I relayed my experiences of the past few days. I told her about Ryan taking off angry, finding Scott in the meadow beaten and bruised, and how I finally blew up at him. We raised our glasses and toasted each other's little victories. "Here's to us, the better of the two sexes."

The next day I woke up hung over and feeling raw. We rushed around gathering up our things and set out for the airport. After finally making it through security, we checked in and I headed for the nearest gift shop. My stomach was in knots thanks to our "girl's night out". I bought some aspirin and joined Monica who was looking as rough as I was.

We didn't have long to wait before we began boarding the flight. We took our seats, stowed our bags, and fell asleep. I didn't realize it was more than halfway through the flight until Monica tapped my shoulder, brining me back to life. "We missed the first drink cart, but I managed to grab some water when I went to the bathroom." She said. My mouth was too dry to say thanks, so I gave her a look of appreciation and took a few careful sips.

"God that was good! Thanks." I put the cap back on the bottle and set it down beside me. "Monica, I'm worried that Ryan's gonna be pissed at me for taking off." I turned to her for comfort.

"You're right, he'll go ballistic, but he'll get over it and forgive you...and me I hope." She bit her lip and looked back to me. "My poor brother! We've put him through hell these past few days haven't we?" She giggled and I couldn't help but join her in the joke. "I can just see him now, sitting in the office finding our note. He'll crumple it up and throw it at the wall. He'll cuss up a storm and then grab the phone and call everyone he can think of to ask if they know where we are." She rested her head back and looked up. "Right about now he's realized he can't get through to Scott, so he'll probably go pick him up."

"You think they'll figure out where we're going?" I grabbed the water and took a big swig.

"I doubt it, even if Ryan does figure it out, he won't let Scott come anywhere near me." She closed her eyes, "Don't worry Tess, they don't have a clue. You should sit back and think of this as a vacation." She reached out and patted my hand.

I knew she was right, I just had to get into the right frame of mind. I tried to convince myself to relax and not worry about the guys or how I had completely screwed up my grandfather's last wishes. I didn't give a damn about the money; the whole idea of me being trapped alone in a cabin to write a stupid book was insane. I was gonna live my life my way and not by the constraints of a damned Family Trust. Following Monica's lead, I reclined my seat and closed my eyes.

I woke up when I heard the bump of the lunch cart pass our row. I was starving and even airplane food sounded great. I was happy to find the quality of the food much better than I had experienced before. My excitement began to bubble to the surface as we got closer to landing. It didn't matter that Monica had already made up an itinerary; I was gonna have a great time no matter what she had planned or where we were going. I was away from the cabin and away from the men. My heart did ache for Ryan, but I was too wrapped up in the adventure to let it consume me.

I spent the rest of the flight listening to the radio and watching the movie. When we finally did land, we took a smaller plane and flew to Maui. Monica knew exactly where she wanted to go…I didn't question, I just followed her instructions.

We got adjoining rooms in a nice big resort right on the beach. "You want to rest or do you want to come with me to check out the tree house resort I told you about?"

I stood at the window taking in the grand sight of the ocean. "You go ahead; I wanna head down to the beach." I turned to face her hoping she wasn't hurt that I didn't wanna go.

Smiling, she tossed an envelope of traveler's checks on the bed. "Here…you may need to buy a little "somethin somethin" to make the trip worth while." She flipped her hair dramatically and closed the door. I turned back and stared out the window. It was gorgeous and I wished Ryan could be with me to enjoy the moment. Not wanting to stand there all day pining for him, I grabbed the money and headed down to the lobby. The gift shop was nice but too expensive. As much as I had traveled, I knew the best deals could be found where the residents shop. I hailed a cab and told the driver to take me to a store where he would go.

I found myself right in the middle of town surrounded by small shops and lots of people. It felt great to be swept up in the crowd. I went from store to store buying small trinkets and a few outfits. I came upon a jewelry store and decided to get something nice for Ryan. I found a gold chain and I knew would look great against his bare chest. I never saw him wear any kind of jewelry, but it didn't matter.

Not wanting to get too bogged down with packages, I took another cab back to the resort and tossed my treasures on the bed amazed I still had a large sum of money left. A knock on the door had me skipping across the room, I stopped before turning the handle, "Who is it?" I questioned.

"It's Monica...you mind if I come in for a bit?" I opened the door and she headed straight for my pile of bags. "My God girl, when you go shopping, you don't mess around. She picked up the items and began to laugh as she lifted a large sun hat high in the air. "We'll have to get this sucker its own room." She tossed it into a chair and draped herself across the bed, picking through the rest of the bags.

"You're a skilled shopper Tess; I think that will come in handy if we get the resort idea going." She looked backwards as her head stretched over the edge of the bed. "I got some great ideas today; feel like sitting on the beach and talking about them?"

"What a good idea...I'll get dressed and meet you down stairs in five minutes." She jumped up and ran out the door. I put on the bathing suit I bought in LA and gazed into the mirror. I'd completely forgotten about the cut on my knee. It had become worse thanks to my neglect. I stood there and looked down at the swollen red gash surrounded by a purple bruise. I knew I wouldn't feel comfortable walking around with the battle wound showing, so I grabbed a large scarf from one of the bags on the bed and wrapped it around my waist letting the fringe cover it.

I heard Monica get on the elevator. Giving myself one last look over, I grabbed the big floppy hat and headed out the door. We walked along watching the people in the water. Remaining silent, we took it all in, the air, the warm sun, smell of the ocean and the noise from the surfers. I never realized it before, but in a small way, Monica had been secluded too. She may have had a little more human interaction then I did, but she had been stuck in the woods the same as me.

Sitting on the beach watching the sun set, she told me about the tree house resort and the other ideas she had come up with. It all started to come into focus and I could see the charm of her plan. Not only would it add a little more life to the cabin, it would also give me an income. I closed my eyes as she spoke and was able to picture it all clearly. "I think after a week of tropical bliss, if you're ready…we should go back and start getting this plan in motion." My heart sank when I remembered I had run away.

"Well…" I said as I leaned back on my elbow, "I don't know if I'm gonna have the chance to get anything in motion after what I've done…the conditions of my grandfather's will stated that I had to stay at the cabin for a year."

She bolted straight up; "Well they wouldn't fault you for a little technicality. It's only a week and then you'll be back and I'll do what ever I have to do to help."

The week went by too fast and before I knew it we were heading back to reality. I cringed at the thought of going back, but what I was more concerned about was Ryan. I'd only seen him pissed one time and that was more than enough for me. During the trip, I tried to come up with an excuse I could rehearse before seeing him. Everything I thought up sounded stupid and irrational…I'd have to find something more than words to make him understand and forgive me.

It was late in the day when we finally drove up to his house. To my surprise it looked almost like the cabin. I shrugged my shoulders thinking that it must be a popular design for the area. When we cautiously opened the door, we found ourselves standing face to face with both the guys. Scott's face was filled with concern as he looked intently at Monica, but Ryan's face was as stern as the day he flattened Scott. He looked away from me and grabbed Monica by the shoulders. "You…are going to keep your mouth shut and listen to what I have to say with out one word passing your lips." She stood there looking as shocked as a child who had just had her butt slapped.

He turned to me, "And you…just sit there and wait until I get this whole mess cleared up." Monica and I sat close to each other on the couch; she reached over and took my hand giving it a squeeze to show her support.

Scott sat down in a wing backed chair against the wall as Ryan paced in front of us. "Let me make one thing very clear! I'll be doing the talking here tonight…Not you, you or even you." He pointed to each one of us in turn.

"I have a shit load of apologizing to do and I am not happy that I have to do it, but I have no choice…it's the only way to help mend these damn fences." He raked his hand through his hair. "Tess, I am sorry I stormed out that day not telling you a damn thing and leaving you with that." He pointed; tossing a disgusted look towards Scott. "But to go running off in the night…was just…stupid." He leaned over and looked me straight in the eye and repeated, "Stupid," he straightened up.

"Scott, I am sorry for beating the shit out of you before I let you tell me the whole story." He leaned over and held out his hand. Scott uncrossed his arms, reached out and shook his hand.

"And you…my sister, my own flesh and blood." He put his hands to his chest, "I'm sorry for all the names I called you when I found out you had left." He turned his back to us rubbing his chin, "Although, I was proud of your creativity and the sneakiness of it all."

Whirling around he surveyed our faces. "Now, to clear the air." He knelt in front of Monica. "Scott was telling the truth, Mon. He didn't have anything to do with that bitch. I talked to the maid and she saw the whole thing. Becca heard you coming and made her move just when she knew you'd catch them. So my dear sister, I think you need to get off your ass and take him back before he bolts." The bond between them must have been strong. As I watched her search his eyes wildly finally trusting his words, a smile crossed her lips. Tears streaming down her face, she stood in front of her husband. As he rose, he scooped her up in his arms and carried her out of the room.

I turned and watched them disappear behind a door, happy they were reconciled. Ryan cleared his throat as I shifted back to face him. The warmth in his eyes, as he spoke with Monica, left and I was sitting in front of one very angry guy. "Tess, I've got no right to be mad at you but I am. You scared the living crap out of me not knowing what the hell happened to you or what made you leave the way you did." He stood up and began to pace again. "I didn't know if something had happened between you and Scott or if you were pissed at me…I was freaked out!" I watched him as he paced looking down at the floor.

He sat down beside me and I looked deep into his soul. He wasn't mad, he was scared. I could feel him tremble as he tried to gather his courage to finish his speech. He began to breathe quickly as if he was trying to tell me something, but had lost the words. I leaned forward and rested my lips upon his as he wrapped his arms around my waist. I closed my eyes and melted into his kiss.

CHAPTER NINTEEN

Neither one of us managed to say another word the entire night. We kissed passionately and fell asleep on the couch. Waking up in his arms was still as magical as the first time. I opened my eyes to see he was looking down smiling at me.

"Hi there handsome," I said, smiling back. His eyes studied mine and leaned over to brush a light kiss on my nose.

"What am I gonna do you with you? I don't know what kind of trouble your little adventure has caused, but tell me what you want to do and I'll stand behind what ever decision you make. " His expression turned serious to let me know he was being honest.

"I guess I've gotta go back and finish my book." I reached up and pulled him to my lips. Kissing him deep as I pressed myself against his body. "I don't wanna go, but I have a commitment." I could feel his passion rising as I held him tighter. He slowed our kiss and tried to pull away.

"Well, if you must go back… now isn't the time to tangle me in your woman's web of lust and passion." He raised up and rolled off the couch. I stretched my arms above my head and moaned in frustration before sitting up to watch him straighten his clothes. Behind the door, we heard muffled voices and then a playful scream and giggle. We looked at each other and began to laugh.

"Hope you two are decent, we're coming out." Scott yelled out. "Honey, I think they can hear us out there." He deliberately talked loudly to be the clown he always was. Jiggling the knob for dramatic affect, he swung the door open and leapt into the room. "Well now,

I see you guys didn't kill each other." He raised his hands above his head. "So all is right with the world." Monica came behind him and smacked his butt as she passed.

He brought his hands down and shot her a playful look of pain. "Damn, what's with women and ass slapping?" He looked over to Ryan standing in front of me laughing.

"I know what you mean. I build a windmill for this woman to make her life a little more comfortable and what do I get for all my hard work? A permanent hand print on my cheek." I stood up and wrapped my hands around his back and rubbed his butt.

"As I recall, you were rewarded in other ways too." I smiled as he closed his arms around me.

"Whoa, too much information!" Scott held up his hands acting like he was shielding himself from the sight of us in each other's arms. Walking over to the couch he crossed his arms and nudged Ryan. "I think the women should rustle us up some grub."

From the kitchen, Monica hollered out "Neanderthals! Tess, can you come here? I can't seem to find the rat poison." Letting out a giggle, I gave Ryan one last kiss and headed in to help her.

We made a wonderful breakfast of omelets, bacon and toast. The guys ate like it was the first meal they had in days. We sat there and watched in amusement as they enjoyed themselves. Too busy shoveling the food in their mouths, they weren't able to talk, but were able to make the usual grunting noises. Catching on to us laughing at them, they gave each other a knowing look and went into a routine of grunting like cavemen.

Raising his fork making bits of egg fly in the air, Scott grunted "Food, good food. Must show happiness to wife for making fire hot to make food." He leaned over, licked Monica on the cheek, and went back to his food. Ryan, playing along belched out, "Oh, not wife, but good woman to make food hot. Must show thank you for hard work in kitchen." Thinking I was gonna get a slobbery tongue on my check too, I closed my eyes and tensed. Suddenly he swept me up in his arm and dipped me dramatically before delivering a warm gentle kiss and then he licked my face.

Wiping my check, I sat back in the chair. I looked over at Monica and we started to laugh as the guys went back to shoveling the food in their mouths. I had never met anyone so into playing around. Deciding it wouldn't be smart to sit there much longer for fear we'd be covered in food by the time they were done, we got up and started to clean the kitchen.

Throwing a towel on the table, Monica grabbed my hand and looked over at the guys. "No Tess, we cooked…so they can clean." They looked up at each other shrugged and went back to eating like pigs. "Let's have coffee in the other room."

I sank into the deep cushions of the chair closest to the fire. The house was warm and comforting. It was the exactly the same as the cabin at the lake, but much homier. It had panel walls lined with art and pictures of people and planes. Over the fireplace was a picture of Ryan's dog, Sarah. My heart flipped as I remembered how torn up he was over her death. I looked to see Monica was also looking up at the portrait.

"I know he misses her, ever since the accident that killed our parents and his fiancé, he never opened up to anyone but that dog…and you." Talking in a low voice so he wouldn't hear her comment.

"I didn't know that, he never mentioned it to me." The pieces to the "Ryan's Life" puzzle began to fall into place. "I guess he'll tell me about it someday."

She let out a short laugh, "I doubt it Tess, that boy's got a lot of pain hidden deep inside that he won't let anyone bring to the surface." She looked over her shoulder to see the guys busy cleaning up the kitchen. Feeling sure they couldn't hear us, she scooted closer and I leaned forward. "To make a long story short…years ago Ryan was engaged to a girl he fell in love with in college. He was flying her to Vegas with our parents when something happened and they crashed. He was the only one who survived. It took a long time before he'd get into a plane after that. He felt it was something he did or didn't do to cause the accident, but the NTSB declared a mechanical failure. Scott finally got him back in the air, but he wouldn't fly. He took him up to the lake one day pretending to set it up for a client. When they got there, he faked some kind of dramatic injury forcing Ryan to fly the plane back." She sat back and took a large gulp of coffee. "Boy was he pissed off when he found out Scott tricked him. He didn't speak to him for a week."

We'd been so caught up talking that we didn't notice they had come into the room. We looked over to see both of them standing by the stairs. Ryan's face showed all the signs that he had heard enough to make him angry. He shook his head and shot Monica a disapproving look.

"Pack it up Tess, I'm taking you back." His voice was cold and it made me tense knowing that he was feeling hurt and betrayed. Monica was close to tears as she realized the mistake she had made.

As I got up, I patted her hand and gave her a comforting smile. "He'll be okay, I'm sure it'll blow over before he gets back." I kissed her check and walked over to Scott who stood there with his head down. I gave him a quick hug and kiss, "See you soon?" Keeping his gaze to the floor he nodded. I grabbed my bag and headed out the door after Ryan.

I found him by the truck, kicking the dirt. "She had no right to tell you that. It's private, damn it!" I stood there not knowing what to say. "Get in, I want to make a stop before we head to base." Not wanting to make things worse, I got in the truck and clutched the bag against my stomach. The tension was thick and uncomfortable. I wanted to say something to try to make it ease up a bit, but knew to keep my mouth shut. As we drove into town he seemed to calm down.

"I just need to run in and get a few things and we'll be off." He didn't look at me when he jumped out and headed into a building that looked like a small curio shop. Waiting for him, I twisted the handle of the bag around my finger trying to find something I could say that wouldn't set him off. He came back carrying a large envelope and some boxes. Tossing the boxes in the back of the truck, he handed me the envelope and settled in beside me.

"I'm sorry. I know this whole thing was strange for you to witness, but what she told you was very private and something I'm not ready to face. I'm sure you have a ton of questions, but I'm begging you not to ask. When and if I'm ready, I'll tell you about it, but not now…it's just too fresh." I placed my hand on his and gave it a squeeze.

"I understand." I wanted to assure him more, but I choked back my words. His body relaxed and he leaned over giving me a peck on the cheek. As we drove to base, I kept my eyes focused on the passing trees pretending to take in the sights. The whole time I wondered what was going through his mind.

Once in the air, we weren't able to talk. He kept his concentration on flying the plane, which I wasn't going to break. The air was choppy and my stomach began to relive breakfast. I had tossed my bag in the back and couldn't get to pills I normally took to settle airsickness. Sure that the stress from the morning didn't help, I tried to concentrate on anything that would take away the urge to throw up. I'd have been mortified if he had to see me get sick.

Relieved to see we were coming up on the lake, I tried to sit back and relax. Knowing the landing was gonna be harder to take than the flight, I took a deep breath, closed my eyes and focused on keeping my breakfast down. I got dizzy as we spiraled in and finally landed. Once we taxied to the dock, my stomach settled. I opened the door before we came to a complete stop and let the air hit my face full force.

"Tess, what are you doing?" He said in panic. Still trying to guide the plane and look over to me at the same time.

"Don't worry, I just needed to get some air. I was getting sick." I looked at him and brushed my hair from my eyes.

A smile crossed his lips; "You should've told me you weren't feeling good, I could have spent the time teasing you about it." Weakly I smiled back.

I didn't help him tie down the plane. I headed straight for the cabin and into the bathroom. I was about to take off my clothes when I noticed something different. The solar shower that hung on a peg was gone and in its place was a new shiny shower that craned up over the wooden stall on a swing arm. I got closer to investigate the wonders of this new feature. Turning the knob slowly, water began to rain down, it looked too inviting. Letting it run, I took off my clothes and stepped in. It felt like taking a shower in the rain. The water was unusually warm.

Cleaned up and completely relaxed, I dried off, got dressed and went into the great room. Ryan was sitting on the couch bouncing the envelope he had against the back of the cushions. "Took you long enough...Like the new shower?"

"Yes, thank you. It takes showering to a whole new level of relaxation." I sat down beside him looking at the packages on the table. "So what's in the boxes?"

"Well...you'll have to wait to know that, we have to talk about some things first." He handed me the envelope and motioned me to open it.

I ran my finger under the flap and grabbed the papers inside. "What's this about?" I looked down at some kind of legal document. I wasn't too familiar with that kind of terminology and as I flipped through the pages I couldn't find a clue what it meant. "Ryan, I have no idea what this is?"

He grabbed the papers, and leaned in close to explain. "These are the papers that make this place yours. I want you to have it. I..." I heard the words but they didn't make sense.

"I thought this was my grandfather's cabin." I lifted my hands pointing to the shelves. "These are his books, there's a letter to him from some woman named Sofia, there's stuff here that I know is his." I ran my hands over my head. "I don't get it?"

"Well, it was his place and then it was my mother's, then it was mine and now I want you to have it." I sat there confused. Realizing he needed to explain a little more, he continued. "This place has a history that took me a year to figure out. When your grandfather first came here, my grandmother was his contractor. She wasn't like other women of her day; she had a free spirit and felt a woman should run her own show. While working on the cabin, they fell in love. He was already engaged to someone else and she didn't want him to break his commitment. She left him and he never finished what they started. He went his way; she went hers. She was Sofia, the woman who wrote the letter." He paused for a moment to let me absorb the story.

"When your grandfather learned she had died, he gave the cabin to my mother and I inherited it when she..." he caught his breath. Fighting back the tears, "well, you can figure out the rest." He got up and went to the storeroom coming back out with a bottle of wine and two glasses.

It all made sense. All the clues were starting to make sense. Suddenly I realized that his mother could have been the love child of Sophia and my grandfather. When he sat back down, he saw the panic in my eyes, shaking his head "No, don't worry…we're not related. My mother's father died in a logging accident years before I was born. Relieved, I sighed and slumped back into the couch.

"This is so much to take in" I stared into the fireplace. "But it does make a lot of sense." I sat up and turned to him. "This whole time I'd been making plans for a resort here and I didn't even own the property."

"Well you do now." He picked up the papers and placed them in my lap. I looked down and shook my head.

"I can't take this from you. It's too much." I handed them back. He stood up and tossed the document on the table.

"Tess, there's more. When you left, Scott was so panicked he called your lawyer to see if you went back to Tucson. By doing that he alerted Jerry to the fact that you broke the terms of the will." He turned back to me surprised to see I was completely calm. "Hey, snap out of it, you lost everything! All this time you spent here and you get shit!" I didn't respond confusing him even more.

He tossed up his hands in defeat. "Ryan, don't worry…I haven't lost everything." I took his hand and brought it to my lips. "I found you didn't I?"

"Tess…" he leaned closer and took me in his arms. "You're an incredible woman." Scooping me up as he rose, and carried me up the stairs where we spent the rest of the night making love.

CHAPTER TWENTY

Ryan was already sitting in the kitchen sipping coffee when I finally crawled out of bed. "Hey there sailor, got another cup of mud for me?" He smiled and motioned me to sit. "This damned radio takes up most of the table. You think we can find it a new home?" Nodding, he didn't say a word but sat looking at me over his cup with a knowing smirk on his face. "Okay, what's the big joke you seem to be amusing yourself with?" I took a sip. He shrugged and looked up to the ceiling. "Well, fine then... don't tell me...I've gotten used to being left in the dark."

"Well, I learned something new about you last night..." he began to laugh. "You snore." Embarrassed, I put my fingers in my coffee and flicked it across the table, splashing his face. "Oh, I see the perfect Tess Kelly doesn't like to know she's a normal human." I sat there and watched him giggle.

"So what do you have planned today? You sticking around or taking off? I guess I don't have to stay here anymore." I shrugged as I looked across at him.

"Well, I plan to stay about a week. I think you should finish what you came here to do. If not for the money, then for your grandfather." He was serious.

"You're right...If you could do me a favor and call base for some more supplies, I promise to try and focus on my writing." I got up and grabbed a piece of paper and pen, bent over the desk and begin to jot down the things I needed. I was running out of girl supplies and laughed to myself when I realized how embarrassing it would be for him to recite the list over the radio to some guy on the other end. Another intimate step in our relationship. I handed him the list, gave him a quick kiss and headed to the bathroom to freshen up.

Finally dressed, I headed back into the kitchen and found Ryan clicking off the radio. Looking over his shoulder, he gave me a smirk "You did that on purpose didn't you?" I bent around letting my wet hair smack his chest.

"Yes I did." He grabbed me and pulled me onto his lap pressing his lips firmly against mine.

"Well, I've some news for you…" he said as he pecked kisses along my neck and shoulders. "Jerry called Scott and said he can write off your little holiday trip as a medical emergency if you're willing to stay. It seems there's a few loop holes he didn't tell you about." I pushed him away and looked into his eyes.

"Are you serious?" He smiled and nodded. "Well that's great…I was willing to accept my fate, but since I've come this far…I might as well go through with it."

"I think you're wise. I'd hate for you to just give up." I jumped up from his lap with a sense of renewal.

"Let's see, October, November, December, January, February, March." Counting on my fingers. "That's only six months, I think I can handle that. It's not like I'm gonna be alone the whole time." Ryan cleared his throat and I turned.

"Well, that's another thing I need to talk to you about…" He stood up and took my hand. "I can only stay a week and then I have to leave for awhile." He bent his head down and turned away to avoid the look on my face.

"You won't be gone for long?" Trying to see the expression on his face. "Ryan, look at me, tell me how long."

"I'm contracted through the winter flying a supply plane for a construction company in South America. I can't break the contract." I could see he was as upset about it.

Trying to be strong I caught his gaze. "I'll be okay. We'll just make the most of the time we have together." I stepped forward and hugged him. His arms reached around and grabbed my hands as he stepped away from me.

"We only have a week and there's a lot we should talk about." He buttoned his shirt and went to the coffee table grabbing the boxes and documents in his arms. "Let's go enjoy the day and get this stuff out of the way." I followed as he led me outside of the cabin. Sitting on the grass, he put the boxes in front of me and placed the legal forms on top.

"When you and Monica took off, we found the papers and plans under your desk. You guys really have a great idea, and I think you should go for it. That's why I want you to sign these and accept ownership of the property." Before I could object, he held up his hand and shot me a serious look. "I want to do this." He adjusted his legs and straddled the boxes. Pushing one aside, he lifted the lid of the other and pulled out a model of a small cabin. "I made this years ago and I think it would make a great addition to your idea." Removing the roof from the model, I saw it was one room similar to a bunkhouse at a dude ranch. "The plans showed the meadow surrounded with small cabins like this one. You could build a lodge where everyone could gather for meals and events. If you contracted someone to clear the trees just a little on both sides of the stream…" He pointed and I looked to see where and what he was talking about. "You'd have a better approach for planes to deliver guests and supplies. The meadow can easily land a chopper, but you may want to reserve that area for something else."

He continued to go over his ideas with enthusiasm. My own excitement about the project began to surface as I listened. When he finished, he looked at me intensely trying to read my reaction. I looked down at the model he had so carefully made.

"I was so worried that you and Scott would hate the idea. Monica thought we'd have to go through a big whole production to get you guys to help us." The grin on my face told him I was jazzed.

"I'm glad I got to show you this. I almost talked myself out of it when Monica pulled her bullshit." He leaned back putting his hand behind his head and gazed up to the sky. "I know I need to smooth things over with her, but I think she should stress on it a little. She thinks she has the right to run everything but needs to be taken down a peg." I bit my lip about to defend her.

I took a moment before deciding to jump in. "It's really not her fault, I kinda pushed her into telling me. I've got no right to poke my nose in your business... I'm sorry." Squinting one eye, he looked over to me.

"It's not your fault Tess, she should've kept her mouth shut and let me tell you. I went through hell trying to over come that accident...it took a lot out of me, but I'm over it for the most part." He looked back up and gave a long sigh.

Propping myself up on my side, I rubbed his chest. "I was planning to marry a girl named Caroline...she was my first love. We dated in college, but split up after a big fight and went our separate ways. It was only a few years later we met up again at a carnival and got back together. At that time, I was still a little wild and liked to take chances. Trying to impress her one-day, showing off my tree climbing skills; I fell on my head. She nursed me back to health and made me promise to settle down."

He grabbed my hand and held it tight to his chest. I could feel his heart pounding. "I don't remember asking her to marry me, but I didn't want to wait, so we hopped in a plane with my folks and headed to Vegas." His eyes stared blindly up at the clouds remembering the details. "I don't know what happened...the engine went dead and we were gliding, next thing I knew the plane was a tangled mess of metal."

His voice became deep as he continued. "Blood was everywhere. I looked over at my father...his eyes were wide open and looked shocked. I thought he was alive, but when I called to him he didn't respond. I couldn't move because the instrument panel was smashed up against my legs. I called out for Caroline and my mother but I heard nothing. I sat there and bawled like a baby before passing out. I must have called out a distress, because when I came to...there was a guy standing over me telling me to hang on. Don't remember much after that...I'm just glad I don't have a picture in my head of Caroline or my mother crushed in the wreckage." He closed his eyes and breathed deep.

I looked away trying to compose myself. His story was so traumatic. I couldn't imagine what that kind of experience would do to someone. The Ryan I knew was reserved and for the most part was strong and playful. My heart ached to comfort him, but I knew it wouldn't help at that moment. With his hand still pressing mine against his chest, I laid down resting my head on his shoulder. He wrapped his arm around me and pulled me close.

A rumble of thunder in the distance woke us. We packed the model back in the box and went back inside. Ryan had a roaring fire going by the time the rain began pelting the roof. I rummaged through the storeroom and gathered up something for us to eat. We ate quietly staring into the flames. I knew he was still reliving the memories as I caught painful expressions cross his face.

To break the tension, I flipped on the stereo and let the music fill the cabin. Giving him some space, I sat down at the desk and began to doodle on a blank sheet of paper. Humming to the music I let the pencil drag across the page, letting it flow with the music. The image began to take shape and I bent down becoming completely wrapped up in it. Leaning back in my chair I looked down at the drawing and saw a pretty good likeness of Ryan.

"I think you really captured my dimples." He rested his hands on my shoulders as I jumped, not realizing he was standing there. "I didn't know you were an artist too."

Still in a daze, I confessed. "I'm not, it's the first time I've ever tried anything like this. I guess I just got lost in my own little world."

Bending over, he kissed my check. "I'm going to head up to bed. Care to join me?" I looked up and nodded

Neither of us were in the mood for passion, it was a night for healing old wounds. He held me and stroked my hair, mumbling as he slept. It reminded me of how he used to cuddle with Sarah.

CHAPTER TWENTY-ONE

Ryan pulled out of his funk as the week pasted quickly. We spent every moment together enjoying what little time we had before he'd leave for the winter. My heart was breaking knowing I wouldn't see him every day. I tried to push it out of my mind and put on a brave façade so we could get lost in each other one last time. Wanting to make our last night special, I dressed in the black satin and lace gown I got for my birthday. I pulled my hair up in a loose bun allowing a few strands to cascade down my back. A pair of rhinestone strappy sandals I bought in Hawaii completed the illusion I was trying to create.

Ryan had lowered the lights; turned on romantic music and set out the meal he had spent a good part of the day preparing. He turned as I walked down the stairs. It had been awhile since I had worn heels and I was worried I'd fall. Gripping the rail, I descended carefully watching my feet. He came over and reached out his hand to guide me to the center of the room. He twirled me around and caught me in his arms. Staring into each other's eyes, we glided around the room.

He gave me one last turn before taking my hand and guided me to the couch. Laying a napkin in my lap, he poured two glasses of wine and handed me one. "Tess, I raise my glass to you. You've brought joy and laughter to my life. For that, I am truly thankful." He tipped his glass to mine. I shook my head smiling. As corny as it was, my heart fluttered at the sincerity in his voice. He guzzled down the whole glass, set it back on the table and took a deep breath.

Realizing he was about to say something important, I put my glass next to his and gave him my full attention.

"You've been so patient with me and I know it hasn't been easy. I keep most of my feelings buried inside when I should be expressing them." He took another deep breath and I began to get anxious to hear what he was trying to say. "I'm going to miss you so much. I think you feel the same way." He looked deep into my eyes. "I want to know that I'll have a place in your heart."

I nodded but was unable to say anything. I didn't want to cut in on his speech. I searched his eyes waiting to hear more. The anticipation was burning in my heart. We held each other's gaze as he leaned forward and kissed me softly. Just as he was about to continue, he bit his lip and leaned over to my glass and took a big swig. I saw his hand tremble as he placed it back on the table. With a nervous giggle, he turned back to me and said; "I wanted to say more, but I can't remember it now."

"We've got all night," trying to calm his nerves "there's no need to rush all our thoughts and feelings in just a few moments." He nodded and poured himself another glass of wine.

"I should really go easy on this stuff, I have to fly tomorrow." I laughed as he drank it down quickly. I'd never seen him nervous before. He was like a teenage boy about to have sex for the first time. I realized I had butterflies in my stomach and knew I wouldn't be able to eat a bite of the food he had worked so hard on.

Quietly I whispered, "I'm gonna miss you." I picked up the fork and began pushing the food around. "You make the days easier to endure and the nights...well...more than words can say." My heart was in my chest as I held back the tears that were making my voice crack. He reached over and took the fork from my hand and turned me to face him. I kept my eyes down staring at his leg. He lifted my chin and I saw that he had tears in his eyes.

"If I had known I was going to meet you this summer, I would never have taken the job. I didn't expected to feel the way I do about you." He dabbed my tears with the napkin. "I thought it would be no problem for me to just leave, but I feel as though my heart is being torn from me."

Bringing my hand to his face, I brushed away his tear. "I want you to know that you have me waiting here for you." I caught my breath holding back another flood of emotions.

My heart was breaking as I let the tears stream down my face. He held me until I finally calmed down. I pulled away gently, grabbing the napkin to wipe my eyes. It was too much hitting me too fast. I felt like a blubbering fool.

"Hungry?" he asked. I shook my head and sat back. "Me either." We sat there for a moment listening to the music. "Come on," he held out his hand. "Dance with me." I kicked off my shoes and took his hand. We held each other tight swaying back and forth. The music switched to a waltz as we stopped. Stepping back a bit, we changed to a traditional dance pose and began to waltz. To my delight, he was a skilled dancer. Guiding me gently around the room and twirling me without skipping a step. I felt lighter then air. As it came to an end, he swung me out and twirled me back into his arms.

My heart was pounding in my chest and we were both a little out of breath. I stared into his eyes completely swept up in the moment. All the emotions we were drowning in earlier, were washed away. Sadness gave way to passion, as we became lost in each other's eyes. In one swift move, he scooped me up into his arms.

He placed me gently on the couch and pushed the table aside. Kneeling, he leaned over kissing me gently as he brought his hand up to my breast. I melted as his lips devoured me. I raised my arms and tangled my fingers in his soft hair. Closing my eyes, I became lost in the tingling running up my spine as he trailed gentle kisses down my neck to the base of my throat. His hand tugged gently at the strap letting it break lose from the lace. He reached up and let the other tear from its threads.

My heart quickened as he slowly pulled the gown down to my waist. I melted further into the couch as his tongue trailed over my skin drawing little circles as he nuzzled my cleavage. I lifted up to help him pull the gown down until I was completely exposed. My eyes still closed, I felt the warmth of his hands glide over my body. It was as if he was trying to memorize every inch with his touch. I could feel his breath hot against my skin as I became more excited by his seduction.

He stood and pulled his shirt over his head. As I watched him get undressed bathed in the glow of the fire, I ran my hands over my stomach trying to keep the tingling sensation from leaving me. He looked down as I caressed myself. I had always been self-conscious, but with him I felt beautiful.

"In this light you look like a goddess...you drive me crazy." I giggled and covered my breasts playfully. "Ahh my dear, no time to be shy, I think I've seen just about every inch of your lovely body." He came back to the couch and laid down pressing me against the cushions. The heat from his body sent shock waves through me. Resting his head in his hand, he trailed his finger gently over my stomach. I watched as his eyes followed the path of his hand. I closed my eyes enjoying each level of passion as he explored my body. I moved beneath him arching my back. I reached my arm around and drew him into me. Holding him tight, I felt his heart pounding. "Open your eyes Tess," His voice was deep. We made love slowly looking deep into each other's eyes until our passion reached its limit.

Laying together, bathed in the after glow, we held each other not wanting to lose the moment. He rolled over to face me. "Tess, I love you..." I was surprised he finally found the words. My heart began to race; I reached up and held his face as my thumb brushed his cheek.

"I love you too." My eyes searched his for confirmation that I truly heard the words. When he kissed me, there was more passion then before. Warmth washed over me as our fevered kiss elevated us to new heights of ecstasy.

"My love...I thought I'd never say those words again, and here we are. Wrapped in each others arms, making love, professing love and in a few short hours...I'll have to leave." He kissed the tip of my nose, "But now that I've finally admitted I love you, I won't feel so bad about leaving."

His words confused me; I was crushed knowing he would be away from me for such a long time. "I wish my heart didn't hurt so much." I kept my tears at bay. I drew in a deep breath and relaxed.

"I guess I'll always have tonight to look back on." I looked up to the rafters hoping I could maintain control.

"Tess, we have each other now. If our love is strong, it'll keep us close even if we're on two different continents." With his hand, he guided my face back to meet his gaze. "You finish that book sweetheart and before you know it, I'll be here to pick you up and take you anywhere you want to go."

"I'll be okay knowing you're coming back." I scooted over letting him lay down to rest his head on my shoulder. I stroked his hair, gazing into the dying flames of the fire as he fell asleep. While he slept, I recounted every moment we had ever shared, reliving them over and over in my mind.

I was still awake when the sunlight bathed the cabin. Ryan slowly opened his eyes, "Good morning lover." He looked up at me and flashed a concerned look. With bloodshot eyes, tear stained face and matted hair, I knew I was no beauty queen.

"I know I must look terrible." I reached up and tried to run my fingers through my hair but they got caught in the tangles.

"I know a cure for that." Getting up from the couch, he picked me up in his arms. I wrapped my hands behind his neck as he carried me to the bathroom. We made love one last time as we showered together; enjoying the feel of the water cascading over us.

Our long good bye lasted through breakfast and down to the dock. Holding each other tight, we professed our love repeatedly. Knowing he had to leave, but neither of us wanting to say good bye. Finally, I stepped back and let him go. He rushed through his preflight and before I knew it, he was gone. My heart sank as I turned and went back to the cabin.

I looked around the room seeing the remains of our last night together. The table still pushed away from the couch, the untouched meals, and the crumpled cushions on the couch. I was tired and heartbroken. Maintaining my composure, I busied myself by cleaning up the mess. Once I had everything back the way it was before, I went up to the loft and cried myself to sleep.

CHAPTER TWENTY-TWO

The days got cold near the end of October and the planes weren't able to fly in every week like they had before. Scott and Monica made a few trips up which helped to break the mind numbing loneliness. The plans for the resort were taking shape and during one meeting, we had figured out finances, marketing, and plan layout. Monica took the plans and the model Ryan had made with her to get things in motion. Scott wasn't happy at first about the idea, but he soon gave in when he discovered he would be contracted to fly in guests and supplies.

Finally in November, I was able to formulate the first sentence of my book. I gave up the idea of outlining before I started to write. Once I let structured writing go, my thoughts poured into the pages. As I completed a chapter, I would step back from the desk and realize the day had flown by. After each little victory, I treated myself to a glass of wine and an hour in the sauna. During my celebrations, I imagined Ryan was with me. Closing my eyes, I'd concentrate on his features, hoping at that moment, he was thinking of me too.

Each morning I woke up to look out frosted windows to the deserted lake wondering when the next plane would come. I kept the radio on most of time allowing the crackling fuzz to connect me to the outside world. Some evenings I'd sit in front of the fire sipping cocoa remembering the warm days of summer in Ryan's arms.

One evening, during a reflective moment, I spotted a box under the shelf next to the fireplace. I'd noticed it before, but never thought to open it. Bringing it to the table, I remembered it was the other box Ryan had brought up before he went away. We never got around to opening it.

I lifted the lid and found a bundle of letters rubber-banded together. At the bottom was a small package wrapped in brown paper and strips of electrical tape. I wrapped my arms around my legs resting my head on my knees staring at the items.

Still in a dramatic mode from writing, I wanted to hold on to the suspense a bit longer to enjoy the anticipation. My mind wondered if I should reveal the contents of the poorly wrapped package or read the letters. My curiosity was too strong, and reached out grabbing the bundle.   I shot the rubber band across the room and leaned against the arm of the couch. Opening the first letter I read:

> *My Dearest Tess,*
>
> *By now I've left and you discovered the box. I hope you didn't wait too long to open it. I've written five letters to help keep you company while I'm gone. As I write this, I have no clue where you and my sneaky sister are. I guess it gives me the perfect chance to sit here and put together this surprise. All I ask is you don't read all the letters in one day. The package you're not allowed to open until Christmas. I know there's no way to make sure you'll keep this promise, so I'll have to trust you. Since you've been gone, I've had time to write down my thoughts and feelings. Shocking I know, me…writing love letters to a woman I've only known a few short months. I'm sure I don't write like you do, with your fancy words and wonderful creativity. I'm just going to write as if you're right here.*
>
> *I hope by now I've told you I love you. I fell in love with you the day I woke up after the splash down in the lake. I remember the look of concern on your face. It was at that moment, you touched my heart. I know I held back, but I had demons to conquer, and that will have to wait for another time; I get too emotional when I think about it.*
>
> *I hope your time at the cabin goes by fast and before we know it, you'll be in my arms. While I'm gone, I'll be*

going nuts thinking about you. I wish I didn't have to go, but a contract's a contract.

If for some stupid reason I haven't told you, as unromantic as this is...here goes...I LOVE YOU! I sure hope you love me too. You'll be in my heart and in my mind now and always.

Ryan

My heart was pounding in my chest. I fought back tears and smiled as I pictured him sitting there writing the letter. He had planned to confess his love even before our romantic night together. It did feel like he was there in a small way. I closed my eyes and held his letter to my heart. Feeling nostalgic, I placed it on the shelf next to the puzzle box. It had become a shrine of interesting mysteries.

Feeling inspired, I sat down and began to write. The words flowed from my brain to my fingers as the typewriter clicked away. Page after page stacked up before I realized that it was getting light outside. I looked up to see it was snowing. I stood up and saw a thick blanket of white covering the lake. I hadn't noticed the biting cold that filled the cabin.

I tossed a few logs in the fireplace, letting the heat penetrate my body. Getting wrapped up in my writing did help to pass the days, but I hardly took the time to stop and eat or do anything else. I knew I'd have to find a way to remember to take breaks. I looked down and realized I was wearing the same clothes I'd put on three days earlier. Throwing my hands in the air completely disgusted with myself; I headed to the bathroom to take a warm shower.

Still chilly after I had washed up, I packed on layers of clothes and went to the kitchen to fire up the wood burning stove knowing the heat would radiate up and make the loft warm for a nap later in the day. I'd gotten used to sleeping during the day and working at night. Once the logs were ablaze, I closed the grate and held my hands close trying to melt the cramping pains in my fingers.

The radio's familiar crackle broke, "Tess, you there?" I ran over grabbing the mic.

"I'm here" I didn't recognize the voice. It was muffled and fuzzy.

"Monica, it's Monica...can you hear me?" Her voice sounded panicked. I got nervous.

"I can hear you...what's wrong?" I held my breath.

"Nothing now, I was worried about you...we know you're probably snowed in so I got worried." I smiled.

"I'm fine. I've been so wrapped up in my work; I didn't even notice the snow until this morning." I sat back and relaxed in the chair.

"I'm glad...it will be another week before we can get up there, you need anything?" Sitting up with excitement, I remembered the clock.

"Yes, I need an alarm clock." I said excitedly in the mic.

"Anything else?" The radio began to crackle more.

"That's it...but I could use a visit." I sat back down and leaned close to the radio.

"We...up...can...giving...no...ice...plane...hel..." The crackling static filled the cabin. I clicked off the radio and drowned in the silence. I sat there and stared at the table running the words I did hear over in my mind. I was sure she said that they would be up for Thanksgiving, there was something about the plane and ice. With Thanksgiving only a week away, I got excited.

I jumped up and opened the door. It was snowing hard and only a hint of the forest poked through the blinding white. I wondered what Ryan was doing at that very moment. I pictured him in the cockpit of his plane flying over the jungles of South America and thinking of me. Rubbing my arms to fend off the cold, I closed the door and headed up to bed. The minute my head hit the pillow, I was out.

The snow stopped the next night allowing me to get outside and wander around the woods during my breaks. It was amazing how alive I felt. The forest bustled with little creatures rummaging for food. I knew not to worry about the bears since they were hibernating, but I heard the wolves howl every night. The snow began to pack, so I took a day away from writing and cleared paths from the front door around to the back of the cabin and into the woods, one down to the dock and then one to the open field where Monica landed the helicopter.

Having the chance to take little sabbaticals helped to keep me grounded; allowing me to write and still take care of myself. I had lost a lot of weight from not eating as much as I used to. Close to finishing my book and with Christmas right around the corner, I was getting excited about finally finding out what was in the package. It took all the restraint I had not to devour the letters Ryan had written or tear open the package he left behind.

Thanksgiving day, I got up early, showered and dressed in the warmest clothes I could find that didn't look like they came out of a rag bag. It was difficult to wash clothes with everything frozen over. There were a few days I didn't have warm water or electricity because I had forgotten to unlock the blades to the windmill. A few uncomfortable days were easy to bear and I was proud for maintaining my emotions about Ryan. Tossing more logs on the fire, I looked around to make sure everything looked perfect. Just then I heard the whirring of the helicopter as it came over the ridge. I ran to the door to watch them land. When the blades slowed, I walked out to greet them. Monica stepped down, beaming. "Tess!" She held out her arms and gave me a warm hug.

"Let's get in out of this cold, Scott can grab the food." We headed inside. "We brought the whole feast, and from the way you look, you can use a good meal." She laughed and wrapped her arm in mine as we walked on.

Scott was unusually quiet as we babbled on like a couple of old hens. Sitting in front of the fire on the floor around the coffee table, we ate turkey and mashed potatoes. After stuffing ourselves full, I convinced them to take the loft and made up the couch for myself. I settled in, laying there wondering what was wrong with Scott. He seemed to be in his own little world. I plotted to get him alone the next day to see if he wanted to talk.

CHAPTER TWENTY-THREE

The next day I got up early and started breakfast. As the smell of fresh coffee brought them down, I fried up some bacon and eggs they had brought. I'd been eating oatmeal for a month and was happy to have a change of flavor. The thought of eggs made my mouth water. Scott was still in a mood as we all sat there and ate quietly.

"How long do you guys get to stay this time?" Trying to break the tense moment.

With his arms crossed over his chest he sat back and let Monica answer, "Well..." she said as she took a large bite. "We've got another storm coming in and thought it would be best to stay until it blows over." She looked up, "You don't mind do you Tess?"

I was happy to know I had a few more days of social interaction. "Are you kidding? I need a break away from this solitude. The book's almost done and I need to step back and reflect a bit on where I want the story to go." Getting up, I grabbed my plate. "You should try out the sauna ...it's very relaxing."

Scott got up and walked out the door. I looked over at Monica who kept her eyes on her plate. I knew it was a private thing between them, but wasn't sure if I could resist asking what's wrong.

"So, what's that all about?" Taking the chance that maybe she wanted to get some things off her chest. I walked over to the picture window and saw him standing on the dock, poking at the ice with a stick. "I've never seen him like this."

"It's a combination of things...He's mad at me for spending so much energy on the resort project and he's pissed at Ryan for some reason, but he won't talk to me about it..." She looked up hopeful. "Maybe you...um...could talk to him?"

Not wanting to let on that I had planned to anyway. "If you think it will help, but I make no promises. Scott's been pretty secretive with me since I came here, but I'll try." I grabbed my coat and headed out to join him. He stood with this head looking down at the packed snow.

"Hey there big guy...feel like escorting me to the meadow? I lost my note book and I think it might be there." I hated to lie to him, but I didn't think he would go otherwise.

He nodded and we headed around the cabin to the path that wound around and through the trees. He watched his feet as we walked, I could almost feel his sadness. "Mind telling me what's wrong? I've never seen you this low before." I looked over at him but he kept walking, head down. "Well, it's okay if you don't want to talk about it, but if there's anything you need to get off your chest or just need someone to blow up at...I'm here."

He grabbed my hand as we walked. His grip was loose as if he was drained of his strength. Once we had reached the meadow, he looked out onto the blinding white blanket of snow that covered what once was a field full of beautiful wild flowers. I tried to step forward but his hand tightened pulling me back where I stood. Behind his crystal blue eyes, I could barely see a spark of the man I once knew. With a jerk, he brought me into his arms and gave me a tight hug. For a quick second, I worried I was about to relive the last memory of the two of us in the meadow.

As he crushed me against him, I looked out to the middle of the field where the old tree stump poked through the snow. Stroking his hair to help comfort him. His body relaxed and he released me. His face was blank of any emotion. I panicked as he fell back crashing into the snow. "Scott, are you okay?" He laughed and began swinging his arms and legs creating a snow angel. "You are such a shit!" Glad he was laughing; I reached out my hand and pulled hard to help him up.

"You should've seen your face when I went down, it was classic." I smacked his arm as he wiped the snow from his face. "At least I feel a little better now. You really know how to pull me out of a mood..." Giving me a sideways glance. "I needed to didn't I?" Still looking shocked, I nodded. He took my hand and we walked over to the stump. I sat down as he walked around crunching the snow beneath his feet.

"I'm pissed, but it's not your fault...and if you don't mind...I want to take you up on your offer to vent." He looked down at me seriously...I nodded my head.

Holding my arms out to my side, "Hit me with your best shot." I smiled hoping it would help ease him a bit. He walked around in circles making a path in the snow as he unloaded his troubles.

"I'm not too thrilled with this resort idea that you and Monica cooked up. I've been trying to get her to settle down so we could start a family. Both businesses are doing pretty good and we live fairly comfortable, but she never takes a break from it. Even when we're alone or away for the weekend, she's off planning one thing or another for the lodge, my tour business or this damned mountain resort..."holding up his hand to me. "No offense Tess."

Assured I wasn't, he continued. "I just want her to be a wife from time to time. I want to have kids and a real life. It's really not that much to ask...I just think I should have some say in our lives together, don't you?" He looked at me hopeful that I would agree. I just shrugged my shoulders not knowing what to say.

"Have you talked to her about the way you feel?" I asked cautiously, not wanting to set him off.

"Yes..." he sighed throwing up his arms in defeat. "She's just damn stubborn, she doesn't want to give up her career and settle down. She wants to wait a few more years."

"Well, doesn't that kind of run in her family? Her grandmother was an independent woman and her mom sounded as though she had a fire in her belly too. Maybe she doesn't realize that she can be both career woman and mother and still have great kids. All she'll need to do is give up some of the responsibility to someone she feels comfortable with. I think you guys need to do some more talking." I pointed my finger at him. "Just be sure you keep your cool or you'll lose her again.

Looking like a punished child, he kicked the snow. "You're right, we'll need to talk things out. I know I've been such an ass to her since I found out Ryan might accept the job offer." My mouth dropped open and he realized that I had no idea what he was talking about. "Don't stress out Tess, it's not a done deal. I'm sure he'll let us know before making any decisions…plus his last letter didn't mention anything about it."

"Letter? You got a letter? Did he send anything for me?" Shaking his head… I stood up quickly and punched him in the arm. "You better be kidding me you ass hole!" With a hurt look on his face, he grabbed his arm and backed away from me.

"Tess, I'm not kidding…he didn't send anything for you, he mentioned you in his letter and told me to make sure you had everything you needed and not to leave you alone for too long." I took a quick step forward and he tripped falling on his ass. "He held his hand in front of his face. "Tess, I'm sorry…I'll send him a letter if you want me to, I have his address."

"What the hell's wrong with men?" Standing over him looking down at his stunned expression. "Doesn't he even think to write to me too?" I began to pace. "I read his love filled letters he wrote before he left, but what about now? Doesn't he hurt as much as I do? Doesn't he even care?" My breath caught in my chest as I thought maybe being apart had a different affect on him than it did me. Maybe he realized that he didn't love me as much as he thought he did. Maybe he came to his senses. "Oh my God Scott…What if I lose him too?"

He got to his feet. "You are such a spaz …Ryan loves you, he told me so. Don't go getting all worked up over nothing." He brushed the snow off his pants and walked over to me. "It's my fault if he takes the damn job…I should've made him a partner instead of keeping him on as a throttle jockey." He held out his hand. "Tell you what…I'll try to work things out with my wife…and you…well, you'll go on loving my best friend and know he's coming back for you." His smile made me realize I got upset over nothing. I took his hand and we walked back along the path. We caught sight of the cabin and saw the steam coming from the vent in the sauna. I flashed him a smile and pushed him forward. Nudging him to join his wife. I walked around the front of the cabin and sat on the porch looking out at the landscape.

I could see my breath, as I looked up to the sky. Large billowy clouds roll up over the ridge and I knew we were in for a chilly night. It began to snow as I headed inside. I wanted to give Scott and Monica some space, but there was no place for me to go. Grabbing a book off the shelf, I laid down on the couch and figured they wouldn't notice me if I kept crouched down. An hour went by before I heard them giggling as they ran in and straight to the bathroom. I smiled to myself as I remembered Ryan and I did the same thing.

I kept reading until they finally surfaced fully clothed. "Tess? You can come out of hiding." Monica laughed as Scott came from behind tickling her. I poked my head up and gave a wave.

"Just catching up on some reading...didn't know you guys had come in." I grinned, trying to hold back my laughter.

"You're such a liar...I'm starving...I think we should have some sandwiches." She headed in storeroom to grab the leftovers.

"Every thing okay?" I questioned Scott once she was out of sight. "Yup...can't beat the power of love" he turned and wiggled his butt singing "I'm just a love machine and I don't want nobody but you..."as he walked into the kitchen to help prepare lunch.

Still laughing at his insane ways, I laid back down and looked at the book I was pretending to read. I held it to my chest as my heart ached for Ryan.

CHAPTER TWENTY-FOUR

The storm kept us snowbound for a week. I did my best to stay out of their way so they could spend as much time alone as possible. I was happy they resolved their issues, but it was hard to see two people so much in love when I was missing Ryan. I read through all the letters except one that I wanted to save for Christmas Day. I knew I'd have to spend the holiday alone if the weather was bad. The last few days with them was spent playing cards, laughing and getting the helicopter ready for it's flight out. Once they were certain the conditions were safe, Monica radioed base as Scott retrieved a few more boxes from the chopper.

"What's all this?" I asked curiously as he placed them on the floor behind the couch.

"Well, we thought that it would be a good idea to put this place in a Holiday mood. We found some Christmas decorations in the attic back home and thought you'd like to have them." He smiled knowing that it was my favorite holiday.

Excitedly, I said, "Yes…you guys rock!" I removed the lids and began pulling out the boxes of ornaments and bundles of garland.

"I'll go out and find a nice tree while you gals set up for a good ol' fashioned decorating party." He tossed me a cassette of Christmas songs and headed out the door.

I sat and organized all the items in front of me. I decided the center of the floor was the perfect place to put the tree. Reaching into the second box, I pulled out the tree stand putting it in the center of large area rug that hid the trap door I found a few months earlier.

Monica turned to see my excitement and giggled. "You look like a kid sitting there all wild eyed." She came over and joined me on the floor to look through all the goodies they'd brought. There was enough to decorate the whole cabin. Excited, we grabbed the pine garland and started wrapping it around the rail all the way up the stairs and across the loft. Satisfied with how it looked, we draped more across the hearth and along the bookshelves letting it droop like festoons. Using silk poinsettia flowers, we accented the garland. The green and red gave the whole place a warm holiday feeling. As we waited for Scott to come back, we made cocoa and popped popcorn.

We set the goodies on the coffee table and pushed the couch up against the bookshelves. The room looked huge, but inviting. "You really need to get more furniture in here. Maybe you can plan out what you'd like and we can get it up here for you." She took a sip and looked around.

"Well, I kinda like having it open, but you're right...it is pretty bare and not great for entertaining. I'd either have to get pieces that need to be assembled or you'd have to fly them in hanging from the chopper." Looking over at her, I pictured in my mind a huge table dangling from her helicopter.

"Well, actually we wouldn't have to go that far...the road that dead ends near the meadow would allow us better access. We have to clear a way to the lake anyway, so we have emergency access for the resort. So you can get as creative as you like with your planning." She turned when we heard Scott struggling at the door.

He was able to steady the large tree in the stand and we trimmed off the odd branches until we were all happy with the shape. We spent the rest of the day draping the tree in blue and silver garland, hanging the mix of wooden and glass ornaments and singing along with the Christmas songs that radiated through the cabin. Before turning in for the night, we stood back, arms wrapped around each other and gazed at the perfect Christmas tree.

I stayed up most of the night watching the firelight sparkle on the ornaments. My heart felt excited like it did when I was a kid waiting on Christmas Eve for Santa. My grandfather had always made that time of year special for all of us. I laid on the couch wondering what Ryan had planned for the holiday. I closed my eyes and concentrated hard trying to send my thoughts to him…trying to will him to come back to me. That night, I sent my Christmas wish out into the night.

Early the next day, Scott and Monica left and I was alone again. I felt lost, not knowing what to do with my time. I didn't want to go back to writing, but there was nothing else to do. The snow was beginning to melt in small patches making it muddy and difficult to walk around the woods.

During one of my mud-soaked walks, I gathered up fallen pine branches and fashioned a wreath to hang on the front door. It rounded out the look and feel of the winter season for me. I got lost in the nostalgia of having an old fashioned mountain Christmas, hoping I didn't have to spend it alone.

The days dragged by as I fought to find new things to occupy my time. I had organized every space in the cabin and even went so far as to alphabetize the food in the storeroom. I made a floor plan laying out my ideas for new furniture and even made a table out of split logs to set the radio on.

Finally giving into to the boredom, I set back to work on my book. Before I started, I set the alarm clock limiting me to two hours. Between sessions, I would sweep pine needles up from beneath the tree, take a sauna or go for short walks in the woods. The weather stayed pretty calm bringing me the hope that Scott and Monica would be able to come back. Those hopes were dashed when only two days before Christmas it began to snow.

Completely bummed, I sat at the desk staring out the window and I pounded out more chapters to my story. I stopped setting the alarm so I would keep going without pausing to remember how upset I was. My story began to take twists and turns as I discovered the characters in the book took on new personalities. In my mind they became my companions as I molded their lives with my imagination.

Early on Christmas Eve, I had finally written myself into a corner. I had writer's block and no inspiration to help me work through it. I took the story too far, pushing the characters beyond their limits and I was stuck. Sitting back, I looked out the window noticing it had finally stopped snowing. It was deep and I knew there would be no way anyone could make it up. I was tired and knew I needed rest.

I went out to the sauna and removed my clothes. Once I had it set up and it started to produce the wonderful steam, I laid back and enjoyed the warm moisture as it cocooned me. Of all the gifts I'd ever received in my life, it was the one I enjoyed the most. I was always amazed at the ingenuity of the concept. It didn't take electricity to run and it kept me wonderfully warm.

Once I felt completely relaxed, I went back inside, threw more logs on the fire and headed up to bed. Even though the sunlight bounced off the snow illuminating the inside of the cabin, I was able to fall asleep the minute my head hit the pillow. My dreams were a tangle of memories and desire. I dreamt I was lying on the bed naked as Ryan caressed my body with his strong hands. My hair wet and perspiration glistening on my skin, I writhed beneath his touch wanting him to explore every inch of my body. I could hear him whisper words of love. "Tess, my love…I missed you…I had to come…my heart couldn't take being away from you any longer." I let the words penetrate my mind, hoping I wouldn't wake up. "Tess, open your eyes babe…" I fought the words wanting to make the dream last as long as possible. He laid down beside me rubbing his hand along my stomach with the lightest touch. "Tess…wake up."

I realized I wasn't dreaming. My body tensed as I opened my eyes. His face came into focus. I looked into his deep blue eyes and smiled. As his lips met mine in a passionate kiss, I wrapped my arms around his back and pressed him against my body. He was real and in my arms. I wanted to hold on tight and never let him go.

"This is the best dream I've ever had…sure would hate to wake up now." He gave a laugh and kissed me again.

"I promise if you get out of bed, I'll still be here." He ran his hand up my leg. "Then again, you do look scrumptious." I laid back and let him caress me until my desire was too much to take.

After we made love, we went down stairs to enjoy something to eat. While I was asleep, he had snuck in the back door and set up a wonderful Christmas Eve dinner. "I won't let you talk me out of eating this time, it took forever for me to get here and I'm starving."

He kissed my hand and led me to the couch. The food wasn't hot, but had stayed warm from the fire. I was still in shock to see him sitting beside me eating.

"How did you get here? The lake's frozen and I didn't hear the helicopter." I took a bite and looked at him.

"Santa," he grinned as I gave him a playful nudge. "Actually I drove up…it's only a day from base, but I made it."

Remembering the access road at the back of the property line "You must've walked an hour to get here... you did that for me?" My eyes began to well up as I turned to him holding my hands to my heart.

"Of course I did…well…not just for you…but for me too…I missed you lover." He leaned over still chewing his food and gave me a kiss on the cheek.

"I made a wish and here you are…could life be any more amazing than this?" I poured myself another glass of wine and sat back, crossing my legs under me.

"I see you haven't opened the package yet…I'm glad…I wanted to be here when you did." He finished his meal and walked over to the shelf where I kept it. He tossed it in the air catching it with both hands and grinning like a wild cat.

"You don't get to see it tonight my dear…you gotta wait till tomorrow."

"That's fine …I have plans for you tonight…so you'll be my Christmas Eve present." I stood up and walked back up the stairs swaying my hips seductively. As he came behind me, his hands went up my legs pushing my nightgown to my waist and over my head. We made love until midnight before falling into a deep sleep.

CHAPTER TWENTY-FIVE

I woke up to the sounds of Christmas music. With butterflies in my stomach I knew there was a present to open and a wonderful man who loved me. I grabbed Ryan's shirt and buried my face in it breathing in his cologne. I put it on and headed down the stairs. "Red flannel never looked so good." He came around the corner greeting me as I stepped onto the landing. "Merry Christmas my love." Grabbing me in his arms he dipped me bringing his lips to mine.

He took my breath away. "You're the best present a girl could ever get for Christmas." He looked down seeing the shirt had opened exposing me to his gaze.

"If we keep you in this position, you may never get a cup of coffee." He smiled bringing me back to my feet. Smacking my butt as I went into the kitchen making me jump. I rubbed my stinging cheek and smiled over my shoulder. "Tess, if you keep walking around half naked, I might go insane."

"Good, I've been going crazy for the past three months…about time someone else took the role of the mountain nut job." When I finally got my coffee, I found it made just the way I like it.

"I bet it's been tough for you…I wrote to Scott and asked him to look in on you as much as he could." Looking at me, he realized it wasn't enough.

"That's something I wanted to talk to you about…you didn't write me one letter while you were gone." I put the cup on the counter and stood with my hands on my hips, trying to look stern.

In an exaggerated Irish accent he winked at me. "Ah my bonnie lass, how could ya think I'd forget ya. I wrote ya letters before I left...I wrote em meself. I pinned fer ya day an night." Placing his hands around my waist as he tried to make me smile. "I happen ta know ya love me Tess, more then the sun love's the sky...more then the stars love the night." He gave me a jiggle and I smiled putting my hands on his ass to give him a squeeze.

"Well...you got me pegged you big ham." Kissing me I could tell he had already had a cup of coffee. No man before could make me melt with just a kiss, but Ryan had complete control over me. I insinuated myself into his body as he let out a deep groan.

"What you do to me blows my mind." He lifted me up, giving me one last kiss before tearing himself away. I buttoned up and followed him into the living room. To my surprise, there were presents under the tree. "Look Tess!" He exclaimed excitedly. "Santa came and brought us presents!" He turned to me pretending to look surprised. "Well, he must have gotten the wrong address...I figured we were both on his naughty list." Smirking as I sat down on the floor looking at all the gifts he had brought.

"Oh no my love...we've been very, very good...well, at least we've been good at something." He gave me a wink and reached for a present. "Being the man of the house, I get to play Santa." He looked at a package that was wrapped with red and silver-stripped foil. "This one says...to Tess...from Monica."

Excited, I grabbed the gift and tore it open. A soft and warm fuzzy blue v-neck sweater was inside. He searched around the pile and lifted up a bag with a white bow. "Oh, that ones for me." Placing it aside he reached for another.

"Hey, wait...why don't you open it?" I reached for the bag as he swatted my hand.

"Nope, I pass out the gifts...when you've opened the last one...then you'll sit there oohing and ahhing over my presents." He shrugged his shoulders. "It's a guy thing...you gotta have testosterone to understand." He ducked as I tossed a wad of wrapping paper at his head.

One by one, he handed me gifts and watched as I opened them. He made the same fake expressions of surprise as I held up each one. Scott's gift to me was a basket of scented soaps and bath stuff, which I knew Monica had picked out. Mary gave me a locket with pictures of my grandfather and me. The gift from the pilots was a flare gun engraved with "Fire if you get lonely". Even Jerry sent up a present, but his was just another ream of paper and a new typewriter ribbon.

Before having to endure the torture of watching Ryan open his gifts, he pushed three paper bags in front of me. Beaming with pride he said, "These are from me...thought you could use a few things." Thrilled that he even went to the trouble, I looked in the first bag and pulled out a white crochet-bathing suite. Smirking I reached in and pulled out a lacy shawl, pair of white lace up sandals and a terry cloth towel. I could see the theme developing. I tossed aside the empty bag and grabbed the next. I found a bottle of suntan lotion, white sunglasses, hair ties and a beach bag. I looked up as he pushed the last bag to me. I pulled out wad after wad of crumpled newspaper until I got to the bottom. I turned it upside down and shook it but it was empty. Worried, I tossed it aside and rummaged through the gift shrapnel as he laughed.

"Here, Tess...this is the real gift." I looked up and saw him holding two plane tickets. Blushing, I smiled and reached out to grab them. He pulled them back quickly. "Wait...before you look you have to give me a kiss." I rolled my eyes and leaned forward giving him a quick peck as I grabbed the tickets. I couldn't believe it...Jamaica...he was going to take me to Jamaica.

Draping myself in his lap I wrapped my arms around his neck and between kisses exclaimed "Thank you, thank you, thank you... I'm going to need this trip after being here for a year." I kissed him deeply to let him know I wasn't just playing around.

"There's more where that came from my dear...but not now..." He pulled away looking excited. "It's my turn...you've had your fun...now you get to watch me have mine." He spread out his legs letting my butt hit the floor as he gathered up his presents. He held me crushed between him and the gifts. He opened them one by one holding them up to me and laughing as he piled each piece in my lap. I reached around behind me, feeling for the present I had stuck in the tree for him.

After he had opened the last one…he pouted playfully. "What's this…no present from my girl?…gee, I bring her the best present she's ever gotten and nothing." Mocking me, he brushed away a fake tear.

"Here ya go, you big baby…I wouldn't forget you…even if there is no mall around for me to go wild." I handed him the present and he ripped it open. Holding the necklace in his hand, he admired the way it glittered against the light.

"A gift from the heart…I love it Tess…Thank you." I took it and reached around his neck to latch it. His hand came up and held it against his chest. "I promise never to take it off." He looked down and kissed me deeply. Holding me in his arms, he began to rock to the music. "Let's get dressed and have some Christmas fun."

I laughed. "We usually get undressed to have fun." He squeezed me tight and brought me to my feet.

"You'd catch your death if we did this naked." He raced up the stairs calling down, "Come on woman…the day is wasting away." I looked around at the mess we made. Presents and wrappers were all over the place. Shaking my head, I wondered what he had in store for me, I got up and followed his lead.

Dressed warmly and waiting by the door, Ryan made me promise not to peek. I closed my eyes and let him lead me outside. He turned and told me to open my eyes. Looking out into the clearing, I saw a sled with a large red bow. Laughing, I spun around to face him. His eyes were filled with excitement. "I couldn't get the horse and sleigh up here, so I got you this instead." He gestured to the sled. Grabbing my arm he pulled me along as we ran to it. He picked up the rope and pulled it to the lake. I stopped dead in my tracks.

"Don't you think that's a bit dangerous?" He turned to see my fear. "We could fall through the ice." I hadn't been on ice in years and even then it was at a skating rink.

"Don't worry Tess, this lake is frozen solid." He jumped onto the ice and went sliding. Catching his balance, he turned smiling confidently. "Don't be a chicken…now who's being a baby?"

Cautiously I walked to the edge and stepped carefully onto the ice. Like a cat with tape on her paws, I moved over to the sled and sat down gently. My heart was pounding as I prayed my weight wouldn't send it through the ice.

Proudly he smiled and began to pull the sled. I relaxed and let myself enjoy the ride. By the middle of the day, Ryan was exhausted and we were both freezing cold.

He hung the sled on the side of the cabin and we went in to get warm. Once on the couch, Ryan passed out. I was still full of energy from the excitement, so I cleaned up the wrapping papers and placed the gifts under the tree. Looking back on the day, it was the best Christmas I'd ever had. In my family, there was always a moment when someone was pissed off for some stupid reason and it spoiled the whole day.

Once everything was neat and tidy, I grabbed some beef stock and veggies from the storeroom and headed into the kitchen to make a delicious stew. It felt good to prepare a home-style meal, which I knew would round off the perfect day. As it cooked on the wood stove, the fragrance wafted through the cabin.

Wondering how long Ryan could sleep, I peeked around the corner to see him sitting up stretching his arms over his head. "Baby, you sure know how to wake me up...and all this time I thought I'd have to be the cook around here."

It was like he had eyes in the back of his head. He knew I was watching him. He turned with a smile motioning me to join him. I walked over, holding a dishtowel across my chest waving it side to side giving him a seductive look. "A way to a man's heart is through his..."

He interrupted. "pants?" I stopped suddenly dropping my mouth open in surprise.

"Typical man thinking with the wrong brain." I snapped the towel in his direction. He pulled me down on his lap.

He sighed. "This has been a great day." He brushed the hair from my eyes as I watched him looking at me lovingly.

"It's perfect and I don't want to ruin it by asking when you're leaving...so...we won't even talk about it...at least not until you let me open my last present." He looked confused.

"What present are you talking about?" I looked over my shoulder at the shelf where the package that I had so patiently waited to open sat.

"Oooh that...well, it will have to wait a little longer...we've got all night before I'll let you get to it." I was about to object when he brought his fingers to my lips. "No arguments...I've made up your mind." He kissed me warmly. "I'm starving and that stew's smelling too good to let it burn."

I got up and tossed the towel. "Well, I guess I better get you fed...you may go wild if you don't get food in your belly."

"Go woman...get in the kitchen and pour your man a nice big bowl." I looked back to see him wave the towel over his head. "Man must eat...woman must cook." I smiled remembering when he and Scott put on a caveman production before he left.

After eating, we sat on the couch looking into the fire. "Tess, I just want to enjoy this moment as long as I can." He let out a sigh. "I know you've got a lot of questions, but right now...let's not think about anything but here and now." He wrapped an arm around me and drew me into his chest. I stretched out and listened to his heartbeat. He rubbed my arm and he stared into the fire. I looked up and knew he had a lot on his mind. His soft touch and the warmth of the fire soon lulled me to sleep. I tried to fight the urge not wanting the day to end, but I gave in.

The feeling of Ryan stroking my hair woke me. The morning light filtered through the trees and I realized I had slept the night away. I looked up to see him just as he was before I dropped off. Staring into the fire with my head in his lap. I gave a sigh of satisfaction causing him to look down. "Hey baby, did you have a nice rest?"

I stretched up my arms, "Yes, but I can see from your blood shot eyes, you didn't." I forced myself up and faced him. "Hope you plan to stick around, I'd hate for you to travel in your condition." I worried as his face twisted with different emotions. "Wanna talk about things?"

"Actually, we have to." He breathed in deeply. "I have some decisions to make." He shifted making himself more comfortable.

"Before we get caught up in talking, I need a cup of mud and something to eat." He nodded as I headed into the kitchen to whip up something quick. The left over stew sat on the counter uncovered and I knew I'd have to throw it out. I grabbed the pot and headed out the back door to toss it in the woods. As I passed the sauna, I discovered how Ryan was able to get to the cabin with the gifts. Parked next to the windmill was an ATV with a small trailer attached to it. He must have driven up in some other vehicle and unloaded it from there. He had put a lot of thought into making the trip and the effort assured me of his love.

Grabbing the usual oatmeal, I went inside to make up a couple bowls for us. I was able to see him still sitting on the couch staring into the fire. He finally got up and stretched. I could tell his body ached from sitting there all night. Heading into the bathroom, he kept his head down as he passed with a hint of despair on his face.

I placed the bowls on the table and sat waiting for him to join me. His oatmeal was cold and I had already finished mine by the time he came out. He sat there and poked at the lumps. I reached for the bowl, "Let me heat that up for you." He grabbed it and began to eat.

"It's fine…I like it cold." He took small bites dragging his teeth over the spoon. I knew he wasn't enjoying it.

"I could make you some eggs if you'd like, I think I still have a few left." I started to get up, but he reached out and stopped me.

"No…this is fine…really." He began to take bigger bites until he got to the bottom of the bowl. Looking up he flashed me a big smile. "Didn't think I'd do it did ya?"

I gathered up the dishes and headed to the sink. "You must really love me to eat that crap." When I turned, his eyes were sad. "What's wrong babe?" I went back and sat down bringing my hands to his face.

His expression turned serious, as he grabbed my hands and brought them down on the table. I searched his eyes worried that he had bad news. "Tess, Taylor told me he let it slip about the job offer in South America." He shook his head. "Before you say a word let me finish." He stopped; gathering his courage. "They offered me a partnership that comes with a really nice salary." He stood up and began pacing. "I haven't accepted the offer...not yet anyway ... there's a lot to consider...the only family I have is here...Monica, Scott and now you."

His frustration began to make him talk faster. He was too conflicted to organize his thoughts. Bringing his hands to his head, he grabbed his hair tight and gave out a yell. Startled by his strange behavior, I tensed and pushed back in my chair.

He looked down and saw the fear on my face. Dropping to his knee, he grabbed my hand. "I'm sorry; I didn't mean to freak you out... I just don't know what to do." The sincerity in his eyes helped me to relax. "I came here to ask how you'd feel if I took the job." Searching my mind, I couldn't find an answer.

Realizing my confusion, he continued. "I must admit, making that kind of money would be great...and I'll have a lot more to offer." He looked deep into my eyes. "If I take the job, I move away leaving everything I have here behind." Pacing once again, "If I stay, I give up the only chance I have to advance my career." My heart was torn as much as his.

I wanted him to stay and go back to being the pilot that captured my heart. I couldn't think of what might happen if he left. What would become of us? I was also torn thinking that if I tried to convince him to stay he would resent me for making him give up something he wanted. I had to find a way to stay neutral.

"Ryan, I don't know how I can help you make this decision. I have no right to make you stay or convince you to go. You've gotta do what makes you happy." He turned suddenly with a hurt look on his face as if I had punched him in the gut.

"No right? You, of all people, have every right! It's because of you I can't make up my damned mind." Shocked that he yelled at me, my blood began to boil.

"Don't yell at me, it's not my fault. I didn't force you to go off to South America and dazzle them with your flyboy skills." I stood up and stormed out of the room.

"That's a shitty attitude Tess! I came here to find out how you would feel either way, to see if we had some kind of future together...and here you are dumping all over me." I turned to him not wanting to pick a fight.

"I love you with all my heart…I don't want you to go but I don't want to keep you from doing something you've always wanted." I saw his face relax as he took me in his arms. "I love you Scott." His eyes turned cold as I realized my Freudian slip. He pushed me away and turned. "Ryan…no…don't go." I put my head in my hands as I heard the door slam as he left the cabin.

He wanted a future with me…I knew he loved me, but it didn't hit me that he wasn't asking my opinion as much as he was trying to ask my permission. I had made the biggest mistake of my life. He was pissed off and hurt. He didn't even let me correct my statement…he just left.

My heart sank as I heard the ATV take off. I ran to the back door and around the sauna just as he was heading down the path to the meadow. Like an idiot, I talked myself out of running after him "Fine, he wants to be an ass…then I'll let him…he'll come back." Mumbling to myself as I went back in to mull over what had happened.

It was a simple slip of the tongue…he should have known that I didn't mean that I was in love with Scott. It was noon and he still hadn't come back. Not wanting to be the one to give in, I kept busy cleaning up the dishes in the sink and sweeping more pine needles from under the tree.

I bent down and ran my fingers along the gifts he gave me. I looked at the tickets and saw they were dated for the first of May. He had put so much thought into it, I felt guilty… I only got him a stupid necklace. At that moment, I remembered the package I had waited so patiently to open. I went to the shelf but it wasn't there. Frantic, I went around the cabin tossing things trying to find it. When I was completely exhausted, I sat on the floor looking around wondering where it could have gone.

The sun began to set and I worried something had happened to him. I bundled up and grabbed the flashlight. As I headed down the path, I walked slow listening for any sound that might have given me a clue to where he was. When I reached the meadow, it was dark. The field was empty. I called out but he didn't answer. I followed the tracks from the ATV across the meadow and down another path until I came to the access road. I'd never been that far away from the cabin before. There was no truck, no ATV and no Ryan. He had left…my shoulders began to heave as I cried.

I turned and headed back. Normally I would have been terrified to be out alone at night, but at that moment, I didn't give a shit about anything. I walked along feeling sorry for myself. I got back to the cabin and paced around not knowing what to do. I'd completely blown the best thing in my life with a few short words. I grabbed the mic and flipped on the radio. I heard only static as I tried to call base. I repeated my call over and over but had no response. A few times, I heard the radio click, but there was no one on the other end. Just in case someone had been listening, I sat down in a chair and talked into the void.

"Just in case anyone can hear me, I want to confess I've made the biggest mistake of my life. I fell in love and in a few short words I pushed him away. If anyone can hear me…tell him I love him…tell him to come back to me…tell him I'm sorry." My voice cracked as the tears rolled down my cheeks. I dropped the mic on the table and let myself have a good cry.

CHAPTER TWENTY-SIX

In my heart, I hoped Ryan would come back. I sat there and sobbed until I couldn't breath. For days I couldn't sleep or eat. I felt empty. I knew I'd blown the one chance I had for happiness. I couldn't concentrate on writing, reading or anything but him. At times I told myself he completely over reacted and may still come back once he calmed down. I tried to justify it from all angles, but nothing seemed to make sense. I wrote him letter after letter pouring my heart out, but wasn't able to write anything I knew would bring him back. Even if I did…it wouldn't matter.

Right before the New Year, Monica arrived with Scott in the helicopter. I stood on the porch as they landed and slowly walked out to greet them. The blades hadn't stopped spinning when Monica jumped out. Before I knew it we were face to face. Anger filled her eyes as she began to tear into me. "Of all the stupid things a woman could ever do." She grabbed my arm and dragged me back to the cabin. Flinging me in on the couch, she stood over me. "He took time off his job and flew all that way to see you…" I tried to explain. "Shut up and listen!" I shut my mouth and looked up at her. "You, right now, have no voice…nothing you could say is going to stop me from laying into to you." Scott walked in as she shot him a look. He turned back around and closed the door behind him.

"Ryan's the only family I've got left…when he came to me and asked what I thought about the job offer, I begged him not to go…like a fool I knew he was in love with you. I hoped the two of you would get married, have babies and live here." She lifted her arms and looked around the room. "He came here to make sure you felt the same way about him. He was all set to ask you to marry him damn it, but he wasn't going to until he knew that you would be with him no matter where he was. He was close to turning down the job and then you went and blew it!" She turned away and began to cry. "Tess, I love you like a sister...I know you love my brother." She swung back around. "Why did you have to reject him?" Drowning in her tears she questioned me painfully with her eyes.

"Monica, I didn't reject him. He never asked me to marry him." Confused she sat down beside me and with the back of her sleeve, wiped the tears from her eyes.

"What do you mean?" She sniffled. "Then why did he take off like that?" She looked around trying to figure it out in her mind.

"It's my fault, one minute he was telling me about the job offer, the next he was asking me what to do and then when I told him that it wasn't my place...I made a slip of the tongue and said "I love you Scott"... He got pissed and took off... I tried to run after him, but it was too late."

She was shocked. "Do you?" I looked up confused. "Do you love my husband?" I shook my head.

"What we had is gone...I love him like a brother and nothing more." I looked up hoping she understood.

Unable to hold back, I let the tears fly and fell into her arms. We sat there and sobbed until we were both out of breath. "I didn't want to tell him to go and lose him and I didn't want to make him stay and resent me for the rest of his life. I was confused...I didn't know what he wanted me to say."

"He didn't mention anything about going with him or being together?" I tried to think back, but could only remember the hurt in his eyes and then his anger. "I don't think so...it was all so bizarre. I was angry that he didn't stay and let me explain. I thought he'd come back and we could work it out." Monica looked stunned as she sat back.

"Tess, I'm sorry...I thought you turned down his proposal. He was so excited about asking you to marry him on Christmas day." I flashed back on the how hard it was for him to admit his feelings for me that first time.

"I fell asleep…it probably gave him the perfect chance to change his mind." I started to cry and couldn't stop. She pulled me into her arms and tried to comfort me. At some point Scott had come back in quietly and walked over to us. He stroked my hair as his wife rocked me in her arms.

I curled up on the couch when they went into the kitchen to talk in muted tones. "What should we do?" I heard Monica say.

"There's nothing we can do honey…he's gone and I have no way to call him." There was a long pause before I heard the radio click on and the familiar fuzz penetrated the cabin. "Miller, its Taylor…take my flights, we'll be back tomorrow…usual flight plan at nine." I'm sure there was more to his call, but I blocked it out as my stomach began to twist. I got up and rushed to the bathroom to get sick.

I took off my clothes and leaned against the shower stall to let the cool water trickle down my back. A soft tap at the door brought my head up. Monica peeked around the door. "Tess? You okay? I'm sorry I got you all worked up." She stepped in and grabbed a towel. "How long since you last ate?" I looked at her with a weak smile. "Collect yourself and come have some tea."

I nodded as she turned and closed the door behind her. Grabbing the soap, I took a proper shower. Once I was toweled off and changed, I emerged from the bathroom still feeling ill. Sitting together on the couch, they looked over at me as I walked across the room and slumped into the chair. "I'm sorry guys, I must look as crappy as I feel."

"It's okay sweetie…here, this might help settle your stomach." She stood placing the tea in my hands.

Scott remained quiet but looked concerned as he watched me take small sips. "I've never seen you like this Tess, it worries me." He said as his voice cracked. He cleared his throat and looked away. The sight of me must have repulsed him. My eyes were swollen and red, my hair was matted and my clothes looked like I had worn them for weeks.

I knew if I tried to talk, I would break down again…so I just sat there and stared into the cup. With a whisper, he asked Monica to leave us alone. She didn't argue as she grabbed her coat and headed out the door.

He stared into the fire and spoke softly. "I heard your radio call that night...I tried to radio back, to let you know I was there. He must have heard you too...every time I tried the mic, someone kept breaking off my call." He turned his head. "He must've given up after the first few times. Once the air was clear I was about to radio back but you didn't answer." Taking in a deep breath, he rested his head on the back of the couch. "If I'd stayed off the radio, he could've answered...I'm so sorry Tess."

I couldn't focus my gaze on anything but the tea. "It's okay, it doesn't matter now. He's gone." I took a deep breath and gathered what little strength I could. "If he loves me...truly loves me, he'll come back."

"And if he doesn't?" He questioned me with a tear in his eye.

"Then his feelings for me weren't as strong as we both thought." My voice was empty and cold. I took another sip. "I'm gonna leave here Scott, I want out...I've had enough...I'm finally giving in." My voice became oddly flat. "I can't sit here day after day in this place full of memories and not go mad."

"Tess, please...don't give up...there's too much for you to loose." He leaned towards me. "It's only a few more months...and you said you're almost finished." His eyes pleaded with me. "Tell me what I can do to help."

It warmed my heart to see him concerned for my future. "Call Jerry and see if there's a way I can leave and finish some place else. I just can't stay here." I choked back my pain. "Anywhere but here."

With renewed hope, he winked at me "I'll see what I can do." He got up and headed out the door to find Monica. I put the cup on the table and went to the shelf where I kept Ryan's letters. I had read all but one. I was tempted to read it, but knowing that it would tear my heart out of my chest, I folded it up tight and put it in my pocket. I went over to the writing desk and looked out the window. Monica and Scott were on the dock holding each other. I wanted to smile, but my melancholy mood wouldn't let me feel any emotion. I felt trapped; more then I'd became used to. Going back to the couch, I grabbed a pillow and flopped onto the billowy cushions.

They tried to give me space, but in the small cabin it was nearly impossible. Monica was able to get me to eat and by the end of the day I began to feel a little stronger. Scott took down the tree that had lost most of its needles. It represented how I felt. Memories dangling on bare limbs exposed for everyone to see.

I began to pack up my clothes and the presents. There was no way they were leaving without me. I gathered up the pages of my book and grabbed the box I found under the floor. As they slept in the loft, I sat on the couch trying to figure out how to get the puzzle box back together.

When the sun came up, I gave up and tossed the pieces on the coffee table. Taking the locket Mary gave me, I put the key from the box on the chain and hung it around my neck. I walked to the window and watched as the sun bathed the ice covered lake. The memories began to flood my brain, but I couldn't cry anymore, my heart was numb.

While they prepared the chopper, I dowsed the fires in the living room and stove. Giving one last look around at the haven that became a romantic getaway and then a prison, I grabbed up my bag and leaned against the door letting it latch behind me. My head rested on the wreath I had made as I looked out at the landscape one last time.

Once we were in the air and heading back to base, I tensed knowing I was making another huge mistake. I made up my mind not to worry about what Jerry would throw at me when he found out. I didn't care about anything. The flight went by fast, as I was lost in my own little world and barely noticed when we landed.

Sitting outside Scott's office, I watched him as he heatedly spoke with Jerry on the phone. He slammed down the receiver, jerked it from the wall and sent it flying across the room. He collected himself before coming to break the news to me.

Looking up, he motioned me to join him. "Tess, you need to stay at the lodge for a few months while we get this thing settled with that jerk of a lawyer. Monica and I will get it ironed out and you'll be able to recoup... I know the last thing you want is to be confined to another place…but at least you won't be alone." I had no response other than to nod my head.

With that, Monica and I drove to the lodge and settled me into the same room I had before. I laid on the bed staring at the ceiling. My mood took over my mind and I didn't care what was happening. I lost the man I loved, my home, my money and my self-respect.

CHAPTER TWENTY-SEVEN

Sick most of the time, I had sunken into a deep depression; not able keep food down. I found comfort in my dreams sleeping most of the day. It consumed me. I knew I had to pull out of it and start thinking about my future. Monica would bring me food and try to get me to go to town or for a walk, but I just wanted to be alone.

About the third week, I finally found the courage to get up and wander down stairs. "Tess, it's great to see you up and about." Monica chimed. "Guess you finally beat that flu bug." She handed some towels to the maid and came over to me. "Feel like heading into town today? I have to pick up the mail." I shrugged and followed her to the truck.

I stared out the window watching the trees pass as she chattered about the plans for the resort. Having forgotten all about it, I didn't know how I would break it to her that there would be no money to get it off the ground. Not wanting to bust her bubble I let her ramble on. When we reached town she went in to grab the mail as I watched the people walking by living their lives. I wanted to tell them they had no right to be happy while I was so miserable. I caught sight of a bookstore just as Monica came out of the post office. I got out of the truck and walked across the street.

"Tess, I'll wait for you here okay?" I raised my hand and waved. Opening the door, I took a deep breath enjoying the smell of new books. It was a small store with a limited collection neatly arranged on shelves around the wall. The young clerk looked up from her book giving me a welcoming nod. I walked along running my fingers over the glossy covers, wondering how many of the authors had ever gone through my kind of pain. I felt connected to them in a small way. At the back of the store was a locked case that held old books. Browsing the titles, I came across one that made my heart race. The corners were tattered, but it was the title that had me excited. "Sofia's Story"

"Excuse me…are these books for sale?" She grabbed a key off a peg behind her and came over.

"Sure are…which one are you interested in?" I pointed out the book and she took it from the case carefully. She couldn't have been more then eighteen, I was fascinated as she ran her fingers over the title lovingly. "It's one of my favorites." She handed me the book. "You're gonna love it."

I followed her to the counter keeping my eyes on the title. It was like my grandfather had guided me to find this new treasure. As she ran my card, I noticed the name of the author…Mack Kelly. I had no idea my grandfather ever wrote a book. Reaching for the locket around my neck, I whispered a soft thank you to him.

"I'm sorry, did you say something?" I smiled shaking my head. She handed me the receipt to sign. As I grabbed my card, she looked down at my signature. "Tess Kelly? Any relation?" I nodded.

"He was my grandfather." I turned to walk out when she stopped me. She came around the counter and held out her hand.

Returning her handshake, I gave her a questioning look. "These letters changed my life."

"Thank you…it means a lot to me to know he touched more then just my life." I turned and left.

Monica was flipping through the mail when I got back in the truck. She looked over and spotted the book. "Find something good?"

"Yes…I think I found the key to our mystery." I held up the book. Her mouth dropped open as she read the title. I lowered it and smiled. "Maybe it has the answers about our grandparents."

As we drove back to the Lodge, I read out loud. The book was a collection of correspondences written between the two. Neither of us wanted to stop reading. We spent the rest of the day in the lobby sitting across from each other passing the book back and forth reading to each other. She read her grandmother's letters and I read my grandfathers. Stopping only long enough to go to the bathroom or grab something to eat. They took us through their entire history, how they met, the project they worked on, the love they found in each others arms, how they parted and even into the lives they had found away from each other. It was well past midnight when we read the last letter.

Sitting by the fire we looked at each other in amazement. Their story was much like my own. I found him, I loved him, I lost him and I'd have to live without him. "God Tess, this is so spooky…I could find my own life in those letters." I looked at her oddly. Her life? It was my life… Suddenly she realized I was thinking the same thing.

"It's so weird that we each found a part of our lives in this book." I bit my finger thinking about what the young clerk said to me. I recited her words out loud; "These letters changed my life." I stared into the fire.

"Wow, that's a quick change of attitude." Realizing she thought I meant my life, I shook my head. "No, not me…it was the girl in the store…these letters changed her life…this book was one of her favorites." I looked down at the title and traced over the words.

"We've got powerful roots Tess, maybe we can both find something here that could change the way we are. Maybe I can learn that I won't lose my independence by starting a family." She got up and stretched.

"You're right…we both can learn something …I think I know exactly what I've got to do." I gave her a hug and headed up to bed cradling the book in my arms. I had to take control of my future. I wasn't going to end up afraid and alone…I was going to fight for what I want, I deserved to be happy.

I began to formulate my plan of attack. The next morning, I woke up and took a long walk in the woods organizing my thoughts. I felt more focused, more alive. The inspiration I had lost came back. I knew I wanted to finish my book and find a way to get Ryan back.

When I got back to the lodge, I asked to borrow a typewriter. Setting up a writing area in my room I began to re-write every page.

I spent most of my time locked up in the room clacking away at the typewriter, only emerging for short breaks to eat and run into town with Monica. By the end of February, I was down to the last few chapters. Knowing there was more to write, I had gone as far as I could at that moment. I bundled up the pages placing them in the bottom of my travel bag and headed down to the lobby.

I ran into Scott at the front desk. "Hey, got some news for me?" He turned and gave me a hug.

"As a matter of fact I do...Jerry won't relent, he wants you back in Tucson to sign some papers...I'm sorry Tess." His concern for my future had him working overtime trying to get Jerry to agree to consider the lodge as my confinement. "Tess, I made some calls and found out a few things about him that might help when you get back." He handed me a folder.

"It's okay Scott, I'm gonna be okay." I bit my lip as I asked. "You think you can do me one last favor?" They both had done so much for me; I hated to ask for more.

"Sure...anything." His said seriously.

"I want you to take me back to the cabin before I leave." I smiled to assure him I was fine with going back.

"Let's go...get what you need and meet me outside." He turned to Monica and gave her a quick kiss.

I gathered up a few things and joined him. Scared and hopeful, we drove to the seadrome. He kept glancing at me trying to figure out what I was planning. I wasn't quite sure myself, so I kept quiet. Once in the air, I wondered if the lake was still frozen over. "Will we be able to land this sucker?" I yelled over the engine.

"Sure thing, went up a week ago to check the pipes to make sure the new plumbing didn't freeze." He pointed as we cleared the ridge. The lake glistened as it reflected the sun. We spiraled down and landed smoothly.

Once docked and secured, we headed up to the cabin. I noticed he had removed the wreath from the door. Determined not to let my emotions get the better of me, I stepped inside and looked around. It was the same as when I left. I put down the bag and took out the book my grand father wrote placing in on the desk.

"So are you going to let me in on this...or do I have to guess?" I smiled reaching in the bag pulling out my book and two envelopes.

"You my friend are gonna help me win back the love of my life." I looked up worried he might object. "That is if you're willing." I grabbed a pencil and wrote across the box of pages. "Tess's Story". I arranged the book on top of the box next to the old typewriter, and propped the envelope with Ryan's name up against it.

Taking Scott's hand, I lead him outside. Handing him the other envelope, I began to explain. "I've loved three men in my life...My grandfather, who's gone...you, who I lost but now love like a brother...and Ryan, who I refuse to let go. I need him in my life, more now then ever before. Make sure he gets this letter...if he loves me, he'll come back here and read both books. If I am really lucky, he'll come down from this mountain and you'll give him this." I pulled out his plane ticket to Jamaica. He'll know where to find me.

He shook his head. "This won't work Tess." He looked me in the eyes. "I've tried to get him to come back...but he's stubborn... He won't talk to me about it." He took my hand.

"Scott, please...mail the letter...I think he'll come back." I kissed his cheek and walked back to the plane.

I spent one more week at the lodge before they drove me to the airport. Monica and I exchanged emotional hugs good bye as she assured me that she'd find a way to get the resort up and running. Scott gave me a tight hug and promised me he would do as I asked.

During the flight back, I felt confident that no matter what was going to happen, I'd be fine. I went through the folder Scott gave me before. He was right, there was good reason to be suspicious of Jerry. The documents he found were full of evidence that he was taking advantage of my family's money. Looking forward to seeing Mary again and spending some time in a warm climate gave me comfort. I took out my notebook and began to journal my thoughts.

Finally in Tucson, I walked through the gate to see her warm smile greet me. I dropped my bag and ran into her arms. It felt good to be home again. "Come on, we've got dinner reservations, and from what I see, you can use a good meal." I laughed as she pinched my stomach. "You have any luggage?" She questioned.

"Just this." I lifted the bag tossing it over my shoulder. "The rest will be shipped to the ranch."

We walked arm in arm down the concourse as she made concerned comments about my dramatic weight loss and filled me in on what was happening in Tucson. I hadn't realized how disconnected from the real world I was. I listened to ever word enjoying the sound of her sing song voice. As we drove along the familiar roads she continued her update of current events.

CHAPTER TWENTY-EIGHT

During dinner, I recounted my adventure. She sat there going through every emotion with me. We were there for hours until we realized they were clearing the tables. She asked every question I had asked myself on the ride out to the ranch. My body was tired from traveling and reliving the past months all in one night. I climbed into bed and buried myself under the cool sheets.

After sleeping in late, I got up and took a bath before heading to the kitchen. All the stress was forgotten as I rummaged around the fridge for something different to eat. Grabbing some cheese and a package of tortillas, I whipped up a quesodilla. I had wolfed down two, before I caught sight of Mary staring at me in amazement.

"You must've starved up there…I've never seen anyone eat that fast in my life." She giggled and walked over to wipe a drip of salsa from my chin.

Laughing at how ridiculous I must have looked. "I missed this kind of food…I got sick of eating oatmeal and veggies."

"Jerry's here sweet heart…he wants to see you in the study." The worried look on her face told me she knew what was about to happen. I kissed her cheek and headed down the hall.

He sat behind the desk organizing the papers he brought. "I see you invested in more botox." I walked over and was about to sit in the chair across from him, but instead perched myself on the corner of the desk. I wasn't gonna give him the chance to intimidate me.

Without an expression, he looked up. "I see you haven't changed your attitude...but I must say you're looking delicious." I think if he could, he would've raised his eyebrows.

"Jerry, you haven't changed one bit...your still a wanker...let's get the shit over with before you make me puke." Looking a bit uncomfortable, he sat up and ruffled the documents.

"Well, you basically pissed away your inheritance...however, you do get something. Your grandfather made it possible for you to get half of what was coming to you. The other half goes back into the trust and will go to your children should you ever have any." He looked up briefly.

Clearing his throat he continued... "Now, you need to sign this confirming I explained the terms in detail...and this one agreeing to the terms." He paused a moment. "And this one so I get paid for my services." He sat back and put his arms over his head.

I gathered up the papers and leafed through them. "You have a copy of the will?" I took the pen from the desk and tapped it against my lips.

He started to look nervous, if that was possible. "Sure do...but we've already gone over it. It's all complicated legal stuff Tess, you won't understand it." I shot him a look.

"Don't patronize me you little weasel." Realizing he wasn't going to be able to pull a fast one, he took it from his brief case and handed it to me. "I'll look these over and get back to you. In the mean time, I'm gonna have Mary freeze the assets to the estate until I understand everything I'm signing." I stood up and leaned over the desk looking him straight in the eye. "Don't look so shocked Jerry...like you said...it's all legal stuff...I probably won't understand a thing...but to be on the safe side, I want to make sure my family's money stays where it is for now."

"Those papers have to be signed Tess...there's no two ways about it." He snapped his case shut and stood looking offended by my actions. "Let the record show that I've been with this family for the past ten years looking after all of you ...this distrust cuts me to the quick." He stormed out of the room and slammed the door behind him.

I walked into the foyer to hear his car peel out of the driveway. Mary came rushing in. "Are you okay?" Looking wide eyed.

"Yes, everything will be fine now." I put my arm around her shoulder and led her into the kitchen.

I picked up the phone and handed it to her. "I need you to contact who ever you have to and freeze the family's accounts." She looked at me confused. "A friend of mine did some checking on old Jerry and I think he's been skimming the family trust fund." She grabbed the phone and made the call. I sat down at the table and read the documents carefully beginning with the will. I read it over once and then again. It was a normal will with no stipulations and no strange clauses or claims. There were letters attached at the end with my grandfather's bizarre requests, but nothing stated that if any of us didn't comply with his wishes we would lose half our inheritance. I sat back not believing anyone could've been so sneaky.

I looked over at Mary sitting with her mouth open; completely stunned. "What a sneaky rat...didn't you get a look at this before?" I shook my head

"How could I've been so stupid...all these years I just signed what ever he put in front of me...I never questioned any of it." I smacked my hand against my head laughing. "Oh, shit...I wonder how much he got away with?" We looked at each other knowingly and headed into the study.

As Mary gathered all the financial papers she could find, I placed a call to the firm Jerry worked for. Not surprised, I found he hadn't been there in years. I told the girl on the other end to connect me with one of the partners. I explained the situation and asked for representation. After I had set an appointment, I helped Mary gather up all we could find.

As we shuffled papers into boxes, she caught sight of the locket she gave me for Christmas. She reached out, "What's the key for Tess?"

"I found it at the cabin, it opened a compartment in the floor where I found a box...unfortunately that too was locked, but the key didn't fit it." I shrugged and tossed more papers in the box.

"I have a key like this one, maybe it will fit." She got up and left the room.

I sat back and looked at the key wondering how many there must have been that looked the same. Leaning back, I looked around the room spying the multitude of art and trophies that decorated the walls and shelves. I let my eyes drift over the memories: an old oar my grandfather claimed had saved his life during a rafting trip, a painting of the red rocks of Sedona, lift tickets from around the world, and photos of my family. All the momentos cataloged the history of my grandfather's life. A man so loved and well traveled gone from the world and only a handful of people knew how wonderful he truly was.

Mary came rushing back in bringing me out of my thoughts. "See, it's exactly the same...Mack gave it to me on our honeymoon and said I would find the lock it belonged to someday." She looked at me hopefully. "You do have the box with you?" I shook my head no.

"It's with the things Monica's shipping." Her excitement deflated as she sat back. "I'm sorry Mary, I didn't think I'd need it right away...It should be here any day."

She sighed. "Well, I guess I can wait a bit longer." She gathered herself up and helped me finish putting the papers in the box.

"We need to head out and get these to town." I stood up and helped her to her feet.

The lawyer was happy to take the case. We learned that Jerry was fired from the firm about the time my grandfather put him on retainer. All too trusting, he never took the time to check his background. The papers he tried to get me to sign would have given him control of the money. The lawyer assured us he would contact the proper authorities and help us settle the estate. Mary was to contact my brother and sister and let them know what was going on. Like me, Jerry had sent them on secluded adventures of their own.

Before heading back to the ranch, we went to the bank and changed all the accounts. By acting quickly, we were able to keep Jerry from getting his hands on any more than he had already taken. He had signature cards on every account attached to the estate. With the documents the lawyer provided us...we were able to do damage control.

After a quick bite, we headed to the mall for a little shopping. It felt good to be back in my own element surrounded by people. A twinge of pain in my heart reminded me I was missing the biggest part of my life. I knew the letter I had Scott mail would bring Ryan to the cabin. I was careful with my wording, reminding him of our times together as I poured out my true feelings for him. I had to keep the faith that his love for me was too strong for him to ignore. It was hard to put it down on paper, our love was more then just words, it was life itself.

Mary would see me zoning and shake me out of it. After we had purchased all that we cared to, we headed back to the ranch. I hoped the boxes had arrived with my things from the cabin. Unfortunately, no packages were left at the front door. Once I had everything put away, I called Monica.

"Tess, is that you?" Her voice rang with excitement.

"Yup...been here a few short days and everything's under control. The resort's a go. I set up an account that you can pull the funds from and I mailed off a check to re-emburse you for the money you loaned me in Hawaii." I could hear her breathing, but she didn't say a word. "Monica...did you hear me?"

Breathlessly, "Yes...I'm just shocked...how did you get the money?"

"Scott gave me a file of info he collected on Jerry and with that and other documents we found here...we were able to file against him...I doubt I'll ever have to see him again." I paused a moment and continued. "Everything's gonna to be okay...so how's everything there?"

She sounded panicked. "You're not going to believe what's happened...Ryan's back." My heart skipped a beat. "Scott took him up to the cabin today and he'll leave him there like you asked." I heard her rustle some papers. "I got a call today from Dr. Whetstone's office asking for you. He wanted to make sure you're eating normal again." She cleared her voice.

"Could you call him and let him know that I'm fine. I starved myself for so long, my stomach couldn't handle food." I felt my side knowing the ribs still showed under my skin. "Heck, I haven't stopped eating since I got back…I must've gained about ten pounds."

"That'll make him feel better…he wanted to send you brochures on anorexia…but I assured him it wasn't that dramatic." She sighed. "I miss you Tess, it's no fun here without you."

"I miss you too Mon…I'll be back, I just need to get things settled here." I took a deep breath and relaxed. "Tell Scott hi for me and keep your fingers crossed and hope Ryan comes around."

I hung up the phone and went to my room. I was getting better and feeling more alive than I had since Christmas. Knowing my letter had reached him the way I wanted it to set my mind at ease and my plans in motion. I knew Monica would jump on the plans and start getting things done…I just had to wait until May and I would find out if Ryan's love was true.

My anxiety ate at my nerves as March rolled around. I wasn't sure if I could wait till May and pondered the idea of leaving early. Since Ryan had received my letter and returned earlier then expected, he'd be back from the cabin a month before I had planned. I kept myself busy going through boxes in my grandfather's office and helping Mary around the ranch.

She had cleared out the old stables and began to take in horses from a local vet who rescued abused and mistreated animals. She had a great plan of starting a day camp for kids and I knew it would be a nice addition to the community. She taught me how to care for the horses and I found that it helped to keep my mind off Ryan.

The problems with Jerry were pushed onto the lawyers and I knew their firm would take care of any challenges. My brother and sister returned to their normal lives and didn't even attempt to contact us. I wasn't too surprised. I hoped someday we would be able to act like a normal family, but I didn't want to try just then. I was sure they were as pissed as I was to find out they had been tricked.

It was late in the month when the boxes from Monica finally arrived. I was at the stables mucking the stalls when Mary rushed in excited holding the key my grandfather gave her. Out of breath, she couldn't get the words out, but I knew what she was trying to say. I tossed the pitchfork and grabbed her arm while running back to the house.

The boxes sat on the floor in the foyer. We sat down on the tile and began to tear at the cardboard. With luck, in the first one, under a bundle of clothes was the box. Handing it to her, she put the key in the lock and it turned with ease. She looked up and giggled.

"It's like finding a buried treasure." She looked down and carefully lifted the lid. Inside we found a book and a picture of my grandfather standing beside the cabin. She looked at it and began to cry. I'd forgotten she was still mourning his death. She always seemed so strong and confident. She took the book in her hands and with a look of confusion turned it so I could read the title. Black with gold letters that simply read… "My Life".

I smiled shaking my head. My grandfather in his wisdom and sense of adventure sent me to the cabin not only to encourage me to write, but to create mysteries that would make being there a little more interesting. He knew I'd find all the clues and come home to solve the puzzle. I may have been expecting something different, but when I saw the smile on Mary's face, I knew it was the perfect treasure.

She touched the raised letters gently. "Now I know why he spent all those nights locked up in the study…and why he took that trip…He must have finished this book before he…" her eyes welled up again as she choked on her words.

I reached out and patted her hand on the book. "He wanted us to find it so we could keep him alive in our hearts…I'll fix you a drink." I got up and went to the kitchen. As I mixed her a cocktail and brewed me some tea, I thought about the planning he had to do for us to find his book. I'm sure one way or another it would have been discovered, but I was amazed at how systematically it worked. I hoped the same magic the cabin held for my grandfather would work for Ryan and me.

I handed Mary her drink as the phone rang.

"Tess? It's Scott" My stomach turned as I heard the seriousness in his voice.

"Hey, what's going on?" I sat down and kicked off my boots, praying he was just calling to say hi.

"I picked up Ryan today and you were right, he asked me where you were. I gave him the ticket, but seeing the date he knows you're not in Jamaica." He took a deep breath. "He's heading for Tucson. I don't know how he'll find the Ranch, but he seems very determined."

Knowing my plans were dashed, I gave in. "It's okay; I'm ready to face what's coming. Did he say anything else?" I held my breath hoping for some positive reaction.

"Well, he didn't say much and seemed a little pissed off...but...I know he still loves you." His voiced softened and he almost laughed. "He kept mumbling something like...damn woman's got me jumpin through hoops." I giggled as he mocked Ryan.

"Promise me one thing Tess...let him blow up if he wants to...I think if you keep your temper in check, he won't bolt again."

"I'll try, but I don't see how that would help...if he wants to go, he'll go. I just hope he read my book while he was there." There was a long pause and I began to get nervous.

"I don't know what you wrote Tess, but I'd like to know if there's something you're not telling me." His suspicion rang in my ears.

"I love him Scott...I try to pretend that I'll be okay if he doesn't want me back, but if I lose him...I'll be crushed." I kept my emotions in check as my stomach turned. Even the thought of losing him made me sick. "Give Monica my love... tell her to start building and I promise to come back soon"

I sat there and stared at the phone, Ryan would show up any day and I had no idea what was gonna happen. I thought I was being smart planning everything out carefully even what I was gonna say. In one phone call, he managed to toss my plans right out the window.

Mary had spent days pouring through the pages of my grandfather's life while I cared for the horses. Needing more to occupy my mind, I decided to clean out the old barn that was at the back of the property. It had been the catchall since my grandfather had bought the place. It was time to clear it out so the ranch could function as it was originally intended. I moved out an old truck and farm equipment that was purchased but never used and cleared out stacks of boxes that would have to be sorted through.

It took me a few days to reach the back of the barn, but when I did, I came across an old friend. It was covered by a tarp and decorated with cobwebs. I smiled remembering the fun I used to have, but then remembered why it ended up abandoned. I whipped the tarp off sending a cloud of dust in the air. Bathed in the dim light of the barn was my 86 blue Sportster that made me feel like the coolest chick in college. Grandfather bought it used and gave it to me for my 18th birthday. I had the thrill of riding it for a year before crashing and never getting up the nerve to ride again. It was still in pretty good condition and I figured with a good wash and a once over from a mechanic, it would run as good as new.

I guided it out of the barn and into the sunlight. She was beautiful…I couldn't help running my hands over the chrome and the metallic blue fender. I was transported in one moment back to my younger years. I'd have never let myself get as serious as I had become in the past months. I wanted that feeling back. I pushed the bike back in the barn and headed to the house to call a mechanic.

Mary was sitting in the kitchen curled up in the bay window looking out onto the grounds. "It's so quiet here…sometimes it drives me nuts!" I knew exactly what she meant. She was feeling as alone as anyone could possibly feel. My heart felt her pain, but I wasn't gonna let it consume me again. I went though that hell already and knew I still had to face more in the near future.

"When you get the day camp up and running, you'll miss this peace and quiet." I picked up the phone and dialed the auto shop's number listed on Mary's board. "Hi, this is Tess Kelly…do you make house calls?" I kept my eye on her as I arranged for him to come out and fix my bike.

"I know the mood your in…I was there not too long ago myself…I think we need to take a trip and have a little fun." Finally tearing her eyes away, she looked up at me and nodded. "Today is your day and you can pick anything you want to do…so let me run and get my bag and we'll head out."

She chose to spend the day in Tombstone looking at all the historic buildings, drinking in all the saloons and shopping in all the tourist traps. It was perfect weather and a mild breeze kept the sun at bay. On the way back, we stopped at a roadside stand and picked up some fresh fruit, pecans and buffalo jerky. As we drove along, we sang obnoxiously to country music on the radio in between bites of jerky and fruits. It was well after dinner when we finally pulled into the gates. All the lights were off and the house looked ominous in the moonlight.

Both our moods were a lot lighter and we enjoyed a nice evening in the courtyard sipping sun tea and telling each other stories we remembered about my grandfather. After she had finally headed to bed, I kicked back in the hammock and let myself relax and enjoy the sweet desert night. If there was one place in the world where I could go to feel grounded it was at the ranch.

Waking up dusted by the morning mist, I stretched out and brushed off the dew. I knew better then to let myself sleep in such a position, but the perfume of the wild flowers lulled me to sleep. I walked quietly through the house and into the kitchen. Mary wasn't up so I went ahead and fixed a quick breakfast before heading out to feed the horses.

Tossing the last flake of hay over the fence, I heard a truck pull up behind me. Worried that it may be Ryan, I was afraid to turn around and look. "Hey...Lady? You got a bike needs fixin?" Relieved I turned around and pointed to the barn.

"I'll be down in just a sec, go on ahead." I gave a pat to one of the mares that poked her head over the fence.

Knowing no one likes to be watched while they work, I took my time heading down to the barn. When I got there, he had it up and running. "Just needed a new battery and a bit of dusting. I gave her a lube and juiced up the tank...she's ready for ya." He wiped his face with a filthy rag and headed back to his truck. "Let her run a bit before you take her out."

He left without asking for payment. I shrugged it off knowing I would get a nice big bill in the mail. I walked around the bike as it idled. Getting on, I balanced it between my legs until I felt comfortable with the weight. Gathering up my courage, I kicked up the stand, pulled down my sunglasses, revved it a bit, slipped it into gear, and took off. My blood rushed quickly through my veins, a little afraid but much more excited than anything else. It felt comfortable, as if I had been riding my entire life. I did a few laps around the barn and headed around the house, down the drive and out to the road. I got lost in the feeling of having the wind slap my face and whip through my hair.

I rode for an hour and headed back to the ranch. Coming down the drive, I caught a glimpse of a rental car parked behind Mary's. I rode around the house along the stables and to the barn. At that moment, Ryan came rushing over shouting. "Tess, get off that thing in your condition." He looked pissed. I stopped and revved the engine a few times before shutting it off.

My legs felt like jelly, but I didn't want to show any weakness. "Sorry...what did you say?" I tossed my matted hair and looked up at him.

"I said..." through gritted teeth. "You shouldn't be on that damn thing in your condition...don't you care about anybody but yourself?"

I raised my eyebrows confused by his words. "What the hell are you talking about?" I dusted off my jeans. "What condition?"

CHAPTER TWENTY-NINE

My heart was pounding in my chest. I tried to hold myself back from rushing into his arms, begging him to take me back. I wanted to stand strong and let him be the one to fall to pieces. His eyes were wild as he searched for some kind of answer. "What do you mean "what condition"? Aren't you pregnant?" As I pushed the bike forward heading into the barn, he grabbed the handles and helped.

I let go and stood there staring in shock. "What the hell gave you that idea?" I shook my head and began to laugh, but suddenly a wave of fear struck me. "Did you come back because you thought I was pregnant?"

He set the bike on its stand and came over to me. "Listen woman, I came here because I wasn't about to let you run me around the world like a dog chasing a bone. We need to talk…wait…I take that back…" He began to walk away "I need to talk…you need to listen and then we'll figure things out from there."

Still in shock, I stood there watching him. His back to me, I could see his shoulders tense. I searched my mind for something to say and remembered my promise to stand my ground and keep my mouth shut. Not wanting to have his anger come out in front of Mary, I cleared my throat and sat down on an old bail of straw. He turned and shrugged. "Okay, you want to talk here…fine…I can do this anywhere."

I squared my shoulders and placed my hands in my lap. "Yes, I thought you were pregnant. What was I suppose to think? I read your book and the last chapters clearly stated that you were sick…depression my ass! Even I could read the signs of early pregnancy." He walked over and stood looking down at me. For one quick moment I felt as small as a person could possibly feel. I manipulated him into coming to find me.

"I was crushed when you didn't think you were important to my life. You acted as if you didn't care what I did or where I went. I thought I meant more to you then that and then when you called me Scott…well that was it..." I bit my lip as he stared deep into my eyes. "I was ready to take that job and never look back after that day. You hurt me as much as any woman ever could." His eyes were cold. He stood up and turned his back to me.

"Driving back to base, I heard you on the radio…but when I called back and you didn't respond…I got it in my head you would be better off without me…so I kept going. Taylor called me everyday trying to talk me into going home…Monica even threatened me a few times." His voice got louder. "You on the other hand didn't do shit…I waited day after day to hear word one from you and nothing… not until it was almost too late. I couldn't sleep some nights trying to figure why you still had feelings for him…Like a fool, I thought that by telling you I loved you…well, that you only thought of me." He looked down and kicked at the dirt.

"It wasn't until you tricked me to going up to the cabin that I discovered how you really felt. I read your book." He looked up again. "It's good Tess, really good…you found a way to make me see things through your eyes…but it's not finished."

He paused for what seemed like forever. "I was ready to play your little game and go chasing after you to Jamaica, but didn't want to give you the satisfaction." Walking over to me with a wicked smile. "You had me wrapped around your pretty little finger, but I'm here to take control of this mess." He pulled me to my feet. "Tell me straight…are you pregnant?" I melted as he gazed into my eyes and realized he was hoping I was.

"No, to my knowledge I'm not pregnant." Disappointed, he turned and walked away. "Ryan, don't go…I wasn't trying to make you think I was having a baby just to get you back…I wanted you to read my story so you could feel how much I love you and how torn up I was when you left." My words caught in my throat.

He stopped and turned. "Tess, it's gonna take time… there's too many emotions for me to handle. I know I've got some things to work on…but don't think you're innocent…we both screwed this up."

"I want you to stay…if you can." I walked over and twisted my finger in his shirt, looked up and pleaded. "Please…I've missed you so much…if you leave now…it'll…"he put his arms around me, but his touch was different. I could feel his tension. I wanted him to hug me tight, lift me off my feet and kiss me passionately, but he remained distant. Even wrapped in his arms I could tell it wouldn't be a fast and easy road back to the way we were.

"I'd like to stay, but we can't just jump in the sack and think everything's will work out fine." I looked up and shook my head.

"I understand." I took his hand and we headed back to the house.

I knew I had to be careful not to push him too fast. It wasn't until then that I noticed he looked as if he hadn't slept in weeks. His clothes were crumpled and his hair was long and shaggy. Showing him to the room next to mine, I let him unpack and rest. I went into the kitchen to get a cup of tea and found Mary sitting at the counter pretending to read the newspaper.

"I guess you've met him?" She looked over the paper and grinned. I could see the knowing twinkle in her eye.

"Yes, he came while you were out on the bike…I must say Tess, you found a nice looking guy…hope he sticks around." She gave me a wink grabbing a note pad and tossed it to me. "You got a call…numbers on the pad…a Dr. Whetstone?"

I picked it up and looked at it. "That is the most attentive Doctor I've ever been to." I tossed the message on the counter and looked over at her. "I went to him when I left the cabin…I was suffering from malnutrition and when I tried to eat I couldn't keep it down." A frightened look crossed her face. "Don't worry, he gave me vitamins and it took awhile, but now I can eat like a pig." Her expression didn't relax. "Mary… please… don't worry about it…you've seen me…I'm fine."

Knowing that it was a dead subject, she smacked her knee. "Okay…subject dropped." She skipped over to the freezer and browsed the packages of meat. "Well, we have company…which is a nice change of pace…so tonight we BBQ." She looked over her shoulder for my approval.

"Need any help?" I looked back down at the note.

"Nope…you know what they say…too many cooks…" grabbing the meat and tossing it on the counter.

"Spoils the soup?" I looked up questioningly.

"Nope…ticks me off." She laughed. "Think you can feed and water the horses for me? Gonna be dark soon and it would make it harder to find my way around."

"Sure" I got up and headed to the stables. It wasn't long before I forgot about the note.

I hadn't realized how quickly the day had passed. When I got to the stables, all the horses were waiting in their stalls for me to toss the hay in the feed bins. I went down the line making sure each one got the right size flake and bucket of feed. It occurred to me that it would be nice to have horses at the cabin, but I'd have to find a way to keep them warm in the winter without compromising their safety. I made a mental note to pitch the idea to Monica. I knew she would find a way to make it happen.

After I was finished, I showered and dressed in a new pair of jeans and a loose shirt. I could smell mesquite as I walked out to the courtyard. Mary was busy tossing steaks on the grill while Ryan was lounging in the hammock. "Pretty comfortable isn't it?" He looked up and smiled.

"I can see the charm in this desert life that you seem to love so much." He kicked off the ground letting the hammock swing a little higher.

"It sucks in the summer…too hot…too dry and then the monsoons hit and it's like living in that sauna you built." I pulled up a chair and faced him.

"I could think of worse places to be stuck." He looked around taking in the landscape.

"Have you seen the whole courtyard or just the view from where you're sitting?" I got up and reached out to help him up.

"I didn't think there was more." He grabbed my hand and hoisted himself out of the hammock.

"This place is very deceiving. The yard slopes slightly so some of the treasures are hidden by the horizon." As I lead him past the fountain, the pool came into view. It looked like a spring coming up from the desert floor. The natural rocks with the cascading waterfall added to the illusion. "It's paradise in the spring and a haven in the summer." I looked over at him to see his reaction.

"This is so cool...you can't even see this from the house...I didn't even see it from the barn." He walked around and looked out on the landscape.

I was hoping he would grab me and get romantic, but I could tell he was doing anything he could to hold back from the temptation. I shoved my hands in my back pockets and dipped my toe in the water. It was cool and inviting, I wanted to jump in, but the sound of the dinner bell rang loud. Startled, I turned quickly and began to fall back teetering on the edge of the pool. Ryan rushed forward and grabbed me.

"Close call, you almost got your new clothes wet." He smiled grabbing a price tag that dangled from my sleeve. He held me steady and gave me a quick peck on the cheek.

I was floored. Giving me a gentle tug, he led me back. Mary had laid out a nice spread of food and we ate as she told Ryan about the plans for the ranch. Pretending to listen, I thought about how powerful that one little kiss was. It gave me tingles and I wanted more. I was off in my own little world barely hearing their voices.

"Tess? Geeze girl...snap out of it...did you hear what I said?" A nudge to my shoulder brought me back to reality.

"What? I'm sorry I got lost in my thoughts." I looked down at my food and realized I had only pushed it around making a mess of my plate. "What did I miss?"

"Well dear, I asked you if you made that call to doctor what's his name." She began to clear the plates. I looked to see Ryan staring at me with a questioning look.

"I'll call him tomorrow...he's probably just doing some kind of follow up to make sure I'm not starving myself." I grabbed the glass of tea in front of me and gulped it down.

"Well, just make sure you do call him…it may seem like nothing to you, but it's not cool to make him worry." Ryan's voice was serious and sent a chill down my spine.

"Okay, gosh." I held up my hand dramatically. "I promise to call the fine doctor first thing in the morning."

Stretching my arms over my head, I yawned and excused myself from the table. I wanted to stay and talk with Ryan, but I could tell it wasn't the right time. He needed a chance to settle in and I wanted to let him make the first move. I went to my room and wrote down everything that had happened hoping to someday incorporate it into my book. I still didn't have the right ending.

I looked up from my journal and noticed it was well after midnight and the house was completely quiet. My body was sore from my ride and the tension of the day's events. I took advantage of the time and headed down to the pool. It looked so inviting earlier and the weather was just warm enough to go for an early morning swim.

It was dark and a bit difficult to navigate the path that wound around the courtyard. After stubbing my toe a few times, my eyes adjusted to the darkness as I found the pool. I shed my clothes and jumped in feet first. Gasping as the cold water shocked my senses, I dipped my head under and let it saturate my hair. Getting used to the cold, I slowly swam to the middle of the pool. Floating on my back I looked up at the star filled sky. I couldn't hear the sounds of the desert with my ears under water. The cool morning air blew over my breast as I closed my eyes trying to imagine the warm sensation of Ryan's kiss. Under the water I could hear the echo of the waterfall as I floated closer to it. I stood up under the falling water letting it cascade down my face. I leaned back against the side of the pool stretching my back along the curved rock enjoying the cold water. I thought my imagination was getting the better of me when I felt the electric shock of hands trailing up my stomach and over my breast. I knew his touch. My eyes flew open to see him staring at his hands as they glided over my body. I was completely under his control as he pulled me to him.

I wrapped my arms around his neck and let him lead me to the middle of the pool. Still too dark, I wasn't able to see his expression, but I could feel the desire in his touch. "I came out here to cool off and there you were raising my temperature again." He brought his head to my shoulder and began to kiss my neck. I melted in his arms as he floated me around the pool. I tangled my fingers in his hair and brought my lips to kiss him with all the passion I had built up inside me. He moaned. I wrapped my legs around his waist as we drifted to the shallow end of the pool.

"Tess, I came here to ease my desire not to fuel it." He kissed me softly and I unwrapped my legs to stand. The water came to my waist and a gust of air sent shivers across my skin. I moved over to the steps and sat down letting the water cover me."I didn't mean to Ryan...I thought I was out here alone." I covered myself with my hands and looked away wishing I could disappear. His rejection brought tears streaming down my face. I felt like a fool.

"Tess, don't." He swam over and reached out. "Don't do this...please, I'm not trying to hurt you...I'm just..." he lifted my chin. "Stupid..."he pulled me into his arms and held me tight. "I'm stupid Tess, I tried to play it cool...but I can't...you've got me under your spell"

I wasn't sure if I heard his words correctly. "You're not just saying that to make me stop crying are you?" I pulled away.

"Tell me what you think." His mouth came down on mine kissing me deeply. My stomach tingled as he glided his hands down my back and drew me into his body. The cold morning air made us both shiver. Taking my hand, he led me up the stairs and out of the pool. He wrapped a towel around his waist before sweeping me up in his arms. I rested my head on his shoulder as he brought me into the house.

He laid me on the bed. "Day by day my love...baby steps" He kissed me again before going to his room where I hoped he would lay there dreaming about me.

CHAPTER THIRTY

The cold air may have numbed our passion, but not my desire for him. I had a restless sleep playing over the night in my mind. He loved me; I could feel it in my heart. He wanted to take it slow so I decided to be patient and not try to push him right out of my life again. I relaxed knowing he was only one room away.

It was noon when I finally rolled out of bed and got dressed. My body was still achy as I padded into the kitchen. Ryan and Mary were sitting at the table having lunch. I walked over to the stove and put the kettle on to make tea.

Mary said, "You look like hell dear, rough night?" I flashed Ryan a smile as he chuckled. She looked to me and then to Ryan confused. "What's the joke?"

I cleared my throat; "I'm fine, just sore from the ride I took yesterday. I'll be okay once I get moving around a bit."

I reached out and grabbed the phone just as it rang. "Tess, its Doctor Whetstone."

"Hi, I was just gonna call you." I bit my lip hoping his call was just a follow up.

"I wanted to see if you were feeling all right. I sent you the results of your tests and wanted to make sure you plan to go to a doctor there for follow up." I broke in.

"I haven't been in town to pick up the mail in awhile." My stomach began to twinge.

"Don't worry about it, I sent another copy to a friend of mine in Oracle. His nurse set up an appointment for you for today. That's why I was so eager to get a hold of you." He assumed I knew what he was talking about as he rattled off the doctor's name and address. "I think you should keep this appointment. He'll let me know how you're doing. Take care Tess, hope to see you again soon."

I hung up the phone and quickly dialed the number he gave me. "Doctor Parker's office, how may I help you?"

"I'm Tess Kelly, I think I've got an appointment today?" I drummed my fingers on the counter impatiently.

"Yes Tess, we have you down for three thirty. Just a check up, but we'll need to re-run the tests that Doctor Whetstone did for you." She sounded too chipper.

I hung up the phone relieved that it was nothing major. I shook my head and smiled.

"What was that about dear?" I looked over finding both of them leaning forward staring at me in anticipation.

"I have to go in for a check up. You think you guys can keep each other company while I'm gone?" The water came to a boil and the kettle began to scream. I shut it off not feeling like tea anymore.

They looked at each other in a panic. "Well, I'd like to see more then just the ranch while I'm here...I'll go with you if you don't mind." His voice cracked as he spoke.

"You just reminded me I haven't checked the mail in weeks. I think we should all go and make a trip of it. We'll be back in enough time to feed the horses." She looked at me hopefully.

I knew they were more curious then I was about my appointment and I wasn't going to get away with a lone trip into town. "Okay, well...I'll drop you both off, go to my appointment and meet up with you later."

They rushed around as I fixed myself something to eat. Barely able to choke down a bite, they dragged me out the door. Before I knew it, we were in the car heading down the road to town. Mary stopped and picked up the mail. I sat in the back watching as she pointed out all the uninteresting places. I caught onto the plan they had concocted when Mary asked where the doctor's office was. Not wanting them hanging out with me during the appointment, I lied and told her it was near the shopping center. Guessing that it was the new medical building across the street, she parked in the mall parking lot and handed me the keys.

"I'll meet you in the restaurant when I'm done, it shouldn't take too long. Maybe you guys can do a little shopping...I think Ryan here needs a pair of boots and maybe some cooler shirts. He could help us fix up the place while he's here" She gave me a hug and grabbed his arm.

I felt guilty about lying, but I knew I didn't want them hanging out while I got poked and prodded. I was surprised to see there wasn't anyone else waiting when I got there. The nurse behind the desk greeted me guessing who I was. I filled out the forms she needed and followed her. She charted my height, weight, temperature and blood pressure before drawing blood. Once in the exam room, she gave me a gown and told me the doctor would be in shortly. I began to feel insecure as I stood in the open back gown looking around the room at all medical posters of the female body. It hit me like a ton of bricks when I realized I was in the office of an OBGYN.

My heart pounded in my chest as I began to hyperventilate. The doctor came in and seeing my condition grabbed a paper bag and held it over my mouth. Rubbing my back he tried to calm me down. "Tess, breath slowly...relax...in...out...there." I began to breathe easier.

Taking the bag away, I looked up at him. "You're not the kind of doctor I expected. I thought this was a regular physical." I brought the bag back to my face and took a few more deep breaths as he realized I had no idea why I was there.

"Take it easy Tess, I'm sure you have some assumptions running through your head...but there's no need for concern." He walked over and began to wash his hands. "Larry and I go way back...he knows I specialize in your type of condition...so he called me to do a follow up."

"I don't understand...I went to him because I suffered from malnutrition...I'm not pregnant." A nervous giggle escaped me. "I think I'd know if I was pregnant... wouldn't I?" I questioned as my eyes began to well up.

"Well, I don't know if you are or not...but that's not why you're here." He slipped on a pair of gloves and gestured for me to sit on the table.

My stomach turned as I did. I hated woman exams...they always made me feel so weird.

"We just need to run all the tests again. You were diagnosed with malnutrition caused by depression. It takes a toll on a woman's body and when you've been hit with it once; there's a fifty- percent chance it can hit you again. I know you're feeling fine now, but we have to make sure that you didn't do any permanent damage to your body." I relaxed feeling silly for jumping to the same conclusion Ryan had.

He gave me a full physical and prescribed some vitamins and an easy exercise program. After a long chat, he assured me I was not pregnant, gave me a fatherly hug and sent me on my way. As I drove back to the mall, a huge wave of relief washed over me like the waterfall had the night before.

When I got to the restaurant, I found Mary and Ryan huddled up in a booth talking intensely not realizing I was standing in front of them. "My word child where have you been?" She scooted out of the booth and hugged me. "We were worried shitless, we went over to the medical building to find that it was still under construction." She held me at arms length as she scolded me. "Don't ever scare me like that again." She hugged me once more, before letting me sit down next to Ryan.

He turned to face me. "So...everything okay?" Pushing a glass of water in front of me.

"Everything's fine, I just have to take some vitamins and get some exercise." I grabbed the glass and drank it down. "He says I'm gonna be weak and achy for awhile, but I'll over come that in no time."

They were both staring at me with odd looks. Feeling a bit strange, I grabbed a menu and pretended to look over the selection. They exchanged glances and then Ryan grabbed the menu from my hands. "Damn it Tess...don't leave us hanging...no more secrets."

"What the hell are you talking about?" I grabbed it back and smacked it down in front of me. I could feel the blood rushing to my face as my temper began to flare.

"Don't try to brush this by me girl…I ran into the doctor back home and he told me you were gonna have a baby." He braced his arms against the table and the back of the booth waiting for me to respond to his accusation.

"For the last time…I'm not pregnant …I am however having some difficulty with stress and my hormones are completely out of whack due to malnutrition…which I might add you're not helping with since you refuse to let me eat…now, if you don't mind." I whipped up the menu as he sat there with his mouth open. I couldn't tell what type of reaction Mary was having but I was sure she looked as shocked as he did.

Hearing my outburst the waitress came over and asked if everything was okay. Lowering the menu, I smiled and looked up. Assuring her that all was fine, I ordered a hamburger and a large beer. When she left, I looked over to see that their expressions hadn't changed.

Calmly, I turned to face him. "Listen, I'm sure there's some kind of cross communication here, but I saw the results of my tests and there was no… I held up my hand. "No indications that I'm pregnant."

"I don't get it…Doctor Whetstone congratulated me…said something about my growing family." It hit us at the same time… our eyes grew wide as we whispered in unison "Monica"

I got excited as he grabbed my hands from the table. "Monica's pregnant…that's what he meant. I must've been in such a zone I didn't hear everything he said." We sat there forgetting Mary looking back and forth from him to me wondering what the hell we were talking about. We began to laugh as we realized how stupid we both had acted.

"Well slap me silly and call me George…I'm completely lost." Mary sat back and shook her head.

As we ate, I explained it all to her. The whole time, Ryan thought I was keeping this big secret from him and come to find out it was his sister. With that settled, we were able to relax and enjoy the rest of the day in town. Ryan purchased a few pairs of jeans, some light cotton shirts and a new pair of boots. The perfect clothes for jobs I planned to have him do.

Once we got back to the ranch, Mary hurried down to the stable to feed the horses. Ryan grabbed all the shopping bags and I followed him down the hall to his room. "You get settled... I've a call to make." I gave his arm a squeeze and went to my room.

I laid on the bed and grabbed the phone. It only rang once when Monica's voice chimed. "Taylor's Lodge, this is Monica"

"You little sneak..." I whispered

"I beg your pardon?" Confused not realizing who was on the other end of the line.

"It's me...Tess...do you realize you had everyone thinking I was having a baby?" There was a long pause as she searched for a response.

"Better you then me...How'd you find out?" Her voice hushed and muffled as if she had her hand over her mouth.

"Doctor Whetstone made some strange comment to Ryan, who assumed he was talking about me...let me tell you girl...it caused a bit of stir on this end...but when he found out it wasn't me "adding to the family"...we just put two and two together. Why didn't you tell me?" I waited patiently for her excuse. Rolling on to my back, I lifted my legs tangling the phone cord around my foot.

"Tess...you and Ryan can't tell Scott!" Not believing what I was hearing, I flopped over on my stomach and gasped.

"What? You haven't told him? Are you nuts?" I could hear her panic as she breathed into the receiver.

"Tess...I don't think I'm ready for this yet...I want a family, but what kind of mother will I be, running the family business?" She began to cry and I could barely understand her words.

"You're gonna make a great mom." I smiled hoping my words would soothe her nerves. She sniffled and I could tell it wasn't helping much.

As we talked, I tried to get her excited about all the fun babies can be. I wasn't an expert, but I had one hell of an imagination. After we rambled on for an hour, she promised to tell Scott and I promised to tell Ryan not to call and let the cat out of the bag. I hung up the phone and heard a tapping at the door.

"Come in" I was trying to untangle the cord from my leg as Ryan peeked around the door.

"Is it safe to enter?" Looking around the room pretending to be scared of the wild unknowns of a woman's domain.

"Enter at your own risk!" I slipped the cord off my foot and put the phone back on the nightstand.

"I figured you were talking to my sister...I didn't want to interrupt the "girl talk", so I listened at the door." He came over to the bed and sat down beside me.

"Then I guess you know that you're suppose to keep this quiet... she doesn't want you running to Scott telling." I looked down at his hand as he drummed his fingers on the bed inching closer and closer to my knee. Knowing he was in a playful mood, I smacked his hand as he turned grabbing me and pinned me to the mattress.

Laughing as the weight of his body crushed me. "Okay Tess... I'll keep my trap shut...but you'll have to find another activity to keep it busy." I looked up to see him smiling.

"Well, I guess I'll have to do what I have to do." His lips met mine in a gentle kiss. "We better be careful, the door's open and Mary will be coming back soon. She may think that were doing the nasty." I said as he nibbled my lip. My choice of words struck a cord and we began to laugh hard. He collapsed on me making it hard to breathe; I pushed him off and jumped off the bed. With my hands on my hips I looked down as he rolled over.

With a sneaky grin, he patted the bed and raised his eyebrow trying to entice me to lay back down. "I don't know...I could get grounded for having a boy in my bedroom."

At that moment, Mary cleared her throat startling us. I turned to see her standing in the doorway looking amused. I laughed and walked over to give her a hug. Ryan jumped off the bed and stood with his hands behind him looking guilty. "It wasn't me Mrs. Kelly, she pushed me down and I fell on the bed." He looked down at his feet and began to toe the floor like a child.

"You guys are nuts." She grabbed him and brought him into our hug. "Come on you two...let's watch some movies." She turned and began to walk quickly down the hall. We followed and enjoyed a nice family night at home.

After a few short weeks and with my help, he had built new paddocks near the stables and painted the barn. We still kept an emotional distance from each other, but he did steal a kiss every now and then. I kept up the hope that we would get back to the way we were. I didn't think too much about the failed marriage proposal and knew not to expect one.

I would go for long rides on my bike to give him and Mary time to get to know each other. They seem connected and grew very close. I would walk into a room and catch them talking intently as if they were plotting something. They always stopped when they saw me. Whenever I asked what they were up to, they'd brush me off with some lame story about planning more for the ranch. Not wanting to butt in, I brushed it off.

The day we finished setting up the barn, Ryan and I had cleaned up and were eating sandwiches in the kitchen. Mary had been gone most of the day in town. She caught us clowning around shoving food into each other's faces. "Don't mean to ruin your fun...but I have a surprise for you guys."

Ryan grabbed my hand and tugged me as he followed her. I couldn't stop laughing. Once in the great room, she stood in front of the couch and gestured for us to sit. Ryan sat at one side and I sat at the other creating a large space between us. Mary looked at us and laughed. "Okay, I can play this game too." She clapped her hands together. "Kids, I'm going out." Ryan looked at me shocked and then smiled. "I got sodas and snacks in the kitchen...there are tons of movies you can watch to keep you out of trouble." Holding up her hand wagging a finger. "I expect you to be on your best behavior." With our pouting faces staring back at her, she tried to keep a straight face. "I will be gone for two days...so you'll be responsible for the horses...if you have any trouble, call Bert"

Realizing she was serious, I stopped playing around. "Where ya going?"

"I have to go to Phoenix to see my kids, it was planned before you came back. I completely forgot about it until I looked at the calendar...I left the number where I'll be if you need me." Giving

Ryan a wink. "I think you'll be in good hands here." She bent down and gave me a kiss and left.

Ryan and I sat on the couch quietly as we heard her car pull away. Looking shyly down at his hands as he twisted his fingers around each other. "Tess...will you be my girlfriend."

"Okay, sure...if you want me to." I followed his lead and began to swing my feet hitting them against the couch.

"Okay..." He jumped up and grabbed the remote. Clicking on the TV he sat back down on the other side of the couch. I looked over to see him staring straight ahead like an excited boy about to watch the movie of the century. He was back...the playful fun loving Ryan I fell in love with. I thought at any moment he would turn and leap over to kiss me, but he kept his eyes glued to the TV.

"Okay, you want to sit there and watch the movie...fine..." I crossed my arms over my chest.

When the movie started, I saw out of the corner of my eye, Ryan inching his way a little closer to me. I did the same. Once we were sitting next to each other in the middle of the couch, he pretended to be nervous. Throwing off his little game, I yawned bring my arm over my head and letting it rest on the couch behind him. He turned to me and grinned. "You brazen hussy!" Grabbing me as he laid back. We kissed wildly, stopping only to catch our breath. The room was getting hot so I lifted myself up, straddled his waist and pulled my shirt over my head.

He looked amused as I reached down and unbuttoned his shirt. I ran my hands over his chest letting my fingers tingle. He grabbed my waist and lifted me slightly to get more comfortable under my weight. He scooted to prop himself against the arm of the couch bringing me along for the ride. I smiled knowing that he was living out an old high school fantasy. Deciding to make it come true, I reached behind me and unhooked my bra lifting it over my head letting it fall from my fingers. I arched my back running my hands through my hair, grinding slowly on his lap. He rolled his head back and moaned. His hands slowly moved up my sides and over my breasts as he matched my rhythm. The fabric of our pants rubbed together creating friction. It was erotic.

The flicker of the TV added to the excitement as we teased each other. "Tess, you're driving me crazy." He sat up and held me tight trying to calm his passion. He let go and dropped back against the couch pulling his legs out from under me. Sitting on my feet, I stretched up and took in a deep breath as I fell back onto the couch. I was exhausted. I straightened my legs and stretched out almost hitting him with my foot.

"Whoa there Tess, no need to punish...I just needed a time out." He grabbed my foot and gave my ankle a kiss.

"Don't start something you can't finish old man...I might have to tie you down and go wild again." I laughed as he got up and wiggled his leg to re-adjust.

Noticing the movie was almost over; I grabbed the remote and rewound the tape. Ryan went into the kitchen and returned with a big bowl of chips and two large glasses full of what looked like soda. He sat down and handed one to me. As I took a sip, I realized it was a very large, very strong rum and coke. I looked at him as he chuckled. I sat there wondering why he stopped, but his words "One day at a time" kept ringing through my head.

We watched the movie, but I was consumed with the burning question. I sucked back two drinks by the time it was over. "Well, I guess we better hit the sack...you gotta get up and feed the horses." He bent down lifted me into his arms. "Looks like you're a bit toasted." I let the rum make my head spin as I looked into his eyes and smiled.

"Yup...half naked drunk woman in your arms and there you are...all strong and man like...what ever should you do with me." I giggled and let my head drop on his shoulder as he carried me to my room. He placed me gently on the bed. My eyes followed him as he bent down and took off my socks. He unbuttoned my pants and moved to the end of the bed. Grabbing my jeans by the cuffs, I lifted up and let him pull them off. I closed my eyes hoping he was going to join me.

I heard him move around the room and felt a blanket cover me. Opening my eyes, I was surprised to see he was about to leave. "Ryan...can I ask a question?"

He came back and sat on the edge of the bed. I reached up as he leaned over for a kiss. "Why'd you stop tonight? Did I do something wrong?"

He smiled as he sat up. "You didn't do anything wrong...in fact, it was perfect. We took anticipation to a whole new level." He kissed my nose and walked out hitting the light switch before closing the door. As my head sunk into the pillows, I mumbled to myself, "Anticipation my butt, sexual frustration's more like it." I feel asleep, knowing he was hell bent on making me suffer.

CHAPTER THIRTY-ONE

I got up early the next day and dragged Ryan out of bed to help me with the chores. By mid morning we had the horses fed, watered, and groomed. It was if we both were working off the sexual tension from the night before. We mucked the stalls and went back to the house where I treated him to a good ol' fashioned ranch breakfast.

"I'm gonna go for a swim...wanna come?" I asked grabbing the last piece of toast.

"Nope, I have some calls to make." He took a sip of coffee and picked up the paper glancing over the front page. Not wanting to push the subject, I left him there.

The water was cold. I dove in and swam the length of the pool until I was under the waterfall. I let the water pour over my head trying to clear the thoughts. With a burst of energy, I pushed off and swam as a fast I could. After I had made several laps, I floated on my back trying to catch my breath. Feeling relaxed, I let myself sink under the water and came up feeling completely refreshed. As I cleared the hair from my eyes, I focused on Ryan standing by the side of the pool looking worried.

"What's wrong?" I asked as I moved to the steps. He reached out and helped me up.

"I have to leave and I want you to come with me." He grabbed the towel and began to dry me off.

"Wait, what's this about? Mary's gone until tomorrow and there's no one here to take care of the horses." He grabbed my hand and led me back to the house.

He was scaring me. When we got to my room I twisted my hand from his grip. "Will you just tell me what the hells going on?" He reached for my bag and tossed it on the bed.

Tossing clothes from my dresser into the bag, he explained. "Monica took off and Scott's freakin out. I think I know where she went, but it would be better if you were there…she trusts you…and I think you're the only one who can bring her back." I ran to the bathroom to change. "I called Mary and explained…Bert said he'd take care of the animals."

I pulled on my jeans and began helping him with my bag. "Okay…okay…go pack." I grabbed a few items from the bathroom and figured that if I forgot anything I could always buy it later. I rushed out and bumped into him coming out of his room.

Bags in hand we headed out the door and got in the rental car. My adrenaline raced making my heart pound in my chest. We didn't speak until we were on the highway heading towards the airport.

"It's going to be difficult to get tickets without having to wait for a flight." He sped up as I saw the desperation in his face.

"No need to worry about that…I'll be flying us there…I called ahead and had one of my buddies gas up and file a plan." Normally it would have taken longer to get to the airport, but Ryan was driving like a bat out of hell.

We parked in front of the executive terminal. Whizzing past the attendants hanging around the gate, I slowed as he headed towards a beautiful Lear jet. He bounded up the stairs. I was about to follow him when a woman dressed in a uniform reached out and grabbed my bag.

"Here Ms. Kelly, let me take that for you. I looked into the cockpit to see Ryan had already started his preflight. A younger man sat beside him going over the checklist with him. I looked up as she took my arm and guided me to a seat. It was only a matter of moments before she secured the door and we began to taxi down the runway.

Once in flight, she came over and offered me a drink. My stomach was in knots from rushing around. Water was the only thing I could think to ask for. She sat down and smiled. "I'm

Susan…my husband Jack is Ryan's Copilot. I must admit we didn't expect to leave Tucson so soon."

"How do you know Ryan?" I sipped carefully as we hit a little turbulence.

"They spent the winter flying together in South America. I didn't meet him until I came back from France." She sat back and looked around the cabin. "Amazing isn't it?"

"Yes, I love the ride" I watched as she took in the grandeur. "I hate puddle jumpers"

We passed the time talking about France and the great places we both had been. She had traveled all over the world and decided when she married Jack; she wanted to spend as much time with him as possible. That's why they were both on the flight. They preferred being on call as opposed to having set schedules.

As we descended, she turned on her professional side and readied the plane for landing. I looked out the window to see we had landed on a private strip in the middle of the woods. There was a small building next to a hanger. As we came to a full stop, she handed me my bag and opened the hatch to release the stairs. Ryan finally emerged from the cockpit and led me across the tarmac.

Giving me only a moment to get used to being on firm ground, he took my hand and we went around the hanger to a jeep. Tossing our bags in the back, we got in and began to drive through the woods on a small dirt road.

He looked over briefly. "You feeling okay?"

"I'm okay…how long until we get to where ever you're taking us?" I looked around trying to get my bearings.

"We're only a few miles from Base. We're gonna take the chopper from there. Didn't you get any sleep on the flight?" I laughed at the thought.

"Are you nuts? I gabbed with Susan the whole trip. It helped to keep my mind off Monica. I would've been stressed out otherwise." I laid my head back and let it bounce against the seat as we raced down the road.

I must have fallen asleep, before I knew it we were stopped right next to the helicopter. The day was almost gone and it was getting dark as we rushed to take off. I managed once again to catch a little nap before he nudged me to look down on the lake. I was surprised to see a ring of lights in the clearing beside the lake.

"I made some improvements last time I was here. Thought it might help with the plans for the resort." He shouted over the noise of the rotor blades.

The cabin was bathed in a warm glow from lanterns scattered about. I looked around to see it had been completely decorated with new furniture that made it look more like a home and less like a shanty. I dropped my bags and walked around touching all the new stuff. I turned to Ryan as he walked over to me. Taking my hand, he stood there gazing into my eyes.

"Tess, I have a confession...I didn't bring you here to find Monica." My stomach began to twist as tears filled my eyes. "I've loved you for almost a year now. I'm not great at expressing my emotions, but I think you know how I feel." He dropped to his knee as the muscles in my back began to twitch. "I've loved you...I've lost you...and now that I've found you, I can't live without you... would you do me the honor of becoming my wife?"

Tears streamed down my face, I couldn't find the words to answer. He looked up hopefully. "I'd like nothing more." I took his face in my hands as he stood. Kissing me warmly, he took my hand and slipped a ring on my finger. I threw my arms around his neck and he lifted me up swinging me around.

"You're an amazing woman." He stepped back and brought my hand to his lips kissing the ring that symbolized his love. "I have one more surprise for you." He led me to the bathroom. "Inside, you will find something to change into...take a shower and get all dolled up...once you're ready...follow the lights along the path in the woods. I'll be waiting for you in the meadow." I shook my head trying to come back to reality.

He drew me into him giving me a passionate kiss. "You're not sorry you said yes are you?" I shook my head and went into the bathroom.

Hanging on the back of the door was a pink satin gown. Trimmed with delicate white pearls at the bust and white lace at the hem. It reminded me of a prom dress, with thin straps and plunging neckline. On the shelf over the sink was a string of pearls, pink roses and a pair of strappy sandals.

After a quick shower, I tried to get as much water as I could out of my hair. I brushed out the tangles and French braided it weaving the small pink roses into the stands. I slipped into the dress and draped the pearls around my neck. Wishing I had a little make up I looked in the mirror once more before opening the door. Pinned to the door leading outside was a long stemmed pink rose dangling a note that said..."follow me". I opened the door and walked around the sauna to the back of the cabin. There were small lights glittering down the path. I walked along being careful not to twist my ankle as I negotiated the twists and turns.

To my surprise, I heard soft music begin to play as I emerged from the woods. I looked up to see small cabins surrounding the meadow. Each one lit with a lantern in the window. I was surprised to see Monica had worked so hard to get them built in such a short amount of time. A long path of lanterns hanging from posts led to the middle of the meadow. Confusion set in when I saw Scott walking between them to meet me. Not saying a word, he held out his arm and led me to the middle of the meadow.

My knees went weak as I realized what was happening. He paused a moment to let me gather my courage. I squared my shoulders and walked on. As my eyes came into focus, I saw Monica, Mary, Susan, Jack and Ryan gathered around the tree stump in the middle of the field. I held back the tears when I saw Mary wiping her own tears from her eyes. Monica gave me a confident nod. Susan smiled as if she knew what I was thinking. Before me, standing behind the stump was a man I had never seen before.

I looked over to Ryan nervously and smiled. My heart welled up as I took a deep breath. Ryan took my hand and we stood facing each other. Staring lovingly into my eyes, I realized that this was what he and Mary had been planning.

"We gather in nature where these two souls first met." I wasn't listening to the words as he spoke, until I heard...

"... take this woman to be your wife? Do you promise to love her, honor her and cherish her until death do you part?"

His gaze set on mine. "I do" the words he spoke sent shivers up my spine.

"Do you Tess; take this man to be you husband? Do you promise to love him, honor him and cherish him until death do you part?"

Lost in his eyes I said. "I do."

"I now pronounce you husband and wife...you may kiss your bride." He pulled me into his arms and dipped me delivering the softest tender kiss.

As he brought me to my feet, I suddenly realized something. "Ryan...I don't...."

Cutting me off he said, "You can't change your mind now woman...you're mine." He smiled as I laughed.

"Fat chance of that happening...but I just realized I don't know your last name."

He looked at me amazed and began to laugh. "Well that make sense...you married me without knowing my name?"

The minister raised his arms. "My friends, I present to you Mr. and Mrs. Ryan."

I shook my head in disbelief. "Your name's Ryan Ryan?"

"No babe, Ryan's my last name and now it's yours." The pieces fell into place. In typical flyboy fashion Scott always called him by his last name.

"So what's your first name?" I grabbed his waist pulling me to him and laughing.

"Matthew...weren't you paying attention? The minister must have said it at least twice." He bent down and kissed me as our family gathered around to congratulate us.

The End

ABOUT THE AUTHOR

Maureen grew up the youngest of five children in a military family. She traveled from state to state during the early years of her life, allowing her the opportunity to experience new places and interesting people. When her father retired and moved the family to Prescott, AZ, she found the hometown she longed for. After attending college, Maureen traveled around the Southwest. She finally settled down in Tucson, AZ where she is employed in sales for residential designs. Being a free spirit, Maureen spends her spare time playing darts, going for evening motorcycle rides and visiting her friends at the local tavern. Inspired by her diverse experiences and unique way of viewing life, she's currently working on her second novel.

Printed in the United States
33816LVS00003B/264

9 781420 801620